Wildflowers

Watertower Press

Baltimore, Maryland
Copyright © 2025

ISBN: 979-8985598254

Wildflowers

MERI ROBIE

Praise for Wildflowers

"A beautiful novel about three vibrant, memorable women who refuse to abandon their passion for music despite their struggles with aging, caretaking, and the frustration of thwarted dreams. Gloria, Honey, and Sian are an inspiring reminder that nothing is over until it's over."
— JANE DELURY, AUTHOR OF *HEDGE* AND *THE BALCONY*

"Drop the needle on this power chord of a novel and feel it pull you in. A resonant story about friendship, songwriting, and serendipity, and about how all of us, even aging country stars, can reinvent ourselves."
— ELISABETH COHEN, AUTHOR OF *THE GLITCH*

"In *Wildflowers*, Meri Robie has created an unforgettable cast of badass women. With this crew you'll come for the music on Friday night and end up staying the whole weekend."
— KATHERINE PICKETT, AWARD-WINNING AUTHOR OF *PERFECT BOUND:*
HOW TO NAVIGATE THE BOOK PUBLISHING PROCESS LIKE A PRO AND
DEBRA LEE WON'T BREAK

"[Meri] Robie's written a crackling tale of womanhood in the music industry, both past and present, and reminds us that you should never count a bad-ass grandma out."
— SARAH HENDESS, AUTHOR OF *SECOND CHANCES IN HOLLYWOOD*

"Wildflowers by Meri Robie is an exhilarating dive into the lives of women musicians in all their ups and downs. Together they discover friendship, create excellent music, and show the doubters what talented, complex women are capable of despite forces working to beat them down. Beautiful song lyrics and feisty dialogue complete the enjoyable reading experience of *Wildflowers."*
— Ruth Ticktin, author of *Around & Around* chapbook and *Was Am Going* poetry & flash

"Meri Robie's wonderful *Wildflowers* puts readers in the room where the music is made, and inside the bodies of women who are of a certain age, underappreciated, and enraged. These realistic characters pop and thrum, and their stories and lives intertwine like, well, music."
— Debra Whittall, whose work has appeared in Moose House Publishing and Nevermore Press

Table of Contents

Part I:

Rip Her To Shreds

"Then do we wonder why others prosper
Living so wicked year after year,
Farther along we'll know all about it;
Farther along we'll understand why."
— FROM THE CHURCH OF GOD HYMN "FARTHER ALONG"

"Some guy said to me: Don't you think you're too old to sing
rock n' roll?

I said: You'd better check with Mick Jagger."
— CHER

Chapter 1

THE MAYOR emerges from the mountain mist, ruffling his mahogany feathers and twisting his neck, to scrutinize the stranger on Gloria's porch. Fred, the Mayor, is no ordinary house chicken. He is large and in charge. He recently ran off a fox and a pair of Mormons—on separate occasions—and he misses nothing in the small community. According to Gloria, the Mayor is the best thing about the new couple who have just moved in to the neighborhood. That and the fact that they haven't bought curtains yet, so she can watch them fighting through the plate-glass window.

Gloria watches as a stylish man in a blazer and orange designer eye-glasses shifts from foot to foot on her white plank porch and appears to reconsider the errand at hand. He holds a notebook fast in his palm, no doubt stuffed with so-called facts about her music career. He checks his watch and peers through the window, shielding his eyes from the morning light to see into the darkness of the house, and Gloria, tucked on her loveseat out of his line of sight, thrills with the danger of being almost seen. He raps loudly on her door, glancing worriedly at the poultry patrol. "Gloria Redmond? It's Collin Stavras, from Dervish magazine? Can I come inside?"

The Mayor squawks twice and cocks his head, aiming his good eye at the man, out of place with his graying dreadlocks and pressed chinos among the broken-down flatbeds and American Patriot signs. The Mayor, however, is befitting of the neighborhood, chest thrust forward, clear in purpose and firm in intent. Unsettled, the stranger looks between the approaching chicken and the doorframe, doing wild calculations about distance and time and self-protection. He huffs and rings the buzzer again, this time with the desperation of someone who has found himself in a horror flick. But her doorbell is disconnected, she made sure of that, and she leans back to watch the scene unfold.

The interloper shifts tactics. "What?" he demands of the bird, widening his arms in an aggressive gesture. Fred squawks again, this time putting some throat into it. Gloria plugs her ears with her fingers in advance of Fred's next move. He is rearing up for a scream.

Gloria is moved by the man's fear but holds herself still. People need to learn when to leave her alone. Plus, it's just a chicken. The Mayor, frustrated with the stranger's defiance, extends his majestic wings. He takes a few steps backward, kicking dust and gravel, and then plunges forward, flapping and gaining enough momentum to lift his heft over the fence and into Gloria's yard. From there, it's just a few hops up the stairs. The man becomes frantic, backing himself against the wall of her porch and knocking with intensity.

Once in range, Fred shrieks, every decibel as loud as Gloria has anticipated, and the man claws at the wall. Fred whips his wings into a frenzy and begins to peck at the stranger's shoes, undoing the laces and indenting whitish scuffs on the brown leather.

"Ms. Redmond!" the man pleads. "Please get this crazy chicken!"

The man hops back and forth, and Gloria watches, until she is afraid he'll hurt the bird. She opens the door, standing barely five feet to the man's point guard height, but no matter—she's handled her share of tall roadies, studio musicians, and executives in her time.

She addresses Fred first, laughing. "That's right—get him!"

Fred stops pecking and flapping and hops toward Gloria, insinuating himself between the stranger and Gloria's door frame.

"He just wants some grub," she says and waves the man off. "And to get rid of you."

The man is still dancing away from Fred, who pecks intermittently, looking to Gloria for approval and treats. "Ms. Redmond? I'm here for..."

"I know. You called about the interview, and I thought I said no."

"You did, but then your manager..."

Gloria throws up her hands. "My manager, my ex-manager, that pile of dirt who is also my ex-husband, is not aware of the complexity of my social calendar. I simply do not have time to regale you with stories." She leans on the doorframe like a movie starlet, lets him wonder what she really wants.

The man squints into the drenching sunlight. It's not yet hot, but the morning's events have clearly been trying. "I'm sorry about the misunderstanding," he says, opening his palms to her. "It's not a feature, just a small piece. I'm personally interested in how you plan to spend your retirement."

"You live in the city?" she asks, though of course he does. Brooklyn, by the looks of him. Clean and tall with his locs twisted into a neat ponytail at the base of his neck. Mid-forties, probably. Cute under all that facial hair.

"Nah, Brooklyn." He has a nice smile.

"That's the city. Queens, the Bronx, Brooklyn—that's the city. Only Staten Island can claim independence."

"Interesting take."

"Don't you dare quote me. The city can go to hell."

"Can I quote *that*?" he asks playfully.

"Why not?" Gloria turns back into her house without inviting him in, coaxing the chicken behind her. The man enters tentatively and closes the door to any other stray, belligerent animals that might emerge from the woods.

The Mayor follows her into the kitchen, squawking once when Gloria opens the fridge door. She closes the door and glares. "Keep it up," she says, gripping the door handle and waiting. The Mayor turns his head, summarily redressed. "That's what I thought." She takes a carton of blueberries, tumbles them into a small china bowl, and puts a vanilla yogurt on the counter for herself. She puts the bowl on the floor and sits on a high stool that brings her face closer to level with the man's.

"You're in my house. Let's dispense with the civilities. What's your name again?"

"Collin. Collin Stavras."

"Great. You write for Dervish?" She peels back the lid on the yogurt.

"Correct." Stavras smiles with a friendly, disarming impression. However, Dervish is not a vanity magazine. Stavras has written a one-eighth-star review of an album before. That is, one-eighth out of ten.

"Well, I'm impressed you found me. So that's the first thing you'll probably write about. This dirt road, my Corolla in the driveway, hicks you met along the way. I lived in New York for thirty years and I never met anyone as nice as the hill people around here."

"Hill people?" Stavras narrows his eyes.

"The people who live here. You know. My neighbors." She jabs a thumb in the direction of their house.

"You get along well with them?" He opens his notebook on the counter and taps his pen on his hand.

"Famously. My neighbors across the street are the proud owners of The Mayor here." The chicken pecks at the empty china, a red imperial pagoda on the base laid bare sans blueberries. Gloria scoops her yogurt and points her spoon vaguely behind her. "That lady back there, she's crazy. Tinfoil-hat crazy. She told me she thinks I'm watching her." She shrugs. "I am, but that's beside the point." She takes a mouthful of yogurt and drags the empty spoon across her tongue.

She breaks into her signature smirk, the one that has graced nearly every album cover he probably researched before this trip: Last Best Shot and Pussycat and Little Woman, all her iconic phases, dimples framed by blond hair and sparkly eyes. She can tell he's charmed.

"You think she's dangerous?" he asks. "You being all alone up here?"

Gloria shrugs. "She once said to me, 'I have a gun.'" Gloria leans forward, conspiratorial. "So I say, 'So do I.'"

He smiles, waiting for her to say more.

"I have a reputation to protect," she offers. "If you know my music, you know what to expect."

"Glad I made it past the sniff test," he says. His body unfolds into an openness she's seen before, a big man trying to show how little he has to hide.

She taps her nose. "I wouldn't say that," she says. "There's a bit of rot you journalists will never quite get rid of."

He coughs uncomfortably and tries a new tack. "So, are you working on a new project? Or is this really retirement?"

"No, not working," she sighs. "I've come here to die. When I kick off, they'll have to drag me out of here, but then the property is willed to a charity down in Galveston." This isn't true, but Gloria wants it to be. She just hasn't gotten around to signing the papers.

"That's very generous, and it's a pretty home," he says. "But I'm not so sure you'll stay put."

She doesn't take the bait. "It's a box. But you know, I'm not the only runaway on this hill. I won't name names, but at least one of my session guitarists lives up here, and who's that guy...?" She snaps her fingers, a trick considering her long kitten-pink nails. "You know, the one who stole all the money in the JP Morgan thing? He works at the kosher pizza place in town. So yeah, I'm hardly alone."

They're about thirty miles from central Manhattan, but it takes at least an hour and a half to get from there to here. The mountain road winds for a long time deep into one-lane roads, some paved and some no more than fire roads, cleared once or twice a year. Her house is at the end of a dirt path, just at the edge of a preservation and trailhead, and has three sets of numbers assigned to it, one according to the postal service, one sequential number according to other houses leading up to it, and one that the GPS apparently thinks it is. She is as lost as she can be in spitting distance from the place where she had built her career. She had to pay more than a million-five for the privilege. And yet, he found her.

"So you are alone up here. Finally split from Len?"

She purses her lips. She's surprised by the sting at the mention of their very public divorce, but after a beat, she shakes her hair back and meets his gaze. "Yes. It is amicable. As amicable as these things ever are," she says.

"Which is to say, it's very amicable on his side, since he kept the house and the car and the ranch, and amicable on my side, since I don't have to see, or smell, that popcorn fart ever again." She smirks, her eyes starry.

"Classy," he says.

She hops off the stool to toss the yogurt in the trash. "You want water? Beer? I'm fresh out of malt liquor though."

Stavras cocks his head as if he didn't hear her correctly.

"What?" she says. "I'm a Steel Reserve girl myself. But I drank the last one last night. You thought I might be a moody wine o'clock bitch?"

He seems distracted and says, "I don't know exactly what type I thought you were, to be honest. I came with questions, not presuppositions."

Gloria shoos the Mayor back out into the neighborhood and returns to find Dory, the raccoon, at the back door, and Stavras, frozen in place in the kitchen, in a staring contest.

"The raccoon just slid the door open," he points, a slight tremor in his extended finger.

"And?" Gloria asks. "You don't like raccoons?"

She scoops a handful of almonds, pours them into the same bowl the Mayor used, and places the bowl on the living room coffee table. Dory lumbers over and moves the bowl to the couch cushion, and then climbs up, settling herself in among pillows and using both hands to scrabble the nuts into her mouth.

"They've got thumbs," says Gloria, wiggling her own. Stavras nods and scratches something in his notebook. Gloria settles herself back on her barstool, but he doesn't sit. From her perch, they are about eye-to-eye, which is how she likes it. He clicks his pen nervously, eyes flicking from time to time at the noshing raccoon, but settles down when Dory leans back in the pillows, belly fully exposed and one foot jacked up to the sky, and sinks into a post-prandial nap. Gloria eats a fistful of almonds and waits for Stavras to turn his attention entirely back to her. What a priss, she thinks. Man can't handle his wildlife. But finally, he opens the conversation he's been banging down her door all morning to have.

She falls into the interview, prepared to talk about some of the big missteps in her career. He seems focused on the now, but she has nothing to offer there. Len is still her manager, yet there's nothing to manage. She's spent, out of the game. She wonders idly what kind of story he'll make out of her tangle of dead ends and non-answers. He'll probably do a "Gloria Redmond Has a Cold" job, describing her swinging pink-frosted toes, the French farm decor, the several cats that slink like long lazing boats around his ankles, distressed maple cabinetry, stylish stemware and plastic mugs with crass sayings, exposed beams and linoleum, bunched daffodils and baskets of silk flowers. She cultivates an exacting mix of cheap and luxurious, and he'll have to rely on what he sees, not what she says, about her life. This looks like a grandmother's dream cabin, a crafter's she-shed, but she is not a grandmother, nor even a mother. Her future is wide open, completely unplanned.

"So no new projects? Really? Not even an offer from AGT or a cameo?"

She shakes her head. "No new projects. I've had it with the life, so there's no point to asking. Can't wait to see what you write about me. 'Sad Old Gloria Finally Put Out to Pasture.'" She uses air quotes as she predicts the headline.

"Actually, do you want to hear the working title?" he asks.

"Hit me."

"'Her Gloria Days,'" he says.

"I do love a pun," she says, fake enthusiasm gushing and her voice going a little over-shrill. She hops off her barstool and heads to the back of the house. "C'mon. I got a job for you. I think there's something dead in my car."

"What?" he says, but he quickly gathers his notebook and follows her out the back door.

She settles into the front seat of her Toyota Corolla in perfect condition and rolls down her window. "I smell it through the air vents, so it's somewhere in the engine."

He leans back and she pops the hood open. As soon as he lifts it, he stumbles back and yowls as if he is being attacked by a bear. Before she can get out of the car, he is sprinting down the road, flailing his arms and screaming in a register that reminded her of some shrieky backup singer Gloria had to axe on her second record.

Gloria doesn't see anything through the sliver of space where the hood separates from the car, so when she circles around to the front and lifts the hood, she sees what made him run. A huge albino boa constrictor, maybe eighteen feet long, blond slashes against the pearl of its skin, is curled up on the engine block like a fat abandoned hose. "Aw, poor baby," she says. It must have been someone's pet. She pokes it with a stick.

Just like a man, she thinks. The dust kicked up by his tires as he sped away was like a desert sandstorm. She works to pry the thing from the engine, getting it all except for some bits of skin. Then she uses vinegar to kill the smell and dumps the creature into a black garbage bag that she hauls out to the green bin that came with the place.

People always disappoint Gloria. Alone, at her age, hauling around trash bags like a teenage boy. Her neighbors should be ashamed. Fred cocks his head as he watches her effort, and even he looks like he might pitch in if he didn't weigh less than her purse.

She surveys her backyard. She's only been living here a month, but it's not a hard life, not what she thought it would be. She could even get something to grow in the bed beside the rocky path where she parks her car. The other night, she watched a bear tear through her neighbor's trash like it was at a rummage sale, sampling old fruit and licking an empty pie plate. People did that to the bear, she thinks. They turned it into a scavenger. She had hoped it would be different out here, different from the selfishness on the New York City streets she'd weathered for decades, but it's the same. Only she hates to see the animals suffer.

She wonders what Stavras will write about her. She dodged every question about her music, so he probably has a running commentary about the chicken, the cigarette butts in the flowerpot on her porch, the front window with lush marijuana buds visible through the curtains. It doesn't matter what she says. He will write about what he sees and make his own caricature of her. There's not much she can do but read about it.

She goes back inside, and the house feels smaller. Her hands are empty. And she's alone. Even the dead snake is gone. She leans back on her buttery couch, a frou-frou jacquard microfiber that matches not just the curtains but the tablecloth and the window seat bench as well. She has spent a fortune having this home perfected before she moved in, managing a string of incompetent and ugly handymen. And now that it's all done, she has to admit, she's bored.

She remembers her last fight with Len. It was just after she'd lost a coveted spot on some ice-skating dance show, and five months after The Voice had turned her down, and nine months after America's Got Talent had said no, and a year after her record company had dropped her. A year before that, she hadn't shown up for a Howard Stern interview after he'd called her tits saggy: She knew they weren't because she'd paid through the nose to keep them properly inflated with saline. But the fight with Len was when hope finally slunk out of her. "You had a good run," he'd said. "Hell, a great run. A lot of ladies stopped performing long before you did."

She was so angry she threw a plate at him. She missed.

Then he said, "I'm moving out."

And she screamed and she screamed until her throat turned raw. When she looked up, he was gone. And that's when she quit on herself.

She unlocks her guitar case now and settles it on her lap. She has promised herself it wouldn't come to this, but music is who she is at heart. She strums a little, the chords finding purchase beneath her calloused fingers. She plucks with her nails, leaning back into an old hymn from her church times. Her voice is tight with disuse, and she flushes with shame at the neglect. But she forces it, grabbing air and pushing it out, letting herself belt it as if she were performing for a cast of thousands. She can see their faces in her mind, and it's only then that the tears come. She left her fans on her terms, but she'll miss them more than anything. When she opens her eyes, Fred crows, whether in empathy or adulation, only he knows.

Chapter 2

IT'S DARK AS a cave when Honey Conaway enters her rowhouse. *Door open, door open, door open*, the alarm chirps. "Of course it is," she grouses. "I'm coming in the damn house." She feels along the wall and pushes a key on the pad to make the numbers light up. She enters the code and the alarm quiets. Once she's in, she can flip the light switches and make the house seem lived in.

If it was a good day, Mama would have already flipped on the switches, so Honey knows today is not a good day.

Herbie Hancocker rushes to Honey, misjudging and running into her leg. He yelps, probably surprising more than hurting himself, and he recovers quickly. The vet said Spaniels were predisposed to eye issues. Herbie needs cataract surgery, and Honey's heart tightens. He is her little prince, and she'd do anything for him, but she has to get her own vision fixed up first. The darkness around her left eye is creeping in and she needs to save up to see a doctor about it. Just one more thing on the long list of to-dos.

Mail is scattered on the floor, and she scoops it and Herbie up at the same time. A few pink envelopes for the water bill, electricity. She'll be able to pay them at the end of the month, just a few more days, and her mother's Social Security check will arrive in that time too. That should be enough to keep going for another month. She remembers that she should implement a digital payment plan for her students so she gets paid more regularly. Mia's niece who is studying business at Coppin offered to set that up. She needs to give Mia a call back anyway. More to-dos, more to do.

"Mama?" she calls. "You awake?" But the tang of weed lets her know her mother is up and moving somewhere in the house. Honey sighs and puts the dog down.

She flicks the lights on as she heads up the stairs, stepping past the one with the rotting creak, until she gets to her mother's room. In the dark, leaning into toward the computer screen, her mother sits, wild-haired and squinting. It's hard for Honey to see in the dark, so she flicks on that light too. Her mother looks up in alarm.

"Mama, you doing okay today? Did you eat?"

"I fixed myself something. We need eggs. They fell out the fridge." Her mother shields her eyes, apparently adjusting to the brightness. Herbie makes it up the stairs and sits at Mama's feet, tail wagging wildly.

"I'll pick some up before rehearsal tonight."

"Rehearsal at church?" Mama loves when Honey is practicing church music. "What are you all rehearsing?"

"'There's a Great Day Coming' and 'Trouble of the World.'"

Mama closes her eyes. "No one can top Mahalia on 'Trouble,' baby."

"Don't I know it," Honey says, smiling ruefully. "But I'm gonna try."

Her mother points at the light switch. "Turn that shit off, baby." She stares into the backlit screen, squinting at something. "I gotta watch this again. I think I get what to do, but I'm not sure how he did it."

"At least put on the desk lamp. You're sitting in the dark."

"The screen's making plenty of light. You better get your eyes checked. You need too much light." Her mother leans back toward the grimy screen. She'd been a custodian for years, but it's as if she took a vow never to clean another thing in her life the minute she retired.

"Sitting in the dark is no good for you, especially with the screen. It messes with your melatonin and circadian rhythm. It's why you can't sleep at night." Honey moves around the room, turning on two lower-light lamps before turning off the overhead. "There. I'll make some proper dinner."

Her mother harrumphs and turns back to the computer.

"What are you doing on there, Mama?"

"Pre-calculus." She turns the screen to Honey who sees a black screen with green, white, and pink letters and numbers. Honey heard of pre-calculus back in high school, but her guidance counselor, noting Honey's aversion to algebra, had warned her away from sciences and math. She remembers graphs of compound interest and lots of letters that stood for numbers.

"Are you fixing to balance our budget, Mama?"

"I been done that kind of math," her mother waves her off. "This is pre-*calculus*. I got variables here. Imaginary numbers." Her mother smiles and turns back to the screen. Honey has no idea what *imaginary* numbers even mean! But her mother is happy messing with the computer program, so Honey will take that as a win today.

It's later than she wanted to get home, but Pastor Blodgett cornered her again, looking her up and down like she was a prime rib. She used to be a prime rib, she thinks, patting her flat belly, but Blodgett is not the man for her. She comes by her solos honestly. Still, it would be nice to have a man to cook for as well as her mother every night.

In the kitchen, a carton of eggs lies spent on the floor in front of the refrigerator. Much of the mess has been licked up by Herbie. She checks to see if she can rescue any eggs, but the potential for dog saliva destroys her trust even in the ones that seem relatively intact. She tosses the carton and wipes up the mess with a towel. So much for omelets. Now she's got to get creative with some sort of stir-fry her mother will harrumph at and reject as rabbit food.

She digs around in the vegetable drawers for an onion, carrot, tofu. Her mother hates the vegetarian diet, but she needs low salt and roughage, and the fatty meat she likes isn't good for her heart. More than once, Honey has found takeout bags of KFC stuffed deep in the bottom of the wastebasket. Her mother has never been big on rules, especially ones from doctors.

After she eats her own serving and prepares another, which she knows her mother will say is too gummy and not salty enough, she places the plate of bright vegetables and rice next to her mother at the computer with a clean fork and napkin. The computer drones with someone explaining lines of equations, all neat and small like rows of teeth. Her mother doesn't look away from the screen, and Honey is piqued that her healthy dinner and hard-earned groceries are no match for the draw of, of all things, pre-calculus.

As Honey gathers the cleansers and rags to clean her mother's commode and run the bath, she mentally prepares her week and stretches her range by singing out her schedule from Monday to Friday. She moves through some more vocal exercises, making a mental note to call the voice agency for more work, and then adding it in song to the schedule, as well as the eye doctor and calling Mia. Not long ago, the pandemic dropped Honey's student rolls and her paid performances to nil, and she's just building back from it. The COVID poison was in their voices those years, and the fastest way to spread it was through projecting droplets of the virus into the air. Whole choruses were infected and people died, singing for joy and companionship, for praise and for purpose. Miss Tiffy, Lon, Pastor Bullock, Miss DeeDee, and that church office assistant, gone like ghosts over the first year, as if they just left out on a long vacation and she heard secondhand about their forever trips to heaven. Along with everyone else, she covered her own instrument with a shroud for years afterward. But now, she savors every note in her church. She's fearless. *Let me die singing*, she thinks. *Let me die happy*. If she ever has to stop singing again, it will be the end for her.

Limber, she takes on the aria from *Death and the Maiden*, moving her shoulders forward and back as she slides from her head to chest voice. It's not as easy as it used to be, but nothing is. She loves the bathroom acoustics and knows it's cheating to fill up this space with her voice. She has to control her power or she'll disturb her neighbors. They won't get so riled up they'll come knocking, but they will turn up their own music so loud she won't be able to hear herself sing. She pushes out the final cadence, dropping from an A to D with power and holding it in the fluorescent lights. The bath is warm, the commode sparkling, and she is surrounded by the smell of lemons and vinegar. She feels warm and clean and ready for the night.

She doesn't have to call for her mother. The end of Honey's aria is all her mother needs to know to start the long trek with her walker from the back room to the bathroom. Honey busies herself with lighting candles and arranging smelly soaps. Then she waits with a washcloth.

Honey's mother had been a firecracker back in the day. She called everyone *baby* and she was legendary at the high school where she worked as the head custodian, Miss Dottie. She joked around with the kids and did this little-old-woman routine, mopping in rooms when the kids told her the teacher was too boring. She'd just shuffle in like she couldn't hear and mop around the teachers' feet. The teachers all knew the gag. They called it "jumping the shark" because the teachers knew their boring lessons had been called out when Miss Dottie showed up.

Dottie used to tell everyone she worked with that Honey was going to be the next Minnie Riperton, the next Diana Ross, the next Leontyne Price, and she bought albums and took Honey to listening parties at her friends' houses when she didn't have a new album herself. Honey wowed the adults with her baby-rich voice, sounding like a grown woman by the time she was twelve. When Honey got into the Baltimore School for the Arts, all the faculty at Dottie's school came out to see Honey's performances, taking up two whole rows in the ballroom and showering her with roses after they ended. Honey was at first embarrassed and then proud of her mother for rallying such a crowd. When Honey got solo performances, her mom's squad would appear there too, and they would hold parties to celebrate even small accomplishments like her backup gigs and the award she won for National Young Artists. These parties were the biggest parties in the world, with crazy loud music and mamas getting down and tattoo artists and trays and trays of food catered by the school's cafeteria workers. Everyone on the block and beyond turned out for Honey. She always felt like a queen.

In the fall of her senior year, Honey won an internship at the London Opera House, but she couldn't afford to get there. Her mother got odd jobs to make ends meet and took in a boarder, Julie or Judy something, who she used to work with, for the extra money and to use as a babysitter for little Barnabas, Honey's brother. But even with the extra funds, it wasn't even near enough for a plane ticket and the cost for lodging. Instead, as soon as she had her diploma, Honey took the money her mother had saved up and moved to New York with her friend Psalm. She had one dream: to sing at the Metropolitan Opera House. But the two of them had failed audition after audition after audition, even for volunteer gigs. The competition was just too intense, and there wasn't much need for a contralto opera singer on Broadway. Psalm wound up getting a job at a public relations agency, and Honey couldn't keep up her rent. Soon Psalm's boyfriend was angling to start a family in the little two-bedroom, which meant Honey needed a different place to sleep. She had been auditioning day and night and making ends meet with a restocking job at Duane Reade, sending money home when she could.

But then it all turned around for Honey. She got a call for backup vocals, and it turned out to be on a track for Elton John, which put wings on her career. Her agent sent her flowers and rang her phone off the hook. Soon she was being requested for backing vocals, and then she was offered her own record deal. Baltimore seemed to retreat farther and farther from her, her mother's and little brother's voices getting smaller and smaller as the bigger and bigger players in the industry took up more space in her life. Too tired to return their calls, she hoped they would trust that she loved them and understood her focus on her career. She bought them a house and sent them money for Bunny's schooling.

But just as she got close enough to the sun to feel the warmth on her skin, her wings melted, and she plummeted back here, to earth, by her mother's side. No one would touch her, and she had earned the moniker "Crazy Conway." People threw things at her on the street, and she was laughed out of interviews. She was on her last $200 when her mother got into a car accident.

Her mother was way too young for retirement, but after the accident, her body was busted from so much hard labor. She was diagnosed with diabetes, a heart murmur, and lupus, on top of the damage to her legs and spine from the accident. Honey found herself busy with their mother's physical needs, and she reached out to her alma mater for teaching contracts while her reputation healed.

Her brother missed her return, but she was so ashamed by her fall from grace that she considered it a blessing. He was off to serve their country at eighteen, and she was saddled with a life sentence restocking adult diapers and gauze pads and baby wipes in her own house.

Her mother is clean but not out of the tub when Honey's phone buzzes. Honey's heart leaps as she sees the name pop up on her screen **maybe: Savion Kimberman.** Her mind floods with love and light as she remembers Savion. He had been a couple years ahead of her in school, but they were in the same department. Honey recalls how, as a freshman, she was paired with him for a duet during the spring concert. He was such a big personality, and she felt like she might disappear next to him, so she wore her hair natural and puffed out to make herself bigger. She applied rose-purple lip color and donned a shimmery blue dress. He was in a purple and blue Nehru jacket and looked fine as hell. Honey's whole gallery were losing their shit while she and Savion led "Ain't No Mountain High Enough" with Honey's boyfriend Damon on drums. Savion thought the cheering was for him and he was eating it up, but when the whole crew rushed Honey at the end of the performance, he saw she was something real.

"Don't worry, baby," her mother had said to him afterward, patting his cheek. "You sing all right too."

Honey smiles at the memory as she ducks into the cold, dark hallway to answer the call. "Savion!"

A woman's voice responds. "Hello, is this Honoria Conaway?"

Honey resettles herself. "Yes, this is she."

"Mr. Kimberman is recording a new album and would be interested in having you in one of the sessions. It's very collaborative, and you would have a lot of artistic control. Would you be interested?"

Honey tries to keep herself from exploding with joy as she ekes out a fraction of her voice. "Yes, please!"

Chapter 3

THIS AIRBNB is supposed to inspire Serafina's next project, but so far, it has been a bust. The pool is leaking into the basement, nearly flooding the rehearsal space, and her collaborator, Michigan, has been called away because his wife went into labor. Everybody's getting pregnant, everyone's getting out of the scene. She's stuck in this mansion alone. She's thinking about a retrospective, but Taylor just did that with her *Eras* tour, and Serafina wants something fresh. She wonders if, after three years in the limelight, it's too early for a retrospective. She's been working all her damn life, so why not drop back to her musical journey? She could start with a video of herself as a four-year-old in a ballerina getup, singing along to the Clash's "I Fought the Law" on her mom's cell phone. After that, guitar lessons, singing lessons…. Boring. She doesn't want to admit it, but her dreams of a retrospective are a giant neon-orange sign that she is completely creatively blocked.

As she looks around the grounds, she knows this place was the wrong choice. She should have rented a fourth-floor walkup in New York City, something fun and loud and gritty and that would strengthen her calves. Instead, she's on this beautiful estate in the middle of Connecticut with nothing around. She can't write about duck ponds or pebble labyrinths. Noey is in Jamaica and Serafina is alone to write this album. She wants to write about her breakup with Dane, but though it's been more than a year, she's not really feeling the ache that usually follows a breakup. They weren't really even together, and now Dane is dating that dude who was on that Nickelodeon show back in the day, and she knows if she writes about him leaving her for a guy, the whole LGBTQ army will be after her for being homophobic. Which she isn't. Obviously. She's just bitter. And she's not feeling intensely enough for Noey to write a new-love album. So she's stuck. What do people write about when they don't have anything going on, when life is just... fine?

She opens her notebook and draws for a bit, writing silly rhyming words that don't go anywhere. She drinks wine and feels sorry for herself, binges *Ugly Betty*, sits on the white leather couch and cries.

Somewhere around two a.m., she wakes, unsure where she is. She is sticking to the white leather and swivels around to find a thermostat. She peels her ass off the furniture and stumbles around, peeking around corners to find some way to drop the temperature. As she scans the room, her gaze falls on a record player that she hadn't noticed before. The Daisy the Great song "Record Player" pops into her head, and she hums the little earworm as she bends down to inspect the machine.

She discovers a stack of albums in a wicker basket under the player and she drags it out to flip through. She loves the way her fingers feel, stepping across the worn cardboard edges. The records all appear to be from the last century, probably a bunch of rejects that you wouldn't keep anywhere but in an Airbnb, more for decor than for utility. But one of the first ones she comes across as she flips through is familiar. She remembers it from her dad's house when she was a little girl, spending hours on his shag rug with earphones on while he fought with his girlfriends or played poker and smoked cigars with his friends. On the album cover is a photo of a blonde woman with high, teased-up hair and a short blue denim mini-dress with white tassels. Serafina's eyes widen to the neon pink scrawl of the title *Last Best Shot*. Gloria! Oh, how as a girl, she loved listening to the inimitable Gloria Redmond.

Serafina slips the record onto the turntable and expertly drops the needle, but no sound comes out. Totally anticlimactic. She has to push a few more buttons on the player to get the sound to come out of both speakers, but it's fuzzy with super-loud pops like her dad's player used to make. She uses her eyebrow brush to dust the needle clean and blows dust off the vinyl. When the needle slips back into the groove, the first slashing guitar licks shriek into the air, followed by Gloria's signature clean soprano warble. Damn, that woman can sing.

Serafina takes another gulp of wine and rummages through her purse for one of the blunts she tucked in before she left. For the next thirty minutes, blazing up, she tunes her own airy voice along the bright, throaty edge of Gloria's country pop voice, finding pockets to harmonize and spaces where they are so in tune she can barely tell them apart.

"I should do a fucking duet album," she says aloud, loving the sound of her own voice blasting a new idea into the room. She says it again, and the more times she says it, the clearer it is to her. "With only the baddest-ass women I can think of."

Serafina googles Gloria as she finishes the first bottle of wine. She finds a recent article in *Dervish*: Apparently Gloria is living in upstate New York. Serafina giggles as she scrolls through Gloria's antics—a dead boa constrictor, a chicken, a shotgun. Up to her old tricks. As Serafina trawls through the article, she learns about how Gloria was pulled over doing 45 in a go-cart, how she talked her way into a photo shoot with Margaret Thatcher, how she cohabitates with a raccoon she taught to use the back door to come and go as it pleases. With each story, Serafina laughs uproariously. "I've got to get this bitch to sing with me," she smiles and laughs. Even Gloria's song lyrics betray her wit.

You can come back lately, but you better come back a man,
'cause I'm one lovely lady,
and you're beer
in an empty can.

She starts a list of other badass legends she'd like to partner with.

Gloria Redmond - obvi, the QUEEN!
Pat Benatar - total badass
Belinda Carlisle and Jane
Sian Harper - crashed the Rock & Roll Hall of Fame - classic!
That Riot Grrl girl
Joan Baez - yasss, preach!
Madonna, of course!
Joni Mitchell - what was she radical for?
Bonnie Raitt - too country?
Kim Deal? Kelley Deal? - whichever one was the drunk.
Anny Jeffers - kicked a horse once, right?
MAREN MORRIS
Liz Phair - badass songs at least
freaking Courtney Love
Queen Latifah?
Gaga got kicked out of a Mets game
Missy Elliott
Selena (did she die?)

Serafina tosses the notepad onto the tight weave carpet. She can call her manager, Jorge, in the morning and talk it over with him.

She flips through the other albums in the bin, hunting other hidden treasures. A whole lotta nothing, other than the Gloria album. Serafina spends the night scrolling through her phone to figure out which of these artists are still performing, living, dead, off the grid, or too old to perform. She has a healthy list by the end and a plan for action.

In the violent sunlight unmitigated by blinds, Serafina wakes with a raging headache, but she is so pleased with the work she did while she was completely blitzed, it barely matters. She drinks a vitamin C mix and slaps a hangover patch on her arm and tries to sit as still as she can. The house is illuminated and gorgeous, the lawn outside beckoning for a picnic lunch or a meditation session, or even sunbathing. It's a perfect day, and she doesn't want to waste it, and she wants to do some songwriting. But she can't bear the sun just yet, so she closes the shades to avoid regret.

The wicker basket is still sitting in the middle of the room, records fanned out around her. She wants to make a record, not a CD or playlist, but a real record. Vinyl is coming back. And it would be a tribute to the women on the album. In the daylight, the pink scrawl on Gloria's album looks tacky, and the songs contain too much '80s overproduction. Still, Gloria's voice has always been true. That and her legs. Woman doesn't have a lick of cellulite on her.

Serafina's cell phone buzzes and she sees it's Jorge. She grabs up the phone and it slips out of her hand, hitting the glass table at just the right angle so that a huge crack splinters out.

"Dammit!" She extracts her phone from the spiky glass and stabs the answer button. "Hey you. I just fucked up the table. But I have a genius idea."

"Yes, you sent many texts last night," he says. "Many texts."

"Sorry. I was excited." She feels chided, but she's too embarrassed to see what she sent him. She does remember, at one point, suggesting a trio with Whitney Houston and Billie Eilish, and winces.

"Why don't you tell me about your plan?" He gives her all his attention and listens patiently to her plan, asking careful questions about permissions, venues, the appearance of collabs with some of the women on the deeper fringes. He sets the record straight on some of her assumptions, and she surreptitiously fact-checks him. He is right about the Deal twins. Where did she hear so much negative shit about them? She keeps them on the list though.

"Serafina, sweetheart," he asks, patiently. "Why this? Why now?"

He's the only older man she'd let call her *sweetheart* because he has an earnest attentiveness that she craves, but she wishes he would just trust her. "What do you mean? It's fucking brilliant!" She rubs her finger against the spidery crack of the table, relishing the sharp prick digging into her skin.

"I don't think it's a bad plan, but it ought to come from somewhere. It needs an origin. What's the story we want to tell with this album?"

She chews her lip, thinking. "What's wrong with just celebrating women's badassery? Isn't that the story?" Her finger is bleeding. She uses the blood to dip into where the glass splintered creating a splatter.

"It can be," he says. "But you keep using the word 'badass' like it's self-explanatory. Are you trying to redeem these women by having them partner with you? Bring them into the spotlight?"

"Yeah, I guess." She hasn't really considered that the album would send any kind of message. "Look, I made an album cover already," she says and sends a photo of the bloody table to him. "What do you think?"

His phone dings and he is quiet for a minute. "Jesus," he says. "Serafina, this is a gimmick. You can't make an album out of a glass table with blood on it. I mean, I want you to think about the optics of hiring seasoned musicians just so you can do duets with them. You don't want this to be a charity album, or like you want to give them an energy shot of your mojo. For most of them, they won't consider this a comeback, and in fact, many won't want to make a comeback. Several of these women have been facing other issues—bankruptcy, domestic abuse, dependency. I mean, just think about it."

"So you don't want me to give them a chance?"

He sighs. "I guess I'm just asking, a chance at what? Your coattails are not that long. Consider the fact that instead of you being the draw, you being the one they will be indebted to, you should think about how you would honor each one. These are some really talented and celebrated women. They're not party tricks."

Serafina knows he's right, but she's not sure what he's right about. She sees how, if she could switch places with any one of them, they would jump at the chance to be on her next album, but maybe it's just for the wrong reasons.

"So you're saying it's like the, what was it... Live Aid, or Farm Aid, or whatever, for past heroines of rock?"

He sighs. She can tell she's not getting it, and she's getting mad at herself. She presses her palm into the table until the glass does shatter and her hand is full of red cuts. It stings, but that's the point. She holds her fist tight, trying not to freak out and concentrates through the pain. "Let me do this. I need something like this right now. It is... it just fucking feels right."

He says, "Okay, you seem most excited about Gloria. I heard you talk about how cool she is and that you loved her music as a child. What was it about her music that got you through? What did you connect to?"

Serafina's mind returns to that den with the shaggy carpet, the green glass barware, and the smell of cigars seeping through the panel door to the other room where her dad was. She hadn't gotten along with her dad back then. He talked to her gruffly when she had questions about her body. Like, one day, she was bleeding from her butthole and she told him about it, terrified of what he would say. He shrugged. "Probably hemorrhoids," and that was it. He didn't get her medicine, didn't take her to a doctor, didn't ask any questions. She could have been butt-raped, but he was just super incurious.

And so she'd tried to get his attention. She tried all kinds of things like staying out late and bringing boys up to her room, but no matter how late or drunk or sluttily dressed she was when she came home, he just wanted to talk to her about her singing career, about the money she was making, about her next fucked-up gig. He was only interested in her making him money, and that's all she really was good for, she knew.

She'd longed for a mother at that time. She wanted a woman who would tell her the truth about her body, why things did what they did. What to do when her pee was too yellow, or not yellow enough, how to fix the sores inside her mouth, to take ibuprofen just before her cycle, how to floss so her teeth didn't hurt in the morning, how to get safe birth control pills or even what red flags she should watch for with boys. She felt like she didn't know anything and her friends' mothers seemed to arm their little girls with truckloads of knowledge, about their bodies and men's bodies, and feelings, and outbursts, and what was okay to think and what wasn't okay to think.

And so when she discovered Gloria, she felt like she was getting the lowdown. Like Gloria was sharing the facts of life in every song. She sang about wanting a man who could handle a little blood during sex in "Seeing Red":

And when you saw red, your look didn't disarrange.
You didn't lose your head, 'cause sheets can be changed...

She also broached the subject of hygiene in her most popular song, "The Five Items." Every girl Serafina knew growing up could whine like Gloria did in her spoken-word pout and then name those five items.

You wanna see, lover?
You wanna see them five items in my purse?
Let's take a look, shall we?
I got lipstick, roll-on, mascara, tampon,
and a little black Colt in a pocket in the back.

There was even a hand-clapping game that went with it. Her songs told about men who ought not be worth a woman's time, how to treat a woman right, and about believing in yourself when no one else seems to notice you.

And Gloria's song, "Stone," which just seemed to speak directly to Serafina about losing her mother:

You weren't there when I turned to stone.

Something about that tight loss, that feeling of acute emptiness, the sting and throb of what Serafina's sliced-up palm felt like right now—that feeling of turning to stone was what made her feel closest to Gloria. Gloria knew what it was like to lose a daughter—she was somehow certain of this. Gloria could have been her substitute mother in that moment when Serafina drank her in through the headphones on that shag rug. Gloria had been speaking directly to Serafina, this little stone goddess Daddy sold for her precious ore.

"Mothers," Serafina chokes out, surprising herself with the emotion that has welled up in her. "They're the mothers I didn't have."

"There you go!" She could hear Jorge's smile through the receiver. "Now you have a reason to call them together to make an album. They brought you up! Now, sweetie. Now we make a plan!"

Chapter 4

"A MOTHERS album? Are you fucking kidding me? Do I look like I wanted to be anyone's mother? Fuck no! Fuck her, and fuck no." Gloria is holding a wine glass so hard it cracks, shooting a shard of glass into her thumb. "Ouch, goddamn it! I'll call you back."

She puts down the phone and sucks the shard out of her finger. She rinses the flesh. It's not a deep cut, but what is Len thinking bringing her this basic project with a twenty-eight-year-old cheerleader? The phone buzzes again and she stabs the answer button and then puts it on speaker.

"I'm bleeding over here. Let me call you back."

"I thought you stopped bleeding years ago." Gloria can hear Len's *heh-heh-heh* as he cracks himself up.

"And you want to know why I divorced you."

"I know why you divorced me. And I know why you still answer my calls."

"Don't flatter yourself." She wraps a paper towel around her finger and presses on it. "Plus seriously, I got glass in my finger." She hears the punchline in her head and mouths it as he says it: "You'll never play piano again."

"I'd FaceTime you, but you're gonna have to extend your screen," she says.

"Why?"

"To see how far back my eyes are rolling."

He clears his throat. Probably smoking again. "So what can it hurt? You could use the publicity."

"The last thing I want is publicity. I moved here to avoid publicity."

"You moved to Orange County. You don't want to be out of the news cycle, or at least not as far out of it as you pretend. You did the interview with *Dervish*, with Stavras. I read it."

"You sicced him on me. I tried to talk him to death, but he wouldn't leave." She opens the curtains and sees a couple on their way past her house, taking pictures. She waves her fingers at them and smiles but closes the curtains just as the guy lifts his phone for a picture.

"The snake was a nice touch," says Len. "Classic."

Gloria blushes. "It was a lot of snake. And I actually felt bad about it. Probably a perfectly nice pet."

"Eh, you can't live without attention. I bet everyone on your block is talking about you."

"What 'block?' The house is on a dirt road." She taps her fingernails on the counter. She knows he's right. Since she moved up here, hikers seem to have discovered a convenient trail that runs right by her house, and she has found herself putting on makeup to do the gardening. "All right, but none of this Mother shit."

"Not *her* mother. Like the mother of women in rock. A matriarch."

"Ugh, that's even worse." She spits out the word: "*Matriarch*. Makes me think of a woman with iron tits and a steel-gray bob."

"Okay, so what about *Mama*. That can be sexy. You've been called a hot mama before? I'm pretty sure I've called you a hot mama in the heat of passion."

"If you have, and if you've called it 'the heat of passion,' it hasn't done shit for me. Just thinking of all this is making my cooch dry up like a bone."

He is waiting for her to say yes, but she's not enjoying making him wait. This flirting is already dead old, and she wants him to hang up and not bother her again. "Fine. Come back to me with *Mama*. I can make that work. Text me a list of the other 'Mamas' who say yes, and if I hate any one of them, I'm out."

"It's a deal. I knew you'd make the right move." She can hear him shuffling papers, knows he's thinking about his cut. But she's tired. That's why she came out here, to get away from his slick-Rick deals and sweet talk. Sure, she can fly to LA or wherever, sing a bit, and collect a check. Then she can still die in this house when it's time and fuck around until then. It's possible. Just means she'll be able to spend a little more money on whatever she wants. She tries to picture the little pink French soaps she likes and a new wraparound dress. She could do this one last favor.

Gloria is going over the *Dervish* article with a Sharpie, crossing out parts she doesn't like. When she's done, the whole thing is just a weird little poem.

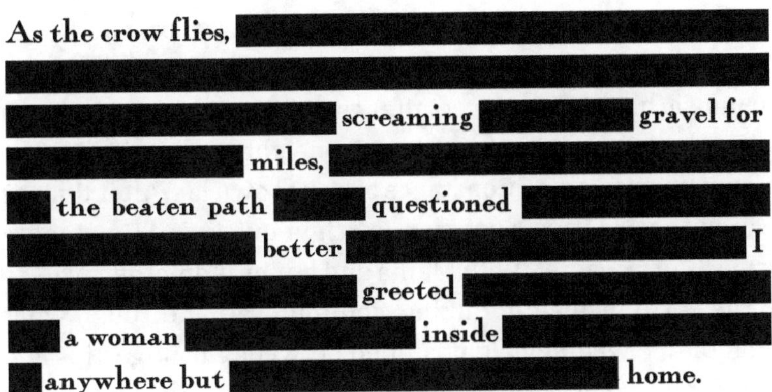

She caps the Sharpie and admires her handiwork. Checks her makeup and adjusts how low her space-kitty button-down fits over her ass. She grabs her spade and steps into her wellies to dig up the potatoes that are finally leafy enough to be pulled.

The dirt reminds her of her grandmother. Gloria conjures her in stolid memories as she tears into the earth. When she'd worked with her grandmother in the garden, Gloria could usually see her mother on the phone and drinking wine in the kitchen or standing on the porch, monitoring the hard womanly work happening over vegetables she wanted no part of, having given up caring for another child who would break her heart. Gloria and her grandmother would kneel in the dirt, breaking up clods with the edges of their trowels, working out some sort of anger, Gloria's nascent and her grandmother's crystallized, on the hard clay clumps. When nothing Gloria planted would grow, her grandmother would announce the fault well into the season. "You didn't plant it in the light" or "The soil here doesn't drain enough." Only once did Gloria suggest she could have used some advice, and that occasion was all it took for her to learn an important lesson about blame.

She assumes she and her grandmother would have had a fabulous relationship if her grandmother had gotten to see her sing or perform. Her grandmother had taught Gloria guitar, had taught Gloria's mother guitar, taught it to anyone who would listen and try to learn. Gloria doesn't have a clear memory of learning to sing, just the constant harmonizing in her house. She, her sisters Marjorie and Constance, and her brother Don. Cooking, cleaning, ironing, joking around, all of it was done to song.

The music had only stopped after the violence to Constance, and the street justice that ended with the nasty neighbor shot dead. Mama and Daddy split up over it, and Constance took her own life. After that, because they were of age, Marjorie got married right quick, and Don took a job in California. Gloria was left with Mama and her grandmother, who dug and dug in the earth instead of talking, communicating through what grew and what didn't, what felt right rubbed between the fingertips and what felt mealy and wrong, what smelled true, even if it was dank or sour, and what smelled toxic, even if it was sweet or light. Gloria learned the rules of life from her grandmother, while her mother smirked and watched over from the window, half waiting for Gloria to turn soft and man-crazy. Gloria never let herself turn. She grew up stone-hard, never letting a man see a flash of weakness, nothing a blade couldn't fix.

She lets herself hum a few lines, seeing how the sound mixes with the heavy work, if she can suss out a rhythm that her voice can steady and ease. She finds herself first landing in Patsy Cline territory, warming her vocal cords with "Anytime," which doesn't demand nearly as much of her range as "Crazy" or "I Fall to Pieces." She warms up further with another song from Dolly Parton called "Wildflowers." It feels right, turning soil and splitting the tiny little tangled roots of her seedlings while singing about flowers that don't care where they grow. The last frost on this mountain appears to be over, so she has hope that at least something will thrive in the rocks and loamy earth. But she also hopes to find something she didn't plant that makes its way into her garden just as it pleases. If she likes the look of it and if it gets along with others, she'll be happy to make space for it and nurture it along with her own tiny green columbine and vervain and frostweed and okra seedlings. If not, she won't feel bad turning it out onto the stone path to dry up in the sun. The way of the world, as it is with the plant kingdom, so it is in the human kingdom. Don't be an asshole and you'll always have a place to lay your body down.

Her voice is stretching and she leans her neck back to get some sun on it. It's not a warm day, and her hands are growing frosty and stiff, but she feels good. She sings one of her own songs then, a ballad she wrote about losing a child, but only she knows what the lyrics mean. Most people think it's about her sister, but she remembers the flush of her womb and the potential of life in it, the devastation of its failure. She would be hard inside because she couldn't bear to be the earth, couldn't bear to be fragile enough to crack open and make space for another thing to live briefly and give up on her, taking her love down with it.

We had big dreams, the two of us,
Just a rainbow on the sea.
A trick, and a glimmer of light
And you just ceased to be.

But I didn't decide to be alone.
You weren't there when I turned to stone.

She's singing full-throated now, twisting the trowel into the dirt, carving out cylinders for her little dirt pots, when she feels a familiar warmth, the attention of an audience. About a dozen onlookers have amassed near the fence, walking slowly. A few are clearly filming her with their cameras. As much as she loves herself an audience, she has to nip this in the bud, lest she become a red dot on some sightseer's travel map somewhere. All a leech needs is to get one little sucker into your skin and pretty soon, you're working for free.

"Ain't you boiled onions never heard of privacy?" she yells, angling her trowel like a knife. Several of them hurry on, holding their hands up in some sort of apology. One woman yells out, "We miss you, Gloria," and Gloria's cheeks burn with the pride of it. Most of them have dispersed, but one ogler just smirks over his phone, not even looking up from his screen. He's wearing a flannel and chinos and looks like one of those assholes who owns a yacht but takes his kids camping because he's too cheap to take them somewhere nice.

She picks up a rock and hurls it at him. He doesn't register what is happening right away, and it catches him in the shoulder, making him drop his phone.

"Ow! Fuck! You crazy bitch!"

"I'm crazy? I'll sue you so hard for invasion of privacy that you..." but she is stopped by another presence.

George, a guy in his fifties who lives down the way, is wearing a militia-grade vest, camouflage cap, and a civilian camouflage shirt tightly hugging his ample stomach. Gloria can sense how hard he's breathing by the steam billowing from his beard. When she'd first met him, George had seemed eccentric, goofy, a little fringey. She invited him in, and they smoked a bowl, and she sprayed him with a pine cleaner and vinegar mix so he could hide his post-high from his wife. Gloria detected the prepper in him, but not the killer. He's holding a rifle and pointing it at Mr. Flannel.

"Move along," George says patiently. Gloria isn't fooled into believing that George won't pull the trigger, either out of fear or stupidity, and she's too far away to physically intercede.

The guy puts his hands up. "I got kids. Don't do it, man."

Gloria tracks where the man's eyes are darting. Sure enough, two little kids are about a hundred feet farther along, geared up with backpacks, probably headed up to the public campground about half a mile down the road.

"George…" she says, but she can see George has already registered the kids. He lowers the rifle and his face broadens into a smile.

"Hey, hey boys. I'm just joking." His smile doesn't reach his eyes. Even Gloria takes a step back.

Mr. Flannel plays along but doesn't take his eyes off George. "Luke, Charlie, stay right there. He's just playing a game, but we're finishing up."

The boys don't come closer. Gloria can see how scared they are. She didn't ask for George's protection and doesn't think she needs it. But she's been around guys like George before, and she knows how to play along.

George lays the gun on the ground. "Game's over." He puts the rifle down on the ground and lifts his hands. Ultimately, he looks scarier to Gloria, broader and less jolly, and now his uneven smile makes his face straight-up terrifying.

Gloria pipes in, making sure the threat isn't lost on the father. "Yeah, your dad lost the game. He can go home and practice not being a dick."

Mr. Flannel gives her a discreet middle finger and hustles off with his probably broken cellphone to scramble up the mountain with the boys. He shucks on his own backpack, and the three of them disappear down the trail to have a shitty camping trip that's already ruined and is likely to get worse due to bears and the cold. He should have just taken them to Disney.

"You all right, Miss Gloria?"

"Never better, George. Put the gun away." She thinks to say more, but later, once her mind is right again.

George gives a civilian salute and hustles back to his ratty old rancher with the peeling siding. Maybe he should take up another hobby, she thinks. Like taking care of his own shit first.

She comes back inside and warms up her hands in lukewarm water, breathing to settle her stomach after the near firefight. She doesn't know George well enough to sense whether the hiker was in real danger, or if it was just a threat, if the gun was loaded or just a prop. She doesn't want to find out.

After her nerves settle, she picks up the song where she left off, just to get herself back to a full, even calm. Inside the house, she hears how her voice reverberates in the high ceilings, how it sounds like a prayer, or not really a prayer, but like gospel music. She hopes some higher power does have the measure of this work down here on earth. Men have always been throwing around too much power, and she's so damned tired of keeping them in check with her wit and sass.

Maybe she will do this Serafina thing. What could it hurt? She's getting sick of this place already. Maybe she will take a listen to Serafina to see if they might vibe. Gloria wonders whether she does have just one more teeny comeback left in her.

Chapter 5

HONEY PRESSES forward down the gleaming produce aisle, her trip out to the county Walmart practically a vacation. She walks slowly, considering avocados she knows she won't get to before they go bad. She likes the brightness of the place, the overhead lighting that makes the vegetables seem fresher and less dingy. Her phone buzzes with an unfamiliar number, and she considers whether it might be Savion's people. It's not a New York exchange, so she sends it to voicemail. She's been getting plenty of calls these days for recording work for commercials and backup tracks, but she doesn't trust the gig-work site she's been using, not since the unpleasantness with that Candy Cotton band and the check that had never arrived, the sheepish, *They didn't take any of your tracks for the song* excuse, as if it weren't the recording fee that had been negotiated. And then her discovery of those laid tracks on the songs of at least six other artists. She doesn't negotiate with chop shops, and she doesn't want to be paid nothing for contributing to an untold number of works of art she'll stumble over only later and whose creators she will never have the funds to bring a lawsuit against. She is not a volunteer, and she should be paid fairly.

But the work is skimpy, and though the Blessed Heaven Revival performance had been a blast, they'd sent the fat old fart Reverend Blodgett to sweat and haw over how tithing was down this year and contributions were not what they had projected, and blah, blah, blah. Honey doesn't like to be unkind, but one must mind not to be taken advantage of. She knows just as well as any of the hardworking and underpaid women who preceded her in the music business to put her purse on the piano and wait until the payment is inside the bag. Only then do you share your gift. Honey had taken half up front, and she's glad she got that down payment, because according to Reverend Blodgett, the rest of her payment was sitting in the kingdom of heaven.

So that leaves the school, and though she hustles from choral classes to individual sessions, at the end of the week, all collected, minus her set-aside taxes, she pays the necessities: mortgage, gas, electric, cell phone bill, internet, cable, house phone, car insurance, house insurance, mom insurance. Then come the checks to the hospitals for what Medicaid doesn't cover. Then a little bit for Mama's medical marijuana, and a twenty-dollar bill for her own spending money. The rest is what is left for food and emergencies.

Earlier, she saw that her mother had dropped another whole carton of eggs trying to tug it out of the fridge, so Honey had to mop it up. She blamed herself for putting it on the upper shelf. Maybe, she thinks now, she should put a couple eggs in a bowl so her mother can get to them and break only two at a time, but then she risks breaking a porcelain bowl every day. Her mother can't help it, negotiating the walker and the stairs, trying to feed herself during Honey's long days away. She ought to call the Medicaid people again and see if she can get a home health aide or at least a visiting nurse. The doctors are cagey about Mama's condition though. They seem to think that she can fend for herself on less than what Honey knows Mama needs. If any one of them would come trade shoes with Honey for a day, she knows they would write up all kinds of paperwork to get Mama a good deal more medical care, if only to keep the cranky old woman quiet.

Honey already spent all of last week's food money on Monday preparing for the week, so she has fourteen luxurious spending dollars left to replace the eggs. The cheapest dozen she finds on the shelf is on sale, so she grabs it and carefully inspects each egg before latching the carton and placing it in the cart. That will leave her with a little more than ten dollars, and she resolves to hold that back so she'll have more next week, though she knows it will never happen. Before Friday, that ten will be gone, plus interest on whatever she is forgetting about or needs to fix or replace.

She's so tired of this particular hustle. Part of her wants to just get a regular old job with a regular old paycheck, something with spreadsheets—not like she has any idea how to work one—or something where her title would be Assistant such-and-such. The secretary at her representation agency, for instance, has a title like *Assistant Representation Agent* or *Assistant Talent Agent.* Honey could do a job like that, take phone calls from out-of-work artists and lie her face off to them, tell them how important they are and then wait for days or months to cut the check, hold them back from work just enough until the agent knows they'll be desperate for their next job, so desperate they'll work with shady clients or sing on crappy, overproduced pap. Or, as she has done in the past, deliberately mimic someone else's singing voice to get the effect of that person of greater fame onto the album.

Ghostsinging. The first time, when she'd been coached into echoing Nina Simone, it was subtle, a couple suggestions for phrasing, some "Give me some anger under it, some power," from the engineer. Before she knew it, he shouted excitedly, "That's right, I love me some Mississippi goddamn!" She heard herself in that sacred space and woke up to this grinning white boy giving her a thumbs-up and then rolling her into the next line. She cracked in that moment, realizing the weight of it, the blasphemy, the betrayal of what she was doing. She flailed around for some way to disguise it. She had to finish out the song to match what he'd captured, and as soon as she got it and he called it a wrap, the shame struck her like a slash of fire across her face. She marched out to the parking lot in a heat of shame and rage. She cried in the front seat, telling herself she'd been tricked and bamboozled and that it had happened to so many people along the way that it was just her time. She constructed a sorry-ass justification that since Nina had passed, it was in her memory, a tribute of sorts. But that was only to find some small way to forgive herself, because she knew if she didn't forgive herself, she was going to drive her car off a bridge. She knew she needed to get herself clean of what had happened.

"Never again," she told her tear-streaked face in the rearview mirror. "Never again will you let them do that to you or to Nina. Or any other woman who has earned her right to own her art. Never again."

So when she later found herself in a similar recording booth, the engineer coaching her toward a specific sound, she sleuthed it out. He was looking for the warm naïveté of Tracy Chapman. On the next beat, she opened her eyes and deadpanned, note for note, the first two lines of "Fast Car."

Dumbass white boy actually clapped for her. "Yes, you know exactly what I mean! Just like that, only use the lyrics on the sheet, like we practiced."

She balled up the paper and dropped the crumpled lyrics on the floor. "You want Tracy Chapman? Hire Tracy Chapman."

She wishes the story had ended with her leaving the studio, riding off on her high horse and becoming a genius in her own right. But it didn't. Like everything else in the music business, the vision was negotiated, the lyrics flattened back onto the desk, so she could sound "Tracy Chapman-esque," but not mimic the voice exactly. One more dirty little concession in a filthy, filthy industry.

So today, when her agent Gregor called, somehow clearly aware how much she was hurting for money, she didn't even ask whether it was an impression of a signature voice, or an a cappella performance to be chopped up for sounds and samples, or a four-part harmony created by one voice—her own. She said yes. And now, standing here in the grocery, with the promise of another check and the dream of working with Savion on something she could creatively co-construct, something that would maybe even let her rebuild her name, perhaps dare to strive for that freedom of fame she'd once so nearly had, she is able to breathe just a little bit because if her mother drops the eggs again, she might have a little more than a $10 buffer to get her through the rest of the week.

After another demoralizing session where she sings out the phone number to an online betting site at least eighty times before the client finally
calls it "not so damned operatic" that he can use it, she's on her way to
Savion's gig. They did pay her in cash, and while she was in the studio, the
engineer, knowing Honey well enough to know she'd say yes to just about
anything, tacked on an emergency recording for some little theme song
for a television pilot, not even the track they'll use for the eventual show.
So she has a cool two hundred in her pocket and a date with an old friend.

Savion had given her the address for a recording studio in Chelsea,
somewhere in a nondescript medium-rise. As always, New York immediately senses her cash and makes a grab at it. What she saved on dis-
count bus fare into New York, she has spent on a costly taxi to make her
appointment. She is sitting on a folding chair beside an empty desk in a
quiet room. The elevator sped her to the right floor, but no one opened
the door when she knocked, so she went in, and here she is. On a desk
is a half-drained smoothie melting into some paperwork, and the only
noise is the frequent five-rings of the telephone before, she assumes,
voicemail picks up. These come in small bursts sometimes, three or four
calls back-to-back, and she can effortlessly imagine herself on the other
side, fretting over a check or some bad press or whatever. This is where
those calls go, she knows. Nowhere.

Not a soul has even acknowledged Honey is here or given her any
sheet music or even a sense of what she'll be singing. The details in the
email were skimpy, and there was an empty file as an attachment, so she's
wholly unprepared. Her response to the email went unanswered. She is
in the right place, she hopes, but it's possible, based on how disorganized
this whole plan is, that this isn't the right place or right time.

She has rescheduled a lesson back at the school to get here on time,
and she's kicking herself because the child, Nala, is a prodigy, and if Honey
could be anywhere right now, she'd prefer to be in a room coaching that
voice that slips along notes and octaves as if oiled. The child has natural
talent, but not control, and her last voice coach was too strict, scaring her.
Honey always softens her eyes and creates a warm, inviting space with

candles for the child, for the voice to find its ideal expression, *breath-sound-sustain-close*. Together, they move through transitions and ranges. She and Nala both leave the hour as new people, ready for the world to work on them taking its toll on their voices and their souls.

And this foolishness today is the exact opposite of where she wants to be. She crosses and uncrosses her legs, tries to remain alert. She had once been dressed down for reading a book while she waited outside a recording studio, as if *she* were distracted and disorganized, so now she stares straight ahead and waits. The chairs are uncomfortable, the radiator is letting out a cranky whine punctuated by haunting knocks, and the lack of decor on the walls is unsettling, considering this is, ostensibly, a music agent's office.

Suddenly there is a flurry of action as a pale, frantic woman dashes into the room, swipes the smoothie into a trash can, and grabs the papers under it. "Oh my God!" She jumps, clutching her chest, as if Honey is an axe-murderer lying in wait. "Why are you in my office?" she gasps, eyes bulging and lips pursing. "Oh, are you Honey? We were waiting for you. Come on!"

Honey follows the woman's twitchy backside down the hall, thinking of the impertinence of calling Honey by only her first name, when she doesn't know this woman from Eve. As they round a corner, she hears his voice, and a warm joy slides across her heart.

"Ms. Honey Conaway! Can it be?" He sports a luminous broad grin and opens his arms to receive her. "It makes my day to see you, not looking a day older than when we last saw each other!"

He looks just the same. Well, no—he is graying, but he looks fit and fine. Memories of high school, when she was one of the brightest stars in a shimmering galaxy, flood her soul nerve. It makes her feel good all over just to see him. She unravels in his attention, feeling her back loosen and her hair somehow feel more lusher and more perfect. People around him whisper, probably about who she is and, possibly, about what happened to her back in the day. Before she knows it, she is swept into an entourage, following briskly down the hall, and she feels important, part of something big, though how she fits in is a mystery.

"It's so good to see you, Savion!" She pushes away her suspicions and gives him all her attention. "I heard you need a little backup vocal?"

"Oh, have you heard the track? Yes! I cannot wait to hear you rock it!"

She panics. Should she tell him she didn't get the music? She doesn't want to get anyone here in trouble or make any enemies. Before she can even form an answer to his question, other people with more expedient questions insinuate themselves forward to grab his attention. Then Savion is ushering people into the recording room, a grand, beautiful space with huge windows that have a view of the East River. The piano is glowing from inside, and the room is golden wood artistically dappled with soundproofing material, and the whole space feels like a warm brown leather jacket. It's as if the place had been carved from father's long, beautiful Pontiac sedan in the '70s, before he'd had a heart attack in the street and left her and her mother with her baby brother and mountains of grief. Savion puts his arm around her and whispers, "We made it here, sis. You and me. We're going to *do* this!" And his earnest face draws her out of her reverie and back into the now. It's really happening! She's going to be on his album!

But within minutes, Savion is occupied with all number of logistics in the grand recording studio. Honey casts around, trying to figure out which person would be most likely to have the music she's missing. She homes in on the shivery-looking young white woman whose office Honey had apparently entered without permission. The woman side-eyes her and purses her colorless lips. This is probably the Assistant to the Assistant to the Assistant to the Superstar, and Honey is left with her guidance. The name from the email, *Bella*, pops into Honey's mind.

"Excuse me," Honey tries to ask as nonchalantly as possible, gliding up to the woman. "Are you Bella?"

The woman nods curtly and tries to look over Honey's shoulder to observe the various old friends of Savion settling into an impromptu horns section.

"It's nice to finally meet you." Honey plows forward. "I wanted to ask... I did not, in fact, receive the attachment with the music files. Do you think I could have a moment with it to get prepared?"

It's not unreasonable to ask. She knows it's not unreasonable because it's simply professional courtesy. How is anyone to do a job when they are not prepared? In fact, "a moment" is not nearly enough time, but she wants to please Savion and do this session, so she feels like the request is not at all out of the ordinary.

Which is why, when this Bella gets angry, when her face puckers and twists and twin puffs of air burst from the woman's nostrils in rage, it takes Honey so completely by surprise.

"I sent it a week ago. You didn't even look at it?" Her face is red and, instead of waiting for Honey to respond at all, she turns on her heel and marches over to Savion and taps him on the shoulder. In the din of the instruments tuning, Honey can see Bella pointing at her, and worse, Savion's face falling with disappointment.

Honey feels herself shrinking as he makes his way across the room, Bella hovering around his elbow. "Honey, you're not prepared? You're always prepared. That's why I asked for you."

"The email didn't come through..." she begins.

Bella cuts her off, edging her own body between Honey's and Savion's in some sort of weird protective stance. "She knew my name, and she's here. She's lying! Of course she got the email!"

"I meant," Honey starts, but her eyes are already hot. Other people are staring at them now, and she knows she's causing a scene. "I meant that the attachment didn't come through. I got the email, but not the attachment."

"Why didn't you write back to us?" Savion asks, genuinely, but Honey can see him calculating the risks of moving forward and the costs of this precious studio time. She folds her lips into her teeth. He sighs and says, "Never mind. Let's step outside."

Honey's heart sinks to her stomach. She knows she's being dismissed and the trip has been a huge waste of money and time. But he closes the door carefully once they're in the quiet hallway, away from the bustle of tuning instruments and calls for wires and plugs. Savion turns his face down to her, fatherly or maybe big brotherly. Either way, it takes her breath away and she melts a little in the manly attentiveness. He searches in her eyes, his own pupils roving to command her attention. "Listen, Bella is a bitch, and she's been trashing my whole system since she got here. She's fired as of today. You are still my girl, you hear me?"

Honey bursts into full tears. She is so grateful her Savion is still here, that he still loves her and cares for her. "Thank you. I'm so sorry."

"No sorry, don't be sorry. All that…" He gestures to the recording room. "All that was unnecessary. I'm so sorry to put you through that."

"Okay." She sniffles. She knows she's a soggy mess, and she wipes her nose with the heel of her hand. Then immediately regrets it and looks away in horror at her own slovenliness.

"Okay?" He puts his hand on her chin, and she feels like a child.

"Yes, okay." For so long, all she's wanted is to feel young again, to be the child, to be the one someone else takes care of, and the weight of that desire is nearly too much for her to bear.

He smiles and she smiles, and then they laugh. His brown eyes warm her like liquid love. She nods. She wants to fold herself into his coat pocket and live there.

He produces a handkerchief and she uses it, shoving it into her purse before he can ask for it back. A gentleman, he doesn't argue.

"Honey, you can't sing today. You know that, right? If you're not prepared, I just can't use you, and I've got to get this today. I'm trying not to stitch anything in later. The vibe for this piece… well, the whole purpose was to have you and me in a room together, rocking it, you know?"

So she is being fired. She nods and takes a breath, trying to conceal the hitch in her throat. "Yes, I know."

"Oh, I wish you could be on this piece, but this train has to go without you." He searches her face for a minute. "But wait—I have an idea! I'll be right back. Don't go anywhere, and if Bella comes out of there, don't engage!" He makes slashing gestures with his hands, and she lets out a single laugh she can't hold back before sinking back into her despair.

She looks down the hallway. This is not the recording studio of her prime, but it could have been. She remembers how her own gold record proudly hung in the hallway at home. She was easily Grammy-bound then, and everyone knew it. The memory makes her uneasy, but it also relaxes her. She's been here before and she's been through the worst of it. Whatever is next, it can't be that bad. The memory of her father that surged up from the yellow leather, the blond wood and cool decor, that must have been a sign. It has to get better. Or at least, she just has to believe it will.

Savion comes bounding back toward her with a piece of paper flapping in his fist. "Here." He's not out of breath, but he does need to get his air back before the session, so he holds up a finger. He takes three deep breaths and she joins in. They make it a practice, and they're smiling by the end of the third.

"Look, this is a contract." He stabs at the paper with his thumb. "You don't have to sign it, but I know that Serafina is looking for established artists—only women—to do a duets album. And I just made sure you're on the list. You know Serafina, right?"

Serafina? *The* Serafina? Honey can't turn on the radio or walk through a mall without hearing at least a few snatches of her music. She's one of the few musicians working who is actually making money from downloads *and* album sales. It's like working with Aretha or Madonna or Bowie! Honey can barely find words. "Me? Serafina would want me on her album?"

Savion cocks his head sweetly and puts his hands on her shoulders. "Baby, you have no idea of your worth, do you?"

"I don't know, but Savion, I hope you do!" They share a quick hug, and he ducks back into the studio.

And just then she realizes that, aside from the piece of paper in her hands, she has no idea what to do next. So she reads it from top to bottom, signs it, and waits patiently on the floor of the hallway for Savion to be finished in the studio so she can ask him where on earth she is supposed to turn it in when it's complete. She pokes around on her phone to find something to read, but her eyes are tired and the darkness limits her visual field. She closes her eyes and dreams of what it might be like, what kind of duet she might do with the great Serafina.

Over time, she hears, thinly and through the door, the lush composition, the energy and fire, the synergy of the esteemed musicians Savion has collected and kept close. To think she was one of them, and she's missed her chance. Her heart aches and tears, aches and tears, with a raging desire to be just inside that room with him, with all of them, where that horrible witch Bella is and Honey is pointedly not.

When the session is over and people emerge, sweaty and smiling, they nearly trip over Honey's extended legs. She pulls her ankles under her, making herself smaller. Savion spies her. He is flushed and warm, and he crouches down next to her.

"What'd I miss?" she asks, trying to keep her smile from cracking.

"The creation of the world." He looks up to the ceiling. "I wish," he puts a fist to his mouth. "Honey, I wish you could have seen it."

"Me too, Savion." She pushes the paper at him, kisses him on the cheek, and says nothing else to him or anyone else, nothing at all for the rest of the day, that whole long trip home alone.

Chapter 6

SERAFINA IS DOING her best writing, possibly ever. She feels good, productive, and strong. She has been crafting new songs and reading up on her duets matches, singing along to their albums and generating lists of old standards that might work, though she's still not crazy about that idea. Her own voice has never been better and she's not leaning on autotune so much. Even that engineer Richie says so, and he's usually the only one who gives her real feedback, so she trusts him over everyone else. She's even singing around the apartment, real singing. She knows her voice can handle it.

Noey is sprawled on the couch in her underwear, her back tanned and glowing from her recent trip to Jamaica for her friend's bachelorette party. Serafina crawls onto Noey's back and presses her own body down. At first Noey hums. Serafina licks along the tan line. Noey tastes like caramel and salt. Soon Noey squirms and protests, "Baby, get off! I can't breathe!"

"Oh, I'll get off all right," Serafina says and wiggles her body. She is bigger than Noey, but she is bustier. Her boobs start to hurt pressed into Noey's lungs. "Just say please."

"Please!"

Serafina rolls off, laughing. "You're always so serious after you travel."

Noey bats her eyes. "Because I always have to go alone because you're always working and it's always a shit time without you. Everyone is like, *why didn't you bring Serafina?*"

"Right, and we've discussed this. With me, it's like, *oh, Serafina, Serafina!* And I have to fend everyone off so I can have some human time with just my baby, and then everyone thinks I'm a bitch. It's easier this way."

"Easier for you." Noey turns back to the book she has been reading. Serafina rubs the silk of Noey's panties, kisses Noey's neck. She can't get enough of Noey's skin. Noey uses some almond butter lotion that actually tastes good. Finally, Noey slips in her bookmark and sits up, letting Serafina climb into her lap. They move against one another, but Serafina realizes Noey's not really into it, just tolerating her grind.

"What's up, love?" Serafina tilts Noey's chin up to look in her eyes. It's just a flicker, but she sees it. "What?" she asks more sternly. "Did you fuck someone?"

"No!" Noey protests. "Never. I told you. I don't cheat."

"Okay, so what is it?"

"It's nothing. Let's kiss." She purses her lips and reaches up, but Serafina holds Noey's hands back and waits. "It's really nothing," Noey insists.

"Tell me what's going on."

"I don't really know. I just miss you when you're busy, I guess."

She and Noey have been together for only about twelve weeks. Serafina knows because she has put a heart on the calendar for their upcoming six-month anniversary. But what Serafina knows about Noemie Valentin is much more than she lets on. She met Noey a year ago and had a dossier created on her before she ever even tried to get close. Noey is not a serial cheater, and she doesn't go in for any shady stuff. They had her checked for prostitution, scams, theft, and even shoplifting. She's squeaky clean. Whatever Noey is worried about is personal, which means it's something about Serafina. Maybe Noey's having second thoughts, or maybe she's already seeing someone else.

The blade of jealousy twists a little in Serafina's mind. She thinks of her own body, so huge next to Noey's tiny, perfect one, and feels like a giant monster. That one little nick in her ego is enough to allow self-hatred to flood her senses.

"Okay, well if I'm so fat and ugly and annoying and you don't want to fuck me, I'll just go into my room and write." Serafina stands, feeling as ugly as she described. She is bloated and she hasn't done her skin care in two days. She wouldn't want to fuck herself. She walks to the window and watches the flow of traffic uptown, the clumps of people hustling in the crosswalks, the death-defying bike messengers zipping around parked trucks. So many people out there. She doesn't have to be stuck with anyone, but she doesn't want any of them. She aches for this one who doesn't love her anymore. She aches for Noey to close the gap between the couch and the window. Her skin feels magnetized by want to Noey's touch, lovingly presented in apology.

Instead, Noey picks up a pillow and covers her chest with it. "Oh-em-gee. You are such a child sometimes. I don't understand these temper tantrums!"

Serafina whirls. "Temper tantrums?"

"Yes, you do this. You say, *Oh, let's mess around.* Then you see me think something, or you *think* you see me think something, and then you get like this." Noey has dropped the pillow and is standing now, her cute warm belly jiggling with the wild hand gestures. Serafina almost forgets to think about herself and is overcome with desire.

"I do, don't I?" Serafina asks coyly, anticipation flooding her senses.

"Yes. All the time." Noey shakes her head, her sleek black hair draping like a curtain over her eyes. Serafina likes her like this, a little bee-stung. That adorable pout.

"I'll stop. I promise. I'll be better to you." Serafina closes in, putting her hands on Noey's waist. "Are we making up now?"

Noey nods, looking away and unsmiling. She turns her face back to Serafina, lips firm. "I'm serious. Don't think for me. If my thoughts are ready to share, I will share them. If they are private, I have my reasons."

Serafina nods too, but she's not listening. She takes in Noey's smell, the feel of Noey's body under her fingertips. She leans down and wraps her hand around the small warm hill covered by Noey's silk panties, and the minute Serafina's tongue touches Noey's, she swears she can feel the waves lapping along a Jamaican shoreline.

The buzzer to the apartment goes off and Serafina is still tangled in the sheets when she realizes what time it is.

"Fuck, fuck, fuck! Anny Jeffers!"

Noey groans. "I wish you wouldn't do potty mouth."

"Fucking Anny Jeffers!" Serafina hisses and runs into the living room. Clad only in a towel, she holds the buzzer for five full seconds to signal the security guard to let Anny up. She hopes it's enough. Then she dashes back into the bedroom.

"*The* Anny Jeffers! Folk legend. She's coming here for a songwriting session. She's got to be seventy years old now, and I don't want to keep her waiting. Throw something on!"

They scramble into their clothes, and Serafina smears what's left of her makeup into place, tangles her hair into a messy bun. Noey, in her little red skirt and black top, looks like she is ready for the club, as always. Not a hair out of place.

"I'll just stay in the bedroom," she says. "On the iPad. Watching Netflix."

"That's perfect, baby." Serafina kisses her on the cheek and heads into the hallway to let in one of the greatest folksingers of all time. On her way out, Serafina sees it again, that flash of questioning in Noey's face, a distance, or a desire, maybe to be somewhere else. But before Serafina can catch it and make sense of it, Noey climbs onto the bed, crosses her legs, and pops in earbuds. She smiles and waves at Serafina, and Serafina shivers the negativity out of her head with a cleansing breath.

Anny has a handsome weathered glow with long steel-gray hair and laughing eyes. She's wearing a pair of vintage Levi's and a scalloped flower top and stands tough and a little bowlegged. It makes Serafina a little hot for her. "Serafina, in the flesh!" Anny says. "I almost didn't believe you were a real person!"

Anny is probably referring to Serafina's brand persona, a hypersexualized robot warrior who processes human emotions vividly in her songs. Her big record, *Transwomanism*, is a concept album in which she is a plastic humanoid with a steel beating heart and exaggerated sex organs. In all of her videos, she is stylized to look like an avatar with glossy skin and dead eyes. She received some political flak for the album title, since she, it was pointed out to her a great number of times, is not a trans woman. But all publicity is good publicity, and she found herself talking about the album on talk shows and in interviews, defending the term as it applied to trans people, which was mostly a bunch of bullet points her agent and publicist threw together about supporting the trans community. Her last album, *Carbon Form*, the one that went platinum and held onto the number one spot for twenty-two weeks, suggests she is a completely AI entity. All the songs are about not having a body, or wishing to have a body, or wanting others to shed their bodies and join her. The videos for that one disappear her into just a single body part or a voice.

In one video, the one for the title track, just her stylized foot appears to command others to take on military roles and sacrifice themselves, and at the end, the foot is blown up in a cloud of smoke. And Serafina's earlier album is even further removed from reality. In that one, all the songs are in some way related to the unconscious state.

The biggest hit, and the one that has made her a millionaire, "Cobalt Blue," is loosely about her last miserable breakup that had sent her into a deep spiral. Coming out of it, she'd imagined just breaking down into tiny little subatomic particles and bits and bytes into the universe. When she shared this vision with her songwriter, they started riffing on it, and when they landed on the hook for *"I saw you... Cobalt Blue,"* they both knew it was going to be big.

But since then, memes and rumors and conspiracies have suggested that Serafina is not real at all, that she is some sort of CGI or AI or whatever, or even a science experiment. Jorge kind of likes to "percolate the buzz a bit," as he says, so they haven't scheduled that many tours, and those few cost upwards of hundreds per ticket, with lots of radio giveaways to make sure it's more equitable and she's not accused of elitism.

"I'm very real, I can assure you." Without thinking, Serafina turns to show her very human butt, slaps it, and smiles.

Anny's mouth drops open like she isn't sure what to make of it, and then she leans back. "Oooh, you're a hoot! I'm gonna like you!"

Serafina has worried about this meeting because Anny's voice in her youth may have been compatible enough with Serafina's to make it work, but she worried that they won't sound good together with Anny's advanced voice. Serafina's flat robotic sound creates the auditory interest, and she needs a partner who comes with something pretty, something to soothe the ear after her roughness. Some singers have made the switch from an unusual or eclectic persona to singing ballads and standards, like Billie Eilish and Queen Latifah and Cyndi Lauper, but Serafina isn't ready to abandon her persona and has been relying on her partner to pick up the straight-man aspects so she can add her weirdness. For the next two hours, Anny and Serafina prove Serafina's hypothesis that they are completely incompatible singers. The songs she has been harmonizing to on Anny's album are from prior to Anny's bout with throat cancer. Somehow, Anny has been able to claw back her singing career, but her new voice is gravelly and low and pitted like a hard road. Serafina will have to drop to a mezzo-soprano to harmonize at all, and either way, it's going to be tricky. She hasn't listened to Anny's richer comeback sound, and she kicks herself.

Anny plucks and twangs at her guitar, rambling along on story songs, and while Serafina tries to be polite, she doesn't want to do any old country ditty. She knows the lyrics to a few of the standards, like "Silver Threads and Golden Needles" and "Achy Breaky Heart," but her and Anny's phrasing are vastly different, and even Serafina's cleanest open notes contrast in a creepy way to Anny's throaty depth. As much as they try to adjust, each is unflattering to the other woman's sound. Serafina sounds like she took a drag from a helium balloon, and Anny sounds progressively more like a bullfrog. They try to separate into verses, shift keys and register, but it's just not working. They laugh and shake their heads at each chorus, try again, decide the next try is worse.

When Anny finally puts down her guitar, she says, "Girl, I don't think this is gonna work out. We sound like shit." As she shakes her head,

Serafina feels ragged, worn through, like the woman rode her and is ready to take more. She's not sure how Anny is still upright.

Serafina offers to make some tea, worn and hyperconscious of poor confined Noey in the bedroom bingeing *Glee* again. She takes the long way to the kitchen and pops her head in and asks Noey, "Did you hear any of that?"

Noey shakes her head and points to the earbuds. She gives a thumbs-up and hopeful smile. "Is it going great?"

"It's like trying to sing with Bob Dylan out there."

Noey's face crumples. "Ew."

"Yeah." Serafina nods. "Anyway, shouldn't take too much longer. You okay in here?"

"You bet! Take your time."

Serafina returns to the couch with two mugs of tea. She wants to say how much she loves Anny's albums, but she doesn't.

Anny leans back and takes in Serafina. "Let me ask you: Why did you choose me?"

Serafina's response includes words like *icon* and *genius* and *trailblazer*, but Anny's eyes are as glazed as doughnuts. Anny cuts off Serafina's babble. "You know, you don't need to be a patronizing little bitch. I'm still selling out venues."

"You? That—that's amazing!" Serafina regrets the words as soon as they're out of her mouth. She does sound like a patronizing little bitch.

"Yeah. Mostly, my audience is made of old friends or new acolytes, or just people waiting for me to die. Everyone wants to see me before I go. But I'll take every last gig I can before I kick off, you know?" She stage-whispers. "I'm a Leo."

"Me too!" Serafina giggles and gushes. Though really, she's on the cusp with Cancer.

Anny seems to be chewing on a question for a minute. "When Jerry told me about this project, he said that the theme is about mothers. You mean mothers, like mothers of rock or mothers of folk or mothers of what exactly?"

"I don't really know," Serafina admits. "I just know that I wanted to honor the women who came before me. I didn't have a female role model growing up, and I got a lot from female singers. Like, you know, when I was little, Tori Amos and Sinéad O'Connor gave me all this confidence in being a woman and standing up for yourself after being made small. And Gloria Redmond gave me advice on men and you know, periods and stuff. She was really the catalyst for this idea."

"Gloria was the catalyst? Huh."

"Why? What's wrong with Gloria?"

"Nothing is wrong with Gloria. It's just, there's nothing maternal about her."

"Well, she never had children, but..."

"No, I mean, she's not warm or loving. She's only ever been out for herself. I think she may have wanted to be a mother, but she told me that she'd rather shoot bullets than shoot babies out of her hoo-hoo."

Serafina laughs. "I've heard that quote."

"Yeah, well, she told me that when she fired me from a project for being pregnant with Cassidy. She told me that I should get rid of the kid if I wanted to be on her album because it was fucking up my voice."

"Was it?"

Anny is incredulous. "Of course it was, but that's not the point! Women have to stick together in this business. You don't force a peer to have to choose between work and a child. That's insane." Anny peers at Serafina. "Did she agree to this project yet?"

Serafina doesn't answer but gives her a knowing smirk and rolls her eyes, and they both laugh.

"I knew it! Well, don't wait around for her!" Anny stands and rubs her blistered hands on the denim weave of her jeans. "And now, this old froggy voice is gonna lose me this job too. Oh well!"

Serafina suddenly wants it to work. She wants it so badly. In her mind, Anny has become the keystone to the album, and she's not sure how she'll ever move forward. She considers offering a songwriting credit, or somehow adding another voice to the mix to find some shared harmony, but she can't envision it. It will either sound like Serafina is showing off and Anny is beyond help, or like Anny is singing a completely different song and Serafina is clueless.

"I don't get it. Tony Bennett has been able to put together like fifty duets albums. How does he do it?" Serafina grouses.

Anny chortles. "Because he's Tony fucking Bennett!" She seems to sense Serafina's pity and turns her mouth down. "Look, baby. I survived cancer and a rattlesnake of a husband who left me during chemo for a twenty-two-year-old. My next six months of concerts are sold out. I'm gonna be all right."

"You're right," Serafina nods, blinking rapidly, suddenly desperate and nearly electrically charged remembering the warm, loving arms waiting for her in her bedroom. "Yeah, it's not gonna work."

But Serafina now has an opening. If it won't work with Anny, Jorge has been pushing hard on some punk singer from the mid-nineties who hit her stride the year Serafina was born. Maybe she could take Anny's place.

"Hey, do you know Sian Star?"

Anny leans way back as if Serafina has taken a swing at her and then rights herself. "Dang, Sian Harper! I don't know if the woman is in jail or rehab, or maybe both. That's Sian Harper for you. Last I heard she was heading to Alabama to be with her daughter. Might be a conservatorship situation. I dunno." Anny peers at Serafina. "You got Sian Harper to commit to your record? You met her yet?"

"No, it was just a suggestion from my manager. Apparently Sian Star's manager is keen to get her projects."

"She can't be a great musical 'mother' if you've never heard of her!" Anny laughs. "Take a listen to the Whirlygirls. You've heard of them? She was their lead singer. And she had a bit of a solo career that was much better in my opinion. But she's also one of the craziest broads I ever did know in this industry. I swear I've seen her piss on the windshield of a police car. Or at least I think I have. I'm so old I'm not sure I haven't pissed on a police car at some point." Anny cackles and slaps her leg. "Well, I hope she hasn't screwed up her voice as badly as all this."

Anny points to her own throat, and the vulnerability of the gesture tears at Serafina's soul. Impulsively, she puts a hand on Anny's shoulder, and Anny gently removes Serafina's hand and holds it. Serafina sees a cool glaze settle over Anny, and Serafina senses that a window that might have been open has just been closed.

"Hey, no hard feelings. Really. I've been here before, and you'll be here again. Sometimes, it just doesn't work for whatever reason. Don't worry your pretty head about this. It's just one more splash of mud on our skirts on the roadside of life. But let me say, I got two things out of today: One, you are a fine, fine singer and I'm impressed as hell by what I heard today. You don't need to hide behind a robot or whatever persona because the talent God already gave you as a human woman is enough with shovels to spare. And two, I'm gonna tell everyone that when I questioned whether you're a real live girl, you showed me your ass as proof." Anny squeezes Serafina's hand and lets it drop. Then she leans in for an angular, but kind, hug. "And I'll see that ass again at the Grammys. You watch."

Serafina laughs genuinely, and a freedom flows through her. Her laugh roils over, and Anny's grin broadens. This *Mothers* album is going to be something, Serafina is sure of it, sure she needs it more than any other project she's done in her life, if only to bring her closer to the magic Anny Jeffers has brought into her home today, the magic Serafina first felt listening to Gloria dish in those old '80s songs.

In the morning, she calls Jorge and recounts the session with Anny.

"It was a disaster. It didn't work at all. You should have heard it! I didn't know a duet could thin out my own sound so much!"

"Hey, hey. I have good news, sweetheart—great news! Have you ever heard of the fantastic, amazing, gorgeous R&B singer, Ms. Honey Conaway?"

Chapter 7

GLORIA HASN'T found a song yet she likes by the little tramp, Serafina. All this pleading and whining, and what is this genderbending robot nonsense? Gloria has always come at music tits first, ample rump behind, all woman in between. She's never tried to sing like a man, play like a man, or do anything in her career like a man, let alone a robot or some sort of disembodied political voice. It's too damn artsy. The tunes aren't all that bad. There are some good hooks, but nothing compared to Gloria's music. Gloria's own musical "mothers" were women who sang while cooking or washing dishes or putting up the laundry, women who sang on their way to church or on their way home. Not that she doesn't appreciate art. She gets all her paintings from local artists at fairs, looks the artists in their eyes. As modern lingo has it, she *sees* them. She validates them. That's how she deals with art.

It's the overproduction that irritates her. She wonders how this Serafina sounds live.

She clicks one of the "(live)" songs on YouTube, something called "Carbon Form." The video is grainy and streaky, definitely captured live, and probably totally illegal. Gloria squints to see a young woman much like her own younger self, breasts and hips and a gold mane of hair, eyelashes that probably tickle the third row of the audience when she blinks. There's a yowl at the beginning that is throaty and sexy and catches Gloria off guard. This isn't in the album version. The drums are steady and militant, and instead of guitar backup, she's accompanied by keys and orchestra strings. It's creepy. It sounds otherworldly, but Gloria can hear the thread of it, the melody. She presses pause and grabs her banjo, picks it out, toggling back and forth to land the tune.

She can't make out the lyrics from the grainy video, so when she feels like she's got the tempo right, she looks them up and reads along as she plays.

In the red room, with the printout curtains,
I waited until I was certain
Your noise, your noise.

Down under grief in my heat and ether,
the haunting of a girl you left a seether,
Your noise, your noise.

Your noise, your lies, your noise, your lies.
You'll never find my carbon form in all the harm you've done.
I'm gone, gone, gone.
You'll never know what word is mine, an electric valentine.
I'm none, none, none.

Your noise, your lies, your noise, your lies…

It doesn't make a lick of sense at first, but on the second run-through, Gloria stops in the middle of a verse. "Oh, it's a just a breakup song! I got you, girl."

She changes the tempo so the melody isn't obscured by the marching rhythm and gives it a little more space and air between the lyrics. She drops a little emotional pacing in her phrasing, as if she is telling someone off, but she sees how the structure of the words can't really carry a direct attack. It's almost campy that way. She backs off and delivers just a few of the repeated words with subtle emotion. Then she brightens some of the notes, lifting a peal or letting a twang hold for just a tiny bit longer to indicate the nuance. Her voice sounds oily and rich, not as bright as her pre-menopause days, but honestly it sounds better, seasoned with age, like those covers Johnny Cash did before he died. Age has its own timbre.

When she has it just the way she wants it, she checks her hair and makeup, grabs her phone stand, and arranges herself artfully in front of the beadboard wall with the tree of life tapestry. She got into these "private" performances on social media during the pandemic, and she knows at least a few people will be tickled she's doing this. She opens her account and starts a livestream, tosses her hair, and begins.

"Y'all, I got a call from someone named Serafina. Apparently she's hot shit. I retooled one of her songs, so here goes."

She launches into the song, imagining her rapt little audience listening as she plays. A few pink and red hearts start streaming along the screen, and chat boxes pop up with comments that glow with affection.

She closes her eyes and plays, finding that she actually likes her version. She feels good with this tune in her hands, even if her fingers aren't limber enough and she hits a tiny sour wobble every so often. It takes her back to her amateur days. The whole song feels fresh and young, like she is climbing into a new skin. Her voice flows into the prickly notes until the very end, when she lets the banjo silence and her own warble finishes it off: *Your lies.* She smacks the banjo with her fingertips and says, "Well, that's it!"

She stops the stream and looks back through the comments. People almost immediately called out Serafina in the chat using the hashtag, and it looks like Serafina's verified account joined at the very end.

Gloria is unreasonably flattered. She didn't expect her livestream to make it all the way to Serafina's attention so fast. She's still reading through the comments, noting friends and kind words, when she gets a text from a private number.

It's S. Saw your live. Does that mean you're in???

How did Serafina get her number? Gloria wonders. She responds with a poop emoji. If it's not Serafina, and it's a prank, it's what the jerko deserves. And if it is Serafina, she should learn to take a joke.

The number responds with a crying/laughing emoji.

Gloria responds with an eggplant emoji.

The number responds with a question mark.

Gloria assumes it must be Serafina and realizes she's actually going to fuck this up if she keeps messing around. She texts, **Sorry. Couldn't find the keyboard.**

Serafina responds, **lol.**

Gloria considers whether she's in. With one foot. Maybe even just a toe. She types, **Yeah, I'm in.**

Someone is knocking on her door. She puts her phone on the stand and peers through the drapes. George has a beer in his hand. She opens the door, but not all the way. She is hoping he brought a little weed or something else nice and friendly instead of that crap he pulled with the hiker. Instead, he puts down the beer and pulls off his cap. He worries the brim and shifts his weight like he's going to ask to use the bathroom.

"Does this mean you're gonna record with Serafina now?" he asks. His eyes are huge and eager, and he looks like a giant, fat baby with a beard.

"What's it to you?" asks Gloria, toeing the beer. He picks it up, embarrassed.

"I saw your livestream. I hope you don't mind. I'm such a fan."

She is taken aback. "My livestream! And you hustled right over here. Well, you are quite the fan!"

He looks down, his eyelashes feminine as he blinks in some surprise. "Oh, oh, I'm your fan, for sure, Miss Gloria. I've always been a fan of yours. But I'm also a huge fan of Serafina. It would be awesome to see you two work together." The way he pushes out so much air on "awesome" gives her neck a little crick. He puts his hands up, adding, "It's just a suggestion. I don't want to make any suppositions." His open, earnest face falters a little as he waits in the heated silence for her response.

She takes a huge breath. "George?"

"Yes ma'am?"

"Go home."

"Yes ma'am." George puts on his cap and, nodding, takes his leave. He looks back as he scurries to the yard with three motorcycles, a chainsaw bear sculpture, and his fat, barefoot wife sitting on her porch rocker. The wife waves wildly, as if she understood George's mission and believes it to be a success.

Gloria goes back into the house and turns the bolt without thinking. Even though her neighbors live a cool football field away, this screwworm is getting too close for her comfort. She picks up her phone and sees a mass of texts and Instagram mentions.

"Well, ain't that a kicker," she wonders. "I guess I got to do it now."

Chapter 8

HONEY ARRIVES at Serafina's New York apartment building and gives her name to an overtly suspicious security guard. The guard buzzes Serafina's place and then crosses his arms. They wait, eyeing one another, for a response from the suite.

"I'm here for a job," Honey says to him, feeling the need to explain herself. He looks at her quizzically, and then she realizes she might have just given him more reason to be suspicious. "No, I mean, Serafina called me. I mean, her people called me. Or they called my people. You know what I mean? She's famous, so of course she didn't call me herself. She could have texted. But, you know."

The guard twiddles his pen and looks at her.

"Can you try her apartment again? She is expecting me."

Instead of buzzing, he picks up the phone. "Name?"

"Honey Conaway."

As he waits for an answer, he taps the pen on the marble desk.

Honey can hear a tiny, harried voice on the other end but can't make out what the person is saying.

The guard turns away from Honey as he speaks. "I got a Honey Conway here? She says she has an appointment to see you?"

Honey can hear the plain word "Fuck!" through the phone line, and then a run of high-pitched talk.

"She said to wait." The guard replaces the receiver and looks down at his desk, where nothing is awaiting his gaze. Honey is dismissed.

She looks around the marble reception area. There are no benches or chairs in the space. She's not sure exactly where to wait.

"Over there," he says, and points to a window. "Or come back in about twenty minutes."

"Where would I go for twenty minutes?" she asks. She peers out the window but through the dark glass, she sees only other apartment buildings. Upper East Side. No coffee shops, no Prêt, no Starbucks. She can't even afford the Manhattan prices anyway though.

The guard shrugs and pulls out his phone to occupy himself and to avoid looking at her.

Honey watches the shapes of people hustle by in the cold. It's a particularly bitter March day, four degrees with a wind chill of negative ten. She can't imagine wanting to leave this lobby, though she is overheating a little in her coat. Actually, she realizes she's overheating a lot in her coat. Her face is burning, and she unbuttons the top button, then the second. In a minute, the cold outside looks like exactly where she would want to be.

She sweeps through the revolving door into the blessed freezing air. A light sleet mists her face and neck, and she can't imagine how she ever bundled up so tightly. She pulls her gloves off and puts her chilling hands to her face. She must have been standing there for a minute or two when the heat recedes and she feels her face cool down for real. The sweat under her arms is moist and uncomfortable as a fierce wind rips through her wool coat. She buttons herself up and enters through the revolving door into the lobby, now warm and welcoming.

The guard hasn't looked up from his phone. She wonders if that was a hot flash. What else could it be? She has no idea how much time has passed, so she comes back to the desk.

Before she can say anything, the guard, without looking up from his phone, says, "I'll call back in five minutes. That's when she said to let you up."

"Oh, okay. Thank you."

She retreats to the space near the window, unsure where to put her gaze. Finally, she pulls her phone out of her pocket and checks her messages. A few updates from the church, an upcoming cancellation, a "friendly reminder" about an overdue cell phone bill. She closes the phone and drops it back into her purse.

"Okay, go on up."

"What floor? What apartment?"

"Second bank of elevators, twenty-second floor. It's 22B."

Honey issues her thanks and hustles to the elevators. Partway down the hall, she faces the black closed door of an elevator and reaches to press the button.

"Second bank!" he calls after her, waving her farther down the hallway. She pulls her hand back as if she had been about to press the detonator for a bomb. She feels like such an interloper, and yet, she belongs here. *They* called *her* for this session with Serafina. She has to remind herself that she is not breaking anything, that her talent has value, and that they wanted her.

She finds the second bank and gives him a thumbs-up, but he has already turned back to his phone. She sees her reflection in the gold of the elevator door. Her hair is wild, her clothes wet and rumpled. She closes her eyes until she hears the ding and steps through, trying not to give her appearance a second thought.

A slight woman in a red silk dress opens the door for Honey and invites her in. "I can't believe I'm meeting Honey Conaway! As a girl, I loved *Staircases*. I played that album every day!" She hums a few bars of "Don't Call Me Miss" as if to prove her research.

"Why, thank you," Honey says politely. This woman looks way too young to have played Honey's first record.

"Yes, I just love how you used your gospel roots on these songs! And I love the metaphor of a staircase for all the stages of a woman's life. Such a powerful and lasting message!" The woman is gushing and touching Honey's arm. Honey pulls her papers closer to her chest. Her face feels hot again, but she doesn't know if she's being made fun of.

"Thank you. Are you Serafina?"

"Oh, god no." She covers her mouth. "Sorry, sorry—I know you're religious…"

Honey laughs. "I've heard so much worse."

"No, I'm Noey, Noemie. I'm… I'm just here to let you in. Serafina and Gloria Redmond are meeting in Serafina's office. Come in and have a seat. You are coming from Baltimore? I hope it didn't take you too long."

"No, just three hours on the train. Then the subway uptown. I used to know my way around the city like the back of my hand."

"I bet you did! I bet you have a ton of stories about this place." Noey pads around the space with deft familiarity and talks with a slight French lilt.

"Honestly, I've never felt fully comfortable in New York," Honey admits. "It's a little like tangling with an old lover, you know? You show up and it's like, *Oh, I remember falling in love with you here, and here, and here,* but also you come to remember why you left."

"It's exactly like that. I mean, I love it here, but also, it totally sucks. It's so expensive and no building is ever the right temperature, and people pee on the street. I mean… well, you know."

"I do believe I do." Honey likes this one. She's a little tea cake. Did she say she was Serafina's assistant? She seems at home, like she might have closet space, but this is definitely a living apartment, not a working office. Noey is dressed up but comfortable enough here to have kicked off her shoes at some point and to pad around barefoot, so either they have a warm relationship, or Serafina will be pretty pissed off when she sees the unhygienic presumptiveness of naked feet. Honey would never take off her own shoes in her boss's apartment.

"Can I get you anything? We have tea, soda, water, and I think some coffee beans in the freezer?" She ducks into the kitchen to rummage through the fridge.

"I'm fine!" Honey calls back. Noey continues to call out beverages. "I'm fine!" Honey yells with more gusto.

A door opens across the hall and two women storm into the room glaring daggers at Honey. They look like two versions of the same woman. Both wear blond tousled buns, but one stands about a foot shorter than the other. The tall one, an Amazon with blazing blue eyes, must be Serafina. The short one Honey recognizes right away. Gloria Redmond. The thin line of Gloria's purple lips and her cunning green eyes are a familiar nightmare.

"Can you please," Serafina pushes down air in front of her body with both hands. "Please stop making so much noise?"

Noey rushes out of the kitchen and furiously apologizes. "This is Honey Conaway! I'm sorry, she was waiting downstairs, and she was here at eleven, and that was her appointment, and I'm sorry, I didn't want to disturb you and Gloria."

"God, whatever," Serafina yells and stomps back into the room she came out of, which appears to be a small studio.

Gloria smirks in the wake of Serafina's meltdown. "Gloria Redmond. Glad to make your acquaintance." She stretches out her hand. "So sorry about the mix-up with the schedule. We are just wrapping up."

Honey takes Gloria's hand politely. Gloria holds her own hand limp, as if Honey is meant to kiss it. Honey angles her palm to meet Gloria's and shakes firmly. "Thank you. Nice to meet you. And take your time."

Gloria smiles broadly, perhaps knowingly. She sinks back into the room, her Cheshire grin disappearing into the dark of the closing gap.

Noey whirls to Honey. "I'm so so so so sorry. This is all my fault. Gloria just showed up, and Serafina has been literally obsessing over her. I knew you were coming, but I didn't know how long they would take and I kind of hoped you wouldn't come after all." She claps her hand over her mouth again. Honey is coming to see it as an affectation. "I mean, just that you would reschedule so you wouldn't have to travel all this way and then wait. I mean, it's so rude."

"I completely understand," says Honey, hoping to calm Noemie.

"You don't understand," Noemie sits on the couch with her face in her hands. "I don't like... you don't deserve to be treated that way. You're... you're Honey Conaway!"

Honey takes in Noemie. She must be Serafina's assistant, but she didn't "Yes, miss" or "Yes, ma'am" Serafina, and in fact, Serafina hadn't even acknowledged Noemie during the entire episode. Noemie doesn't look like a sister or other relative. She's slight with definite Asian features, straight black hair and shining black eyes, and not more than a sprig over five foot, while Serafina, now that Honey has seen her, looks like she was assembled in some northern European country out of old ship parts. She can't work out their exact relationship.

"I've been treated worse," Honey says quietly.

"At least Gloria was civil," Noemie says, with a little toss of her head.

Honey is onto that one. "Mm-hm," is her response.

Noemie doesn't seem to hear the noncommitment in it, the spice. Instead, she starts listing types of tea on her fingers, much more quietly, while Honey ruminates on Gloria's response.

Honey doesn't buy Gloria's "pleased to make your acquaintance" act; this is hardly an introduction. The first time she met Gloria, Honey was barely twenty-one, and Gloria was well-lodged in stardom. Honey could forgive the forgetting because not only were they unevenly met in star-power at the time, Gloria was coked off her rocker and threw a microphone and a guitar during the same session. But the second, third, fourth, fifth, sixth, and seventh times they met, Gloria was always on her way down and in deep need of a friend to rescue her from her own worst instincts, and they had shared some moments over time, or so Honey thought. But Honey was likely just a passing ship to Gloria, who was always caught up in her own drama. Honey's voice was on Gloria's third and fourth album, and they'd shared a studio. Of course, Gloria never turned around to notice her backup singers. Well, except to fire them.

Noey curls up on the couch. "So what have you been doing since…" She opens her palm, as if the unspoken breakdown could just rest there in that neat little hand.

"Oh, this and that. I sing with my church."

"I bet they love you there. I'd love to hear you sing gospel."

"You think?" Honey wonders about Noey, what she really knows about music. "What gospel songs do you like?"

"Songs? I don't know any specifically. Wait—when I was in high school, one of the ladies would play gospel music in her office. One of them was really joyful, like Good Day or... wait..." She softly claps and sings, "'Oh Happy Day...'"

Honey knows the one and quietly harmonizes. They sing through the whole chorus, with Noey leading the call and Honey the response.

"Oh, it was a whole thing in high school! Me and all these girls would be clapping and singing all the way to our lockers. Dang, that takes me back!" Noey's eyes sparkle. "Can we do that again, but you lead?"

Honey nods and starts the rumble of the first verse lower than her normal range, just to keep it from being heard in the office. "Oh happy day..." "Happy day!" They lean into each other and clap and sing in harmony, laughing with their eyes and reveling in the joy of it.

The door to the office pops open and Serafina throws back her hair, puts on a bright smile. "Honey, I'm so sorry about that before." She reaches out her hand to shake. "I'm so excited you're here! And I see Noey has been taking good care of you."

Noey beams. "Are you and Gloria finished?"

"Yes." Serafina puts her hands together. "And I can't wait to work with Honey. But I'm afraid I have to be somewhere at noon, and there just isn't enough time today." She grabs her purse. "Do you want some cash for a reimbursement?"

Honey is hungry for that cash. She's being sent home again, and she can't really afford to make another unnecessary trip, not without an advance on this work. A third trip will put her out of range of paying off her credit card on time.

"I'd really rather do it today. I did come all this way, and I brought some ideas."

Serafina cocks her head and purses her lips as if to express how adorable Honey is. Honey sees where this is going.

"I'm out of cash, but Noey can buy you a ticket home, and we can reimburse a next trip. I'm thinking May?"

Honey is livid, but she will not take this woman's money. She wants the money, needs it, but there is no way, and she shouldn't have been messing around with this overgrown teenager anyway. Maybe she can call Savion, tell him it didn't work out, see if he can do something different for her. Her wheels are turning, but she finds herself being ushered into the hallway in a flurry of apologies.

Noey is using both thumbs to work her phone. "You need a ticket to Penn Station, Baltimore, right?"

"I already have a round-trip. I have a Metrocard and can get to Penn on my own. Really, it's no trouble."

"I'm so sorry," Noey says. She seems like she really does care. "I was more excited about you in this project than anyone else. I hope it does work out in May. I really can't wait to hear you sing live."

Honey cries in the elevator, praying no one else gets on. When the doors open, she sends herself back up to the twenty-seventh floor, just so she can cry a little more. The doors open to a similar marble interior with other self-involved rich people living behind other self-involved rich doors. She peers out until the doors close. Then she presses G and uses the gold reflective paneling to clean up her makeup and sort herself out. When she gets back to the main floor, the guard is standing at the elevator door, waiting for her.

"No joyrides," is all he says. Then he returns to the desk.

She is so shocked, it takes a minute for her to step outside the elevator. She feels exposed and nervous. Behind her, the other elevator dings and out steps Gloria, looking refreshed and cheerful.

"Looks like you got yourself some free time in the big city," she says. "Feel like having some lunch?"

Honey shakes her head no, but from everything she knows about Gloria, Gloria has never, ever taken no for an answer. Within a minute, Honey has agreed to a bite at a nearby jerk chicken place, and while she's holding it together on the inside, every piece of her rebuilt heart is losing its purchase and falling into her stomach, and Gloria is chattering the whole way.

Chapter 9

A COLOSSAL waste of time, Gloria thinks as she jabs the down button and waits for the elevator. One car is on the twenty-seventh floor, and the other is on the fourteenth, so either way, she's got to wait.

It's a totally half-baked idea. Serafina doesn't know what she wants and doesn't know how she's going to get it. She has no vision. She thinks she can just invite a bunch of her elders to write songs for her and sell her next album. The bitch doesn't listen, doesn't take criticism, and can't take a goddamned joke. Serafina has about as much talent as Gloria ever had, but Gloria knew when to be charming, and if you deserved respect, she gave respect. Serafina does not have that skill.

Gloria opens her phone and sends another poop emoji to Serafina.

The response comes just as the elevator dings.

Great session! Hope you find your keyboard LOL

Gloria steps into the elevator and presses G. The songs Serafina suggested are such drivel. She and Serafina started out with the revision of "Carbon Form," and Serafina seemed to have been practicing the new phrasing. They honestly sounded great, even if it was on that cheapo Epiphone Serafina had in the corner. Gloria does not need a good guitar. Her grandmother's was always popping strings and the bridge had been reglued hundreds of times. Gloria has more than once credited her own singing power to her need to outsing that sour old guitar. So as she strummed and sang on the Epiphone, Serafina just sat and used the phrasing and cadence Gloria had worked her ass off to create. Then what did she have ready for Gloria? Zilch. Zero. Goose egg.

Serafina blamed it, of course, on not being prepared to receive Gloria on this Tuesday morning. She claimed she was going to schedule Gloria later in the month, after she'd worked up some songs for the catalog, and then she had the gall to blame Gloria for just showing up unannounced. Hardly fucking unannounced! Gloria had said she was coming through text just after the livestream! Serafina had invited her! What did she think was gonna happen? And yes, she didn't call first, but she arrived at a reasonable hour. Who else would show up at a pop star's home at ten-thirty on a Tuesday?

The elevator doors slide open and that woman from upstairs is still in the lobby. She looks like she's been having a good old cry for at least a few minutes. She didn't leave the apartment but a bit ago, so Gloria wonders when she could have gotten all those tears in. Winnie was her name? Sunny? No, maybe Hoochie? Some unprofessional name, Gloria thinks. Probably a backup singer trying to plump up her résumé at the last minute. Gloria has news for her: If it hasn't yet, her voice is gonna drop hard just after the change. Better get her best work in now.

She invites the forlorn thing out to lunch. Can't be all that bad being in the big city. Seems she's come up from Baltimore this morning. Gloria has had some nights in Baltimore! Some mornings too, *hoo*, back in those days! That town can party! She knows of a jerk chicken joint around the way this girl would love, so they head around the block and hop into a taxi to Hell's Kitchen.

"I haven't been in a cab for years," says Hippy or Hoochie-Koochie. The woman is feeling around the seat like it's some sort of Egyptian litter, like she's never seen leather before. The cab lurches forward and the woman grabs the handle above the door. She's still twisting and turning, and Gloria realizes she might be looking for a seat belt.

"Lean back. It's the safest thing," says Gloria. "What was your name again, sweetie?"

The woman hitches a little breath as she smiles. The cab has really gotten to her. "Honey. Honey Conaway."

"Oh, right. Honey. I gotta think of that cereal with the beehive. That's a good way to remember your name. You should use that."

"Mmhmm," says Honey. She seems to be staring at the buildings. Maybe a little intimidated by the city. She's still gripping the door handle and pressing her hand against the back of the driver's seat to brace herself. Gloria felt that way herself, once upon a time.

"You don't come up to New York a lot, do you?"

"About three or four times a year. For jobs, mostly."

Gloria assumes Honey must have a day job. "Oh, what's your line?"

Honey turns full on to face her. "Singing, Gloria. Same as you."

Gloria allows herself a polite little snort. *Same as you.* No one is the same as her. And using her Christian name as if they go way back. If this Honey were the same as her, she would have heard of her before now.

"I see. So do you sing at the front of the stage, or way in the back?"

Now it's Honey's turn to recover from a ladylike jab. They are nearing the restaurant and the cabbie is cutting over to drop them at the curb. Gloria rummages through her bag, but she broke her twenty on a black coffee on the way to Serafina's.

"You got any cash, sweetie? I'll cash app you back."

Honey looks horrified, like she's never paid for a cab before, but she does open her purse and fish out the fare. Gloria is already swiping on her phone. "What's your handle?"

"Pardon?" asks Honey. It is loud, and she's standing in the street.

"Cash app? I want to pay for half the ride."

"Half?" Honey looks dumbfounded. Gloria wonders if she's simple.

"Yes, half the taxi. What's your cash app handle?"

"I don't have one. I don't even know what that is."

Gloria wants to be gracious, but if the woman is going to be stubborn about being repaid, she'll get what she gets. "Well, this place is to die for, so lunch is on me."

Gloria orders a plate of curry shrimp with rice and peas. Honey orders just the rice and peas. She's just skin and bones, and Gloria presses her to order something more.

"You don't like chicken? Why don't you like chicken?"

"Miss Gloria, I happen to be a vegetarian. I will be fine with the rice and peas."

"Oh, *la di dah*. Vegetarian. Hope you didn't step on an ant on the way in here." Gloria is secretly pleased to be addressed as Miss Gloria. She likes feeling young, and *Miss* does the trick.

Honey rolls her eyes as if she is dealing with a child. Gloria smirks. She's getting under Honey's skin.

"Order something else. You can't eat just rice and peas. Have the lemon cake." Gloria turns to the proprietor. "She'll have lemon cake too." Gloria pays for both meals and they make their way to the table.

Once they are settled, Gloria tears into the shrimp. They're delightfully spicy, stinging her upper palate and turning her cheeks warm. "Oooh, these are good today."

Honey pushes the peas around on her plate like she doesn't trust them. She eats single grains of rice with her fork. Gloria tries not to stare because if she does, she knows she'll wind up swiping the damn plate onto the floor. She hates slow, picky eaters.

"So how did you get mixed up in this Serafina thing?" asks Gloria.

"My friend Savion recommended me to the project."

"Savion. Not Savion Kimberman?"

"The very one."

"Oh, he's a beauty, don't you think? How did you meet him?"

"We go way back. We went to high school together, though we were a couple years apart."

"He's what, around fifty this year? So you're like, fifty-two?"

"Forty-six."

Gloria winces. "My mistake." However, she knew she was guessing wrong.

"It's not a big deal. I like my age."

"You look great either way. Skinny, but great. I remember my forties, whoo-eee!"

"And you look great for whatever age you are, Miss Gloria." Honey waves her fork around to indicate the whole of Gloria Redmond, tip to toe.

"Sixty-seven this April."

"Quite a milestone!"

Gloria's face is very red now, she's sure. The heat is a lot. "Can I get some water over here?" she yells back to the counter. A man with a huge Rastafarian cap brings by a glass of ice water. He gives Honey a big smile and then looks at her like she's his aged grandmother.

"Milk, Mother?" he asks. "To cut the spice?"

She shakes her head no, but damn, milk sounds like it's exactly what she needs, so she changes her answer to yes.

He gives her a gap-toothed grin. "Coming right up." Gloria catches Honey stifling her own grin. Honey hasn't taken a full bite of anything yet. Probably too spicy for her ass too, Gloria thinks, self-satisfied with her ability to handle heat.

When he leaves, Honey asks, "Why does he call you *Mother*?"

Gloria fans herself. "Mother Earth, honey. It's my nickname from my fans. Don't you have a nickname?"

"No," says Honey. Gloria can tell that Honey is doing a mental calculation about how this Jamaican goat-slinger can be a fan of Gloria's music. "Well, I did have a nickname for a while, but it wasn't really from my fans."

"Oh? What did they call you?"

"'Cuckoo Conaway.' It was just after the Grammys."

Gloria squints at Honey. "Son of a gun! I remember you." She sees her now, really sees her. Honey turns her own face away, as if trying not to be seen. But even in profile, the memory is triggered: Gloria sees the bloody dress, the spattered face, the wild hair and eyes of the picture that was all over the news that year after she'd attacked Danny Dire, taken out his eye. The woman is a certified crazy person, now prim as a virgin sitting in front of her. Maybe she's on those drugs that level out psychos. But Gloria also realizes that this is the same bitch who'd complained about her name being misspelled on one of Gloria's albums and her producer hounded her for months about it. Now that she's older, Gloria wonders why she resented those calls so much. She would have been fit to be tied if her own name was misspelled on an album, or anywhere really.

"I *do* remember you. You had a gorgeous fucking voice, sweeter than stolen molasses. And what did you do to earn that sobriquet, *Cuckoo*? You were like, walking around half naked, right? Didn't know who you were?"

"No, not exactly."

"You blinded a guy, right?"

Honey shrugs. Gloria would love to know the details, but Honey is shutting down this topic pretty securely.

"Okay, so what happened after that?"

Honey shrugs again. "Baltimore. I got better. I made it work."

"*Cuckoo Conaway*. I remember that. What a shitty nickname."

"Yeah. Yours is way better." Honey hasn't eaten much of her meal at all. She's still nibbling at rice and pushing around the food.

Gloria remembers Danny Dire. She can't say he didn't deserve what he got, and can't say Honey did deserve all that. She wasn't half bad. Had a few hits, and maybe a Grammy, or some sort of industry award. Maybe she wasn't all that crazy. Lord knows there are enough men in the music business to turn a good girl psycho.

A gorgeous milkshake arrives at the table. "For you, Mother."

"Horace, would you please see if you could make some vegetarian food for my friend? She's a vegetarian. If you don't have any here, can you order it from nearby?"

"Of course, Mother." The server winks at Honey. "I know just what to make."

"You don't have to," Honey protests.

"Baby, something's gotta go right for you today. I can tell that I loused up your whole day, and until we started talking, I didn't even realize that I knew you. That you and I have history. So finding you a meal you can actually eat, that's the least I can do."

Honey looks slightly relieved. She puts down her fork and Gloria sips the milkshake, fanning her face and mouth.

"Damn, that's good. Oh, that's real good." She sips until she makes a slurping sound at the bottom of the cup and starts to cackle conspiratorially. Honey covers her mouth, but her eyes are smiling.

A plate of sweet potatoes, collards, rice, and veggie drummies is delivered to the table. "Next door, mother. World-class soul food. All vegetarian. I know you will enjoy it."

Honey smiles. "I guess you're not the only mother in the room," she says, and to Gloria's relief, Honey finally starts to relax into the day.

Chapter 10

"I SHOULD HAVE listened to him." Serafina throws her phone onto the carpet. Tony Bennett's duets are all standards. Barbra Streisand's duets are standards. Even Queen Latifah's duets are standards! What was she thinking trying to write all new songs? And in the styles of her partners? This is a total shitshow.

She has two tracks laid down, and honestly, she doesn't love them. She managed to call Anny back and get her in to do a song in whatever way she wanted, and then Richie tuned the shit out of their voices to get something that sounded halfway decent. The other one was with this early rap artist named Sweetie, and they divided the song into rap and flow. Serafina can't flow on every duet. She has to shine somewhere.

Jorge had told her standards were the way to go, that they could hire some really good songwriters to punch them up. But Serafina couldn't see herself doing an album they play in Ann Taylor or wherever old ladies shop. She didn't want to croon. She wanted to have a powerful, transformative, sexy woman vibe and sing with gusto. Now she knows why this is just not going to work.

And then there's *Instinct*.

A week ago, Jorge got the call for Serafina to audition for a role in a remake of *Basic Instinct*, just called *Instinct*. She rehearsed with Noey, and at the time she felt pretty good about it. She auditioned using a piece from Sharon Stone's character, but she didn't hit it all breathy and sexy the way Stone did. Instead, she played it the way she knows women are these days. They are upfront, they demand consent, and they get the fuck out when the creep level is too high. She barely remembers reading, but she felt great about it when she left. She has been falling ever since. She can't get back on track with songwriting and she is terrified to be offered the role and terrified not to get it.

And fucking Noey. It's the same thing, that flicker of disappointment in her eyes. Serafina is definitely not imagining it. Noey freaked out with joy about the movie opportunity but is still not supporting this duets idea, and Serafina doesn't know why. Relationships are so freaking complicated.

Serafina's next session is on Tuesday. It's supposed to be a make-up session with that woman Honey. She searches up Honey on her music app. Only one album is listed, *Staircases*, and on the cover is a slim Black woman with close-cropped hair and one hand on her stomach, belting out something. She has a white furry boa around her neck and a white tank top, a short white skirt with broad yellow and green stripes on it, and she's standing against a gray concrete wall. It's epic! Serafina kind of wants this album cover for her own wall.

The song with the greatest number of likes is called "Forbidden," so she plays it.

It starts with a playful run of the keys, and Serafina thinks for a moment it will be jazzy, but then the horns and the piano beat down and Honey's voice can be heard in this rousing, everybody-on-your-feet chant with clapping and *Uh-huh* and *Oh yeah*! The beat halts and Honey enters with a smoky rhythmic verse, the instruments picking up pace around her:

It's a secret in my pocket I ain't let on yet
If you lean in real close, you'll never forget
If you're thinking dinner and a movie,
Boy, you'll never know how to woo me.

The sweetest fruit is forbidden

The choicest take is not given
The truest facts are opinion
You're most alive when you're livin'.

The lyrics are ridiculous, but damn, this girl is selling it. It is sexy! She could be singing "Grapes are eighty-four cents a pound!" and you would feel the need to dance. Serafina is, in fact, dancing. On the bed, her legs are kicking and her shoulders are shimmying. Honey is rocking her out.

Serafina smiles in spite of herself and clicks to another song. This one is a little heavier, called "Hellhound On My Trail." She plays it, and this time, she's not dancing. It's compelling, but like most blues songs she hears, it's not really her thing. But then she plays "Don't Call Me Miss," which is a total rocker.

Several of the other songs that have come up for Honey are by other artists, and she sees that, in fact, Honey has been a backup singer on some really powerful hits. She's sung backup for Elton John, Cher, Coldplay, Amy Winehouse, and a whole host of other artists. In fact, it seems she was on at least one of Gloria's albums. The shrieking "Get out / Get out / Get out of my bed" chorus on Gloria's high-powered "Sunrise Cigarette" was all Honey. Serafina is amazed.

It occurs to Serafina that the two were at her place at the same time. Why didn't they say anything? They must have history.

"Noey!" Serafina calls. Noey doesn't answer. She's probably watching something on Netflix. Serafina goes out to the living room, and sure enough Noey is curled up on the couch with an iPad. Serafina peeks over her shoulder and sees she's watching a documentary about the rise of videos on MTV. On the screen, Sheryl Crow is putting on a shoe and talking with an MTV host. Serafina can't hear what's happening, but then Gloria is pictured in one of her videos, sneaking behind a wall and half-lit, the light trained on her singing mouth with red lips. A man falls backward into a swimming pool and a woman blows smoke off the tip of a finger-gun.

Serafina laughs aloud. Startled, Noey jumps, caught like a little baby rabbit, and hugs the iPad to her chest. "Dang, S. Why did you scare me like that?"

"I didn't mean to." Serafina climbs over the back of the couch. "Whatcha watching?"

"MTV documentary. Did you see Gloria there? Isn't she amazing?"

"Yeah, but I couldn't hear it." She twirls a lock of Noey's hair, snuggles closer.

"And you know that Sian Star from the Whirlygirls? Her voice is so good. It reminds me of yours. You really should reach out." Noey uses her finger to scroll back along the video progress bar to find some scene of Sian Star or her band.

Serafina yawns. "Why are you so interested?" she asks. It seems suspicious to her, like Noey is spying, or taking too personal an interest.

"I've always loved music. You know that! It's why I'm so crazy about you." Noey smiles all sparkly. Too much, Serafina thinks. She's playing it up again, hiding something.

"You really have been invested in this project. And I can tell you have something you want to say about it. Why don't you go ahead and say it?"

Noey taps the window to find the stop button and clicks the side of her tablet to darken the screen. She blows a lot of air out of her mouth like she's frustrated. But then she looks up.

"Okay. Okay?"

"Yes, okay. Tell me. I can take it." Serafina moves her feet apart slightly, as if preparing for a hit.

"Okay. Well, you know I love you, right?"

"Yes. And?"

"And you're an amazing artist. And what you create, it's like, really real. Like people in our generation get it. They get it and it speaks to them, and it speaks to me. Like, you gotta know that. But you made this collection of women who did that same thing, but in their own time. And they are like, legendary. They are people who have relationships with other people through their music. And I don't want to be mean, but you're like, really not honoring that." Noey is kneeling on the sofa now, facing Serafina. The iPad is pressed against her belly like a shield.

"What do you mean, not honoring it?"

Noey chews her lip. "I mean, like you're not coming to them for who they are. You're coming at them as a collection of people, like *Oh my god this person*, but really, you need to be like, *You, you are the only person.* There's a difference."

"I'm not sure there is." Serafina feels herself getting warm. She knows she doesn't take correction well, and she's been working on it with her therapist, but this is not an easy correction to take.

"There is, babe. I mean, I might not be saying it the way you can hear it, and I'm sorry about that. I think you should keep being you, keep making your own star brighter, and really see where your career takes you. You don't need to do this duets thing right now. It's a distraction. It's, like, what's the point of it?"

"Mothers. They're my musical mothers. I wouldn't be anything without them. We've been over this."

"I don't think you know what it means to have a mother. No offense!" Noey has her hands up. "I mean, I'm so sorry you grew up without a mother, but you only know like shitty stepmother bitches who didn't really raise you right and were jealous of you. I think that is seeping into this project. You're not letting them sing. It's why it's not working. You're not coming in as equals and blending. Instead, you're like..." Noey is searching for the words.

"I'm dominating?"

"Yeah! You're kind of dominating, but you're also just taking up all the space. That's why I think you need to keep being you, Serafina. You need the whole stage. The *whole* stage." Noey is smiling brightly like this is the best thing in the world, like Serafina needs more stage than anyone.

"So I'm a super selfish fat fucking bitch who cannot handle sharing the spotlight with anyone?"

Noey's face falls. "That's not what I said at all. You always take me in the wrong way."

"I mean, you just told me I need the *whole* stage! What else am I supposed to think?" Serafina makes her body huge by holding out her arms and widening her stance.

"Babe, you're not supposed to think." Serafina winces. Noey tries to recover. "No, I mean, you're not supposed to *over*think. You're supposed to listen."

Serafina flops onto the couch and puts her head in her hands. Noey kneels next to her and brushes Serafina's hair back. It feels really good, even though Serafina doesn't want it to. "All I'm saying is to let this project marinate. Maybe it will happen later. Right now, it's not the right time. It's a weird project for now. Let it sit."

Noey seems to remember something. "Did you get a callback from the film?"

"No, no one texted me."

"Check your voicemail, silly!"

Serafina sees three missed voice messages from a 323 area code. "Oh shit. Who fucking sends voicemails anymore?" She puts the phone to her ear to listen to it replay.

Noey is too excited and starts to bounce on her knees on the couch. "What are they saying? Did you get it?"

Serafina can't believe what she's hearing. "Oh my god, bitch. I got the fucking lead!"

Jorge agrees with canceling the project, but he refuses to make the calls. "This business is 10% talent and 90% *relationships*." He draws the word out, elongating each of its four syllables. "You may need to work with these artists again or need their recommendations. Play nice, Serafina."

So Serafina is procrastinating.

"I'll call Honey," volunteers Noey. "I think I know how to break it to her."

"Call them all for me. Please?" Serafina really doesn't want to do this, and she knows she has to call Anny. She is desperate to just leave Gloria a text. Or better yet, a poop emoji.

"No. You have to do it. You can tell them that the project is on hold, but if you don't speak to each one personally, you'll be a shitty collaborator."

"Arrghh!"

Noey picks up her phone. "We'll do it together." She looks at the contract with Honey's number. "Here we go!" She taps in the numbers and holds the phone to her head. "It's ringing! Go, go!"

"You think any of these bitches give a damn about me? Of course they don't. Why did I even start this stupid project?" Serafina moans.

Noey gives her warning wide eyes. "Hi, this is Noemie Valentin. I'm calling for Ms. Honey Conaway? Yes, thank you. Of course I'll hold." She turns to Serafina and covers the receiver. "She has a house phone!" she stage-whispers and drops her mouth open like she's discovered a cuneiform tablet in her cereal box. Noey wanders out of the room with her phone so they don't sound like they're working a phone bank.

Serafina rolls her eyes and finds Gloria's sheet. Gloria has put up the hardest time of them all, and Serafina will be glad to see her go. She dials the number, and it goes to voicemail.

"Hi Gloria. It's Serafina. I just wanted you to know that I got a part in a movie, so I won't be moving forward with the duets album. You'll be compensated for your time. Please expect a check from my manager, Jorge Castro. Again, I'm so sorry to have to break this news to you, but I wish you luck in your future endeavors."

Not so bad. Her bullshit administrative assistant skills are still sharp from that internship. Serafina gets ready to input the next number when a text pops up on her screen from Gloria.

All the best. Xxoo

From anyone else, it would seem reasonable, but she feels a chill on her neck. She writes back.

You too

The message doesn't go through to say "Delivered" or "Received." Instead, a message pops up.

This number is temporarily out of service.

Noey returns to the living room deflated. "That was really hard. I mean, really hard. She really needed this work." Noey looks destroyed, but Serafina is too angry to deal with Noey's bleeding-heart drama.

Instead, Serafina stares at her phone as if it has just bitten her. "Fucking bitch blocked me!"

Chapter 11

THEY HAVE SENT a check for $200. Honey does some quick calculations: She spent more than one-fifty on each round-trip ticket, three of them in all, including the one for the failed session with Savion, and it turned out the last ticket was nonrefundable. Add to that the subway fares, the stupid-ass taxi fare Gloria never paid her back for, lost wages for two missed voice lessons, and on top of it all, now she's got some chest cough and can't sing, perform, or be around her students for another month. She's out almost a grand.

She won't be able to make the mortgage this month, so she calls the bank. The woman she reaches is receptive and kind, but she says she can only defer the payment for fifteen days. Her mother's Social Security check should be here at the beginning of the month, or on the seventh, tops. She's got $800 and change coming in from clients. She can try to hit up the church again, payment for services rendered.

Or, she thinks, maybe she can appeal to Serafina. In the phone call the other day, Noemie seemed to suggest that the project is on pause. Perhaps there is another project? Or she could sing backup on some session work?

She decides to try. "Screw my courage to the sticking place," she says, quoting one of her favorite Shakespeare plays, and dials Serafina's number. She walks into the kitchen, the room farthest from her mother's room, and tries to keep her voice low as she prepares to negotiate. Or beg.

"Yes, hello?" Serafina answers. She sounds distracted.

"Yes, this is Honey Conaway." Honey squeezes her eyes shut and hopes Serafina will remember her.

"Oh yes! I think Noey talked to you. Did you get the kill fee? Sorry we had to cancel. I only answered because I was expecting a call…"

"Yes, I did. I wanted to ask about that. What is included in that cost? I mean, how is it calculated?"

"Um, I think my manager Jorge can help you with that. I'm not really…"

"Yes, I understand. I saw in the contract that we would be paid a $200 kill fee and any session time, but I only received $200."

The line is quiet for a moment. Serafina's voice comes back through staticky. "But we didn't have any sessions together, so that makes sense, right?"

"Well, we didn't have a session because you were busy during our first appointment because you took Gloria ahead of me."

"Yes, but that's not *my* fault."

Honey can hear bustle upstairs in the house, and she backs herself into the corner behind the fridge, leaning in to whisper. "Well, it's not my fault either. And I did come up for one session, and I bought a ticket for a second one, which I couldn't get refunded." She knows she sounds defensive, but Serafina is in the wrong here.

Serafina huffs. "You should really call my manager. I'm sure he can work something out for you."

"Great! I will. Can you give me his number?" Honey uncaps a pen and scrambles for something to write with.

The line gets scratchy. Serafina sounds far away when she speaks again. "I listened to your music. You're really good. Amazing, actually."

"Thank you." Honey has never been good with compliments. This is a business call, and she fears she's getting sidelined.

"I'm in LA, on set. It's early, but I really don't think there's anything I can do. You should call Jorge."

"I will, if I can just get…"

"And don't sell yourself short."

"I'm trying…" Honey feels her mouth closing around the business argument. She's trying to tell this woman exactly how much she's worth, and it's Serafina who's deflecting. "I just…"

"I'll put in a word for you wherever I go."

"If there's any other project…"

Serafina's voice turns chilly and patronizing. "Honey, let me give you some advice. Don't sound desperate. It's not a good look."

Honey starts to panic. How does she sound? She is desperate. She could lose the house in a month. Her royalties and gig work have dried up and she's canceled on her clients to travel for the collaboration. Serafina is the reason for this mess.

"You said…"

"They're calling me for makeup. I've got to go. Call Jorge."

And the line drops. Again, Honey is alone. She scans the paperwork for Jorge's number. She doesn't even know his last name. She googles "Serafina manager Jorge representative" and gets a lot of press releases but no direct line. She calls the talent agency most associated with Serafina, but no one picks up. She leaves voice messages, and she tries her hardest to sound eager, not desperate, in all four.

The Social Security representative is adamant. "If your mother can work, she should work. She needs to find a job. Just because she has a disability doesn't mean she should get permanent benefits, including replacement income."

"But she doesn't have a job. She can't even get a job."

"That's not what our records say. We see that she has received two paychecks from someplace called UBK Work?"

"That can't be right."

"I suggest you talk with your mother," the representative says firmly.

"I just bathed my mother and helped her to the toilet ten minutes ago. I think I know what my mother is and isn't able to do."

"I'm sure it's a misunderstanding. Talk to your mother."

But it isn't a misunderstanding. Her mother *has* been earning money. Of all things, she's been hired as a part-time code writer. And her first two checks are in their sealed envelopes on her mother's dresser.

"Mama, when on earth did you get a job?"

"About a month ago. It's nothing."

"It's not nothing! You're getting checks! I hope it's more than you were getting from Social Security because they dropped you and you're not getting that money anymore."

"It's probably more. I hope."

"Mama, what kind of job is this?" Honey slits open the envelope and draws out the check. It is written out to her mother, and the payment is $600. She tears open the next one, and that too is $600. "Oh my god, Mama! What kind of work is this?"

"Piecework. They send me little bits of the program that need some patches and I write up the patches. It's simple when you know what to look for."

"Show me, Mama." Honey stares into the filthy screen. She subsumes the desire to fetch the glass cleaner and wipe it down. Instead, she stares through the sticky, gritty screen at a stack of windows, and she's not sure if it's her poor eyesight or the complexity of what she's looking at, but she's barely able to differentiate the various boxes and little figures all over the place. Her mother clicks onto a browser and then hits a few buttons. Before her eyes, all the words on the page disappear and there's a foreign language with symbols in it. Code.

"See here, I did this part." Her mother uses her fingers to indicate a chunk of text about the height of a cupcake. "Before, it didn't show the buttons with the right colors on the screen, and the text was just a bit out of place. So I put the right bits in and uploaded it, and now it's right as rain."

"You got $600 for that?" Honey is amazed.

"No, baby. I got $600 because they sent me hundreds of these. I did as many as I could in 30 hours each week. If they like the work, they send me the check. If they don't like it, they don't. So I make sure they like it."

"How many of these bits do they send you to do?"

"Oh, I don't know. I like doing it. It gives my brain a workout."

Honey notices something about her mother, now that she's opening up about this work: She's happy. She actually looks satisfied and productive. And now that she thinks about it, Honey hasn't smelled the rank stench of weed in a few weeks, at least. Maybe even a few months, since December or so.

After Mama had gotten into the car accident and been forced to retire, she had gotten so depressed. Ever since, she has padded around the house like a madwoman. Her mother dislikes reading, dislikes television, dislikes radio. She only wanted to play games on her phone or watch her pastor's sermons on the computer. So when she told Honey a while back she was doing Khan Academy, Honey thought it was just one more foray into keeping her mind occupied. Now she wonders if her mother has actually taught herself a valuable skill.

"Mama, what am I looking at here? Is this programming?"

"This..." Her mother pokes a cracked yellow nail at the screen. "This is github. I pulled the code from the master branch. I pull to work on it local, but I have to upload to the development server. Then I check it to make sure it looks the way it should."

Honey is floored. "How did you learn all this?"

"I did one of these online courses, but everyone just asks questions online about how to do little things, this or that, and other people answer. So you jump in on the conversation, or you look for someone else's answer. A lot of what you need to know is online, and if it's not, you figure it out, and then you can tell other people."

"Mama, I don't understand a damn thing you're talking about."

Her mother turns to her and gives a dead stare Honey can discern even in the low light of the room. "Honey, I sat in the audience and listened to you sing an aria in German. I didn't understand a damn thing you were singing, but I clapped anyway."

Honey thinks about it. Her mother's checks together, if they come regularly for a month, are a few hundred more than she was getting in disability payments, but she has to work for them, and the money is not guaranteed. Honey looks at her mother's face, full of purpose for the first time in so long. It's not as much as a job like this should pay, she thinks. But maybe her mother has to build up more skills.

"Oh, I am so sorry, Mama. You are right. You deserve applause!" Honey claps and shakes her fists in the air, cheering on her mother's success. As her mother takes a chair bow, Honey does a mental calculation for the month's bills. "Mama, how many more of these checks are you going to get?"

"I don't know. I'm on a trial period. I think if they like me, they'll offer me a job."

Honey holds up one of the checks. "Can I use this to pay the mortgage?"

"Aw, I was hoping to take a Hawaii vacation!" Mama smacks Honey on the leg. "Of course you can! Put the other one in our savings."

"Thank you, Mama. Just remember, they are not sending you Social Security if you keep getting these."

"Why not?" Honey's mother looks askance. "That money is owed to us, isn't it?"

"You work for money, or if you can't, you get the Social Security. You don't get both. That's what the lady on the line said."

"Damn. Okay, well I guess I got a job then. Bring me some of that red wine you got in the cabinet downstairs. We'll celebrate."

Chapter 12

SOMEONE HAS TORN up Gloria's garden. By the looks of it, some wild-life. Even so, it looks calculated, malicious. Evil-hearted. The lettuces are chewed down to the stem, and the peas, which had just flowered, have been uniformly chomped on and then stomped on. Each nascent pod has just a teeny stab wound of feral teeth but has been ripped from the stem, in places torn down with the vine, and moved over with a careless tread. It's enough to drive one batty.

Dory, the raccoon, is eating berries from her bowl when Gloria comes back into the house.

"You saw what happened? Who was it? I'll kill 'em." She shakes her fist and does her best *And your little dog too*, impression. Dory freezes. Her eyes dart to the closed back door and she drops a half-eaten berry. She drags the screen door open with her claw but doesn't bother to close it on her way out.

"I guess I'll just have to figure it out myself," Gloria holds her palms up and looks around at her empty house uber-dramatically, performing for no one. She feels the loneliness of the room. She's no stranger to putting on an act when no one is looking. In fact, she used to practice bits on stage in her living room when she was just coming up. She had different ones for different parts of the country.

East Coast: "I flew into JFK this morning. Just Fucking Kidding, y'all. I rolled out of bed and got here late anyway."

West Coast: "I took the red eye and used blue shadow to make this perfect violet smoky eye." Rapid blinks.

Chicago: While taking jacket off. "City of the big shoulders. Well, now you know I had 'em sewn in."

Texas: "Anyone know where I can get a little piece and quiet?" Finger guns.

Florida: "Mama? You out there?"

That last one was only half a joke. Gloria had been trailing her mother around different states as her mother took up with different losers. She'd given up on finishing high school and brought nothing with her but a go bag and her grandmother's guitar. The last place they lived was out in Jacksonville. Gloria left the night her mother's boyfriend tried to corner and kiss her. She took all her money, her guitar, and a Greyhound to New York City, fully aware she was the last seed in the tree to be scattered to the wind. She stopped waiting for her mother's smirk to appear in the audience, for a note to be sent to her from some usher, for any acknowledgment that her mother had been near the venue. Those first weeks in New York went about as well as can be expected. She was robbed, raped, and taken for a ride, but she did find her way with Jimmy's help. And then Jimmy turned out to be an asshole. And the rest of the shit is in her Wikipedia entry anyway.

She picks up her phone and automatically checks her email and socials. The business with Serafina isn't over yet. She's not so pissed off for herself, because that shit was irritating and she'd rather not record anything with the little limelight hog anyway. It's that Honey really seemed to need the gig. At Serafina's place in the city, Gloria could smell the desperation coming off Honey, the overeagerness in her eyes and the little pushes of her movements toward the office where Serafina held Gloria captive for nearly two hours. Honey wanted the work. She needed the work.

Gloria's not entirely sure it was about money, even. Honey is looking for prestige, for a comeback. Gloria would have given up her spot with Serafina if she'd known, would give Honey the space on the album. She does remember Honey as a hard worker, taking direction on take after take. Or at least she thinks she remembers that as Honey. If she's honest, it could have been any of them. She'd worked with dozens of desperate backup singers over time, most of them Black. Couldn't hurt to throw Honey another bone, now that this nonsense was canceled.

She dials and Len answers. He sounds like he's out of breath. "Are you fucking someone?" she asks.

"Why the hell would I answer the phone if I were in the middle of fucking someone?" he huffs. "I'm on the treadmill."

"Oh yes, going nowhere fast, as always."

"What do you want?"

"The Serafina thing—it's off."

She hears him pressing buttons, probably to stop the machine. "What did you do?"

"Nothing! She canceled it. It's off."

"You can't talk her into it?"

"Len, why would I? *I* had to be talked into it. If you want to turn on your charm and persuade her, call her yourself. I'm just doing you the favor of apprising you that it's a no-go."

"Goddamn it. Did she say why?"

"Something about a movie. She's in Los Angeles now. Or I think she is. I don't know. I blocked her number."

"You blocked her? You blocked Serafina? Really? I can't believe this shit." The sounds behind Len get louder and then quieter. He's likely rearing up for a lecture. "Gloria, she is A-list. A-LIST! You have never been A-list. It is a miracle she considered you at all. I was picturing you at the Grammys, Billboard, American Music Awards, at the Rock & Roll Hall of Fame, Juno, Mercury!"

"Wipe those dollar signs out of your eyes, Len. I'm retired. RETIRED. You can't tell when what you want is different from what I want. That's what the divorce was for, Len. It was a proof of concept. You want all this, and I want a little garden and a tiny house and a place to die quiet and alone." She's tapping her fingers on the counter fiercely.

She has all she wanted from this place. Little heartless beasts who tear up her hard work. Neighbors who spy on her over the fence and through the internet. No one to listen to her as she delivers killer lines to an empty room. She is lonely. She knows it. A heat rises on her neck as she realizes the person she's talked to the most since she's moved up here is her ex-husband, a guy she once threw plates at on the regular. She's lonely, and that's what that feeling at the pit of her stomach is.

"Glo, I know you. I know you better than you know yourself. You're tapping those nails right now, and I can hear it just a tiny bit. And that is your tell. When you tap, you're biding your time, waiting for the right offer. You're saying you're out, but you are always in for the right price."

"Yeah, what's my right price?" Her voice isn't keeping up the gusto because she's already feeling sorry for herself.

"You tell me."

The answer comes quick: Honey. She will work if Honey works, she decides. "I need you to find some work for this woman, another one who was supposed to be part of the project."

"What woman? What's her name?"

"Honey Conaway."

"Conaway? Cuckoo Conaway? The one who lost her damn mind on Danny Dire? No, she's untouchable. Can't do a thing."

"What do you mean? You can do a thing. You can always do a thing. Figure it out. That's my price."

"Why do you want her? Do you know who I have to go up against? I could get you Sian Harper. Her agent just called me and she needs a gig."

"Get me both. I'm feeling charitable. And you should feel lucky I'm doing anything at all. As I said, I expect to die in this house. Peacefully."

She hangs up. She has one more task before she's done with this unpleasantness. She fills a small cardboard mailer with strands of raffia and pink and gold vintage paper, gold leaf with a pattern of baby's breath, $40 a sheet. It looks gorgeous. She closes up the box and writes Serafina's address in loopy script, and then her own return address at the top. Finally, she flips the box right side up and admires her handiwork. She pops the top and into that lovely nest, she drops a little gift for the stubborn, self-centered bitch: a brand-new pink pacifier.

Chapter 13

THEY ALWAYS HAVE stupid craft projects at these things. Parents at the school pay loads of money, on top of tuition, to sit inside the cafeteria on hard plastic benches with the kids, and then they wander around spending more money buying crap their kids made. This one is called Eastertide Carnival Celebration, as if spring in Alabama is just something to heap laudatory nouns upon.

Today the craft project is lacing up gimp in little cardboard shoes to hang on a "shoe tree." It's stupid. Even Carly thinks it's stupid. And she's three.

"Sunny, can I do it like this?" Carly asks Sian, twisting a green strand of gimp around her little pink finger until it turns red and swollen.

"Yes, baby," says Sian, pushing the cardboard shoes out of the way. "We can use the string however we like. We can make bracelets." She demonstrates by putting a string around her scarred wrist, angling the red welt toward the table. Embarrassed, she moves the plastic thread to her neck. "Or necklaces."

Carly's eyes widen and she starts grabbing the plastic string. Sian is braiding a few strands together when Lulu stomps back to the table, hissing. "Mama! Christ!"

Sian looks up, alarmed. Carly is slowly twisting two strings of gimp around her own neck, cutting into the pale folds of flesh.

Lulu unwraps the gimp from Carly's neck and pulls the cardboard shoes over. "I swear, I can't leave you alone with her for two minutes!" Cutting her eyes at her mother, she demonstrates the lacing aspect for Carly.

"If the shit was so dangerous, why did they put it out for kids this age?" Sian huffs.

"Because it's a supervised activity. You are supposed to supervise. What were you doing?" The acid in Lulu's attitude could cut a hole in the floor.

A minute ago, Sian admired her handiwork, which looked like an elegant Celtic knot. Now it just appears like a few cheap bits of plastic bent into loops.

"What's the point of this, Lulu?" There are fat families everywhere at different tables, sitting with obedient toddlers who are crayoning the fuck out of paper or just pre- or post-meltdown. "Why can't we be at your house?"

"You know why," Lulu hisses. And that's true and also not true. Sian has never done anything seriously dangerous at Lulu's house. But also all her nosy neighbors know when Sian is living there, even though she's grown out her mohawk, and they take pictures of her smoking a blunt on the back porch or giving them a finger or flashing a tit. They're here because Lulu thinks Sian won't pull anything in public, but Lulu should know better. Sian's tolerance for bullshit is super low. Any one of these families could be walking out of here with Sian's spit on their face if they disrespect her.

But this is a nice school, so they won't. They'll sit on their asses and glue stupid, cheap beads to stupid, cheap boards and then throw it all out when their kids move out to go to college or to do heroin or to join the army or to kill themselves. And this stupid-ass day will be the thing they cry over and the beads will feel super important. She wants to pitch a fit in the middle of this degeneracy.

"I need a cigarette," says Sian.

"You need to pay attention to your granddaughter. Here. Help her do this one," Lulu shoves another cardboard shoe at Sian as if Sian is not clear on the mission.

Sian drops it and goes back to working on her Celtic knot. A metallic pain stabs her in the groin and she winces, puts her hand to the spot. It's warm. *The stings and daggers of menopause*, she thinks. Or is it slings? Is it daggers? Probably Shakespeare never even thought of menopause. Either way, the stabbing pains have been off and on, though she hasn't had any other signs. Sucks getting older, she thinks. But soon she won't have to deal with blood anymore.

Carly stands next to Sian on the bench and whispers in her ear something very important, something that makes Sian smile. "I want blue hair like you."

Sian whispers back. "I got you, baby."

Lulu's pretty mouth twists with jealousy. "What secrets are you two sharing?" She smooths her jacket under her as she slides in next to Carly and gently wrestles the toddler back to a sitting position. "What is Sunny going to do? What bad thing did she just promise?" Carly, giggling, doesn't tell.

They don't have to meet in public spaces. Even though Lulu had tried for a restraining order on Sian, the judge had disagreed. He said as long as anyone else is around, it's a supervised visit, and as long as Sian doesn't try to get high while her granddaughter is around, she's not under any other constraints. So she can curse, bring a boyfriend around, or drink, within reason. All in all, the judge seemed to be on Sian's side.

The judge might have been a fan.

The judge was actually, probably, most definitely a fan.

So Sian got the better end of the deal, while Lulu spent all her public relations money on the sleazy lawyer. And they both got their picture in the paper, but Sian got honest-to-god interviews out of it. Lulu may or may not have gotten a book deal. Little bitch isn't telling.

Sian has never enjoyed other mothers, especially mothers of preschoolers. All the worrying about perfect little bento boxes and whether

Montessori or Emilia-Reggio was a better fit, or that whole Baby Einstein thing. If Sian could do it over, she'd send Lulu to some sort of boarding school, force her to make her own friends, make her respect her mother more. Actually, she had sent Lulu to boarding school for two years, but that was just while Sian was in rehab, and then back on drugs, and then back in rehab, so Sian didn't really get to enjoy Lulu's time away.

This line of thinking is not helpful, Sian knows. She forces her attention to the craft materials again and this little snugglebug of a granddaughter.

"Those are some nice laces. What are you gonna do with your shoe, baby?"

Carly holds on to Sian as she stands on the bench again. "I'm gonna kick."

Sian's smile broadens. "Yeah, baby. Let's give 'em all some good kicks!" She looks at Lulu as she holds Carly's hands, and they both kick their legs out at the other people who cower, slightly, at their faraway tables. "Rock and roll!" Sian says as she winks, just in time to see the rolling of Lulu's eyes.

"How many days, Ma?" Lulu's count is slightly different from Sian's. "Nineteen?"

"Forty-seven, not counting Graceland."

"Why aren't we counting Graceland?"

"Because it's fucking Graceland. You can't go to Graceland sober. It's like not even allowed. Plus it was weed." Sian gestures with her arms around the auditorium. "Ninety percent of the people in this room smoked weed in the last week."

"Mom, half the people in here are toddlers."

"Contact high. Whatever. I really fucking need a cigarette."

"There's no smoking on campus. There's no smoking in this town, Mom. You have to go to the Kmart in Allen if you want to light up."

"How do you stand this place?" Sian knows that Lulu doesn't have much of a choice though. The only place that had taken her for college with her shitty grades was Auburn. Auburn, Alabama, and then she fell in love in college instead of waiting like a sensible person until she got back to New York. Now Lulu can't leave because she's been co-parenting Carly since her divorce, though co-parenting just seems to mean that her ex-husband takes the kid one weekend a month and gets to harass Lulu if she thinks about leaving the state. And since Sian's last overdose, Sian has become Lulu's other ward. And as much as Sian wants her independence, she knows she's not safe to live alone. Even if she wants to kill everyone who is just trying to help.

Sian is used to feeling uncomfortably visible. She doesn't remember a time when people didn't whisper and point at her, and she came to read their gestures as fawning over her or jawing about her maliciously. These good country folks are not appreciating Sian's tank top or her skinny, strung-out style. They hold their toddlers close when Sian comes by. They may not even recognize her, which is a good thing because she's not up for the hungry eyes of fans today.

Lulu shrugs. "It's mostly okay."

"It's so white it makes my skin crawl."

The carnival is a fundraiser for the school. The children have made art that is pinned to the walls all around. They've also poured candy into jars and decorated the jars with glued-on beads and glitter, and the teachers have taken pictures of the children as they sleep, and these photographs are on the wall. All of this is for sale. The fundraiser also includes a service auction where you can bid on a teacher to take your child out on a picnic, or you can get an hour of legal advice. Sian is finding it hard to want anything here.

"It's not all white." Lulu points to a few families on the edges who look Indian or Pakistani. Sian can't tell. They're sitting by themselves, and that makes Sian feel even sadder.

"It's not a city though. I haven't heard anyone say one word in Spanish since we've been down here."

Sian leans over to Carly and whispers, "Mijita, te amo mucho y solo a ti." Carly beams up at her and plants a kiss on Sian's cheek. Sian ruffles her granddaughter's hair.

"Mom, you're not ready to go back to New York. You think you are, but you're not. It's safer in the South."

"It's not safer in the South for anyone."

"It's safer here for you. If you can't find your connections, if effing crazy Blue is not banging down your door at three in the morning, if Jerry isn't beating the crap out of you or stealing all your money, if the people you talk to are not known only by one moronic street name, then you are safer. Safer from yourself."

She's right, but even without the sickness coming back, life makes her head itch. "I can go into any grocery I want and walk out with a beer and a firearm. You really think it's safer?"

"Mom, please stop scaring me. Just stop."

Sian stands and wanders off, moving her body and taking her mind off the ache in her groin. She might have mistaken it for lust, an ache for penetration, a pressure to be satiated by more pressure and friction. She remembers the days right after she gave birth, how she sometimes sneaked away while baby Lulu slept to rub herself raw, her clitoris feeling stiff and angry, her vagina pulsing insistently. Drugs sometimes settled the hormones, but sometimes made it all worse. Bodies are so freakish, she thinks, and she can stare at the crowd, mentally strip them all naked, and watch them creep around like animals, the men with their oblivious dicks and the women covering their saggy tits and trimmed and lotioned vulvas. *Carnival* is both meat and flesh, carnal and carnivore. All this meat in the room, trussed up and pretending it's clean.

She finds herself critiquing the pinned art like some sort of undergrad. Lots of fingerpainting, which she knows won't last even until the kids graduate high school. The paper is too low quality, and she can smell the egg in the tempera, so it will turn or, at the very least, crack in time. She looks at the children's paintings, and one catches her eye. It's called "Scarecrow," and it has what looks like a cat on a pole and birds that are either pecking at it or just angled in a way to attack it. It's massively intense and Sian immediately wants it. She unpins it, takes it to the cashier, and pays $5 cash. She doesn't carry a purse, so she just holds the painting under her arm as she fixes up her wallet.

She returns to the wall to scan the other art. Carly's painting is just a big black smear. It doesn't seem worth the five bucks to Sian.

Carly runs up to Sian's legs just as she's moving on. "Sunny!" Sian hoists her up and points at Carly's art.

"Can you tell me about this painting?" she asks Carly.

Carly is exhausted. She shakes her head and buries it in Sian's neck. The heft of the child, warm and loving, is reassuring, a sensation to collect for those desperate moments when Sian feels like shit and like killing herself. This is what she's living for. She can't possibly traumatize this baby the way she'd been traumatized. She must keep going. Lulu starts to unpin the picture from the wall.

A teacher steps forward with two well-dressed parents who didn't bring their child. The guy is wearing a long camel-hair coat, and the woman has a chichi purple trench coat draped over her arm, and they're clearly on their way out. No one needs a coat in Alabama in April.

They're looking for a specific picture, and the teacher says, "Oh, I think it was here. It was called 'Scarecrow.' Really interesting piece."

Sian realizes what's happening and turns to hustle out of the place. Lulu senses Sian's panic and looks at Sian suspiciously, knowingly. As Sian adjusts Carly, Lulu snatches the picture from under Sian's arm. "Mom," Lulu hisses. "You can't just steal another kid's artwork!"

"I paid for it. You can ask that bitch over there." Sian points with her elbow at the cashier.

"That picture is not Carly's. You can buy Carly's, but that one belongs to another child."

"It belongs to me. I paid five bucks." Sian tries to grab it back from Lulu's hand, but Lulu is too quick.

Lulu hisses, "You're unbelievable." She turns to the couple and holds out the painting.

"It's art! I'm in an art gallery. I can buy whatever the fuck I want!" Sian hisses back. They're making a scene, which attracts the teacher's attention.

"Oh, there it is," says the teacher. "There must have been a misunderstanding. This one is Carly's." She points at the rejected smeary painting. Even Carly doesn't seem to want to recognize the work as hers.

"I want this one. I paid for this one," says Sian, getting close enough to snatch back the other kid's painting. She tucks it under her arm again, and Carly grunts. "Five dollars."

"Yes," smiles the teacher. "That's Eloine's. And these are Eloine's parents."

"Then they can ask Eloine to paint something else. I paid for this one."

The teacher is smiling wildly, now appealing to Lulu. "Ms. Carson, I hope you understand..."

"Of course we do," says Lulu.

"I hope *you* understand..." says Sian.

The guy in the coat has been puzzling over something for a minute. Suddenly, he snaps his fingers. "Were you in a band back in the nineties? The Whirlygirls?"

Sian rises to her full height and shifts the baby to her other shoulder. She knows exactly how she's going to win this battle, and the war. In all her glory, she smiles, and says, "I was. And I'm taking this painting. When your kid grows up, you can tell her that the Sian Star has her weird-ass fingerpainting on her wall."

She walks out with the baby on her shoulder and the painting in her hand, Lulu trailing her to the parking lot.

"You're unbelievable," Lulu shouts.

"And you're a broken record. You're boring as hell," Sian throws over her shoulder.

"Give me my child right now or I'll have you arrested for kidnapping." Sian keeps walking and Lulu yells after her. "That's what it is: kidnapping. Walking away with another person's child."

Sian stops, her eyes burning. She really is trying, but she can't get work, she is dying for a cigarette or something stronger. Her daughter cannot imagine how it is to live in her body, to hate herself so much, to need something to believe in.

She turns and sees Lulu is stretching out her arms to her child. Lulu's eyes are disappointed, disengaged. She can't even see Sian anymore. She has no empathy left.

"I'm still your mother," Sian says. "You can't get rid of me."

"Mom," Lulu says. "Give me Carly. It's time for us to go."

"You can't get rid of me," Sian says again, less sure. They are halted under a streetlight in the parking lot full of equal numbers of pickup trucks and Priuses. Sian's eyes catch on a bumper sticker that says, "Rock and Roll is the Devil's Music (let's keep it that way!)" She smirks, and Lulu's mouth twists in rage. Even still, Lulu is so beautiful, the love for her daughter twangs Sian's groin again, the place where Lulu was made calling out for her.

"Give me my child or I swear I'll scream."

Sian looks at Carly's drooping eyes, runs a finger over Carly's sweaty hairline, smells the baby shampoo and teething gel tangs in a heady mixture. "I have to go, sweetie." Carly puckers up for a kiss and then leans out to Lulu.

As soon as Carly is in Lulu's arms, Lulu hisses, "Why do you always do this? You're such an embarrassment."

Sian fights all the urges that rise up in her, the urge to grab Carly back, the urge to throw herself into traffic, the urge to stomp off and find a dealer, the urge to pick one of those fleshy dads and take him around the corner and screw his lights out, the urge to steal one of the cars and smash it into any other solid object until it stops running or even explodes in flames. All the urges rise up like aerosol lit by a match, and just as suddenly, they whoosh through her and she stops.

"I love you," she says.

Lulu droops her head to the side and says, "Stop it. Stop the mind games." She walks off with the warm, loving child, headed back to her warm, loving house, leaving Sian stranded in the warm, empty night, humidity like a blanket in the spring evening.

"You can't get rid of me," she whispers. She spies the dad with the camel-hair coat and gives him a little wave. He smiles tentatively and looks back into the dark of the school for his wife. Sian heads into the night, looking for a familiar face or car she recognizes, pretending to enjoy the time alone under the stars and the company of no one but herself. Pickup trucks rumble by, and she smiles at each, acknowledging its own potential for her destruction, each a test she has to pass.

Chapter 14

HONEY WALKS into the hotel and asks at the front desk for the location of the Swan Room. The helpful attendant points her back through the lobby and toward a set of double doors. She winds her way past pink and green wallpaper and flashing cameras on the stucco ceiling. The place gives her the creeps. The vibe is not exactly *The Shining*, more like where you bring your little girls in makeup and false teeth to be paraded around and judged by white men. She hustles along the carpet in her kitten heels and finds the steel door to the room. She pulls it open, releasing a gush of cool air drawn forward with the vacuum of the opening.

Inside the enormous room, three people sit at three different tables. It's clear that they haven't rented this room for anything other than a space. Not even a water jug is in sight. It looks set up for a conference of hundreds, not the small group that's currently waiting for her. A white man, who must be Len, is sitting at one of the tables with his feet up. His hair is silvery, and his face is long and sallow with bags under his eyes. He could have been a good-looking man once, with a round chin and full lips and a straight nose, eyes that may once have held a twinkle or two. He looks more like he'd rather be sucking down drinks at a titty bar than making records. He's kicked back slightly and he drops his feet as he spies her. The other two are staring into their phones, and one of them, Gloria, looks up.

Len stands but doesn't approach. "There she is, the golden girl." He doesn't sound happy to see her. She doesn't feel like a golden girl.

"How much did she cost you, Len?"

"Seven-fifty." He rocks back and forth on his heels and smiles in that I'm-gonna-punch-something-in-a-minute way. He grits his teeth. "Worth every penny, I guess." Honey meant to approach him to shake his hand but stops in her tracks.

"Nice." Gloria nods appreciatively. "Baby, you're worth way more than that," she says to Honey.

"The train ticket was more than two hundred dollars because I had to buy it last minute, and I had to cancel…"

"Nope, don't explain." Gloria stands and waves Len off. She levels her gaze at Honey and reiterates, "You're worth every penny. Way more than seven hundred and fifty ever-loving dollars. So good to see you." Gloria leans in for a hug, which Honey receives. It's surprisingly warm and generous, and Honey intuits that Gloria may be the only one who wants her here. The last time they met, Gloria and she did seem to come to an understanding. Still, she fears she's being set up for something. She's heard the stories about Gloria, and she believes them all.

"I'm sorry I'm late. The rideshare from the station…"

"Must have been a long trip," Len says, and he pulls out a chair at the table where Gloria is sitting—not his own table. "Take a load off."

She sits and puts her purse on the table. "So I hear that this is a new project. You're thinking of a duets album yourself?"

"Not exactly," Gloria replies and grins. "I got something better in mind. Sian, sugar, come on over."

The third person, a tall woman with dyed blue hair that falls below her eyebrows, looks up. Her eyes are ringed with black eyeliner, and her roots are steel-gray. Her sallow skin is richly decorated with tattoos and piercings. She's about Honey's age, gorgeous, and familiar. Honey has the feeling their paths have crossed before, like in grade school. Like she has always existed in Honey's consciousness.

"This is Honey?" the woman asks the floor, and she sticks out her hand for a shake. She doesn't make eye contact and doesn't smile. As she approaches, Honey smells cigarettes, patchouli, and garlic.

"Yes. And you are?"

"Sian." She drops into a chair and rifles through her pocket to draw out a mint. She pops it from the plastic wrapper and crunches it immediately, releasing a cloud of spearmint to envelop them all.

Gloria laughs at Honey. "You've never heard of the Whirlygirls? Seriously?"

Honey is mortified. Of course she has! Sian is a legend. "Oh my goodness! Sian Star! I should have recognized you right off. Of course you are!"

"It's been a minute since I've been relevant." Sian waves her hand around at some invisible world behind her. "At least for music," she laughs. Another wave of mint and cigarettes crashes into Honey's senses. It's not unpleasant, this woman's smell. Or her attitude. She's never met Sian before, but Sian's bad behavior is legendary. Honey's memory of Sian's career is a string of irreverent bubblegummy hits, mostly favored by preteens, and then more mature bad-girl songs with double entendre, followed by a stretch of perp walks, burning of posters, spit hawked on TV cameras, slapped cops, and, if she's remembering correctly, the crashing of a car into the Rock & Roll Hall of Fame.

Honey takes quick stock of the three women in the room, including herself. Two of them are in their late forties and one in her sixties and in retirement. She's not sure what the hook can be that brought her to collaborate with these two. She has never thought for a minute that she would find herself in the same room as Sian Harper, Sian Star, mostly because she thought Sian's career was over. But then, she had thought Gloria's was too.

Oh, shit, she thinks. *That's why we're here.*

And as if reading her mind, Gloria smiles brightly and changes the subject. "Sian, I met Honey just, what, a month ago? Damn, it was cold that day, wasn't it? Anyway, we had a nice lunch, and we talked all about this project we were both involved in. We were going to work with *Serafina*."

She stretches out Serafina's name as if it's the name of an island off the coast of Italy. Len rolls his eyes and scratches at the table idly.

Sian's look betrays that she has heard this spiel before, that Gloria is performing for Honey. Sian also looks like she's dying for a cigarette, or something harder. Honey is getting thirsty for a drink herself, just to take the edge off. But there is no wait staff in sight.

Gloria continues. "But Serafina ran off and took her little project with her, and I gotta say, that whole little affair just whet my appetite. I couldn't stop thinking about getting real creative and making an album. Doesn't that sound good to you?"

Sian, for the first time, looks interested in what Honey has to say. She rests her face in her palm and leans forward slightly across the table.

Honey says quietly, "It sounds scary as hell."

"Let me show you something." Gloria reaches under the table and brings up a record. Honey has seen this one. It's *Trio*, the album by Dolly Parton, Linda Ronstadt, and Emmylou Harris. On the cover, they're all in these cowboy getups. She remembers seeing a video of the three of them cutting out paper hearts and singing.

Gloria starts to hum the tune, "To Know Him Is to Love Him."

Then she asks, "You know that one? It's a great album. We should get together and play it sometime, have ourselves a listening party. But that's not why we're here."

Sian picks up her phone. "I'm not singing any goddamned country music."

"No one asked you to," says Len, afraid he's losing a deal. Gloria gives him one of those looks that just about shuts him back into his little box.

"We aren't making a country album. I'm proposing that we make an album that represents the three of us. On equal terms."

"The three of us," snorts Sian. "Call it *The Three Fuckups*?"

Gloria shakes her head. "That sobriquet cannot be equally applied, I'm afraid."

Honey doesn't really understand the premise of the album. "I don't see what we have in common. Like, what genre would we do? Gloria, you've got all those country ballads about not needing a man. And Sian, your music is like angry rock and roll. Isn't that right? And I've been singing mostly gospel for the last few years. How are we going to find a common theme?"

Gloria laughs. "You ain't never been lonely, pissed off, and prayerful all at the same time? I'm not seeing that there's much difference among the three of us. For example, let's take one of the Whirlygirls' later songs. How about 'The Game.' I always liked that one. You know it, right?"

Honey does. Sian doesn't look like she's listening, but Gloria's playing this right. She may even know what Honey knows about the history of this song, and that might be why she picked it. It's one of the only songs Sian got writing credit on, so it probably means something to her.

"I'll start it off. You all come in when you feel like it and we'll see what we can do together."

I've been down and around
In this one-horse town
Trying to find someone to blame

Honey jumps in tentatively on the next line. She spies Sian sniffling and looking away. The purpose of the room is clearer now, as Gloria trills higher and bolder once she has a singing partner, and the space is needed to capture them all.

But it's not as I thought
The bargain I bought
Just another way to play the game.

Their voices create an eerie sound; Honey's contralto and Gloria's bright soprano dart around each other like two lone insects at night. It's just a few bars, but Honey gets it. She's sung with Gloria before, but it hasn't been on an even keel. When Gloria gives Honey space, they do sound, not really complementary, but more like sisters who know how to share.

Sian can't help but join in, despite her obvious reservations. She closes her eyes and picks up on the chorus. Honey puts more power in, finding a waiting space for her contralto below the twining sopranos of the other women.

It's a game with you baby
Win or lose, cheat or quit
This is it, this is it.

It's a game with you baby
Winners, losers all the same
The same in this brutal game.

It's clear they've got something together. Honey is scraping down deep for the desperation in the "Win or lose" line, one she's always liked, the complicated little run and the drop on *This is it, this is it.* And Gloria is bopping around on those high notes like it's nothing up there, singing like she's just dancing, light as a feather. But the addition of Sian's voice is magical. It's a throaty warble that, as she sings along, picks up raw emotion, loss and some sort of threat. She snarls as she sings, perhaps remembering the subject of the song, or perhaps just ruminating on her own bad luck or bad choices. The three sounds braid beautifully, three perfectly formed whole women, the lives they've lived preparing the road for their voices to unfurl on. Honey is lost in it, wants the song to keep going, but they've landed at a place where none of them is too sure of the lyrics. They start to ad lib and then they break into embarrassed laughter.

Len is smiling like a madman. Honey wishes she had a curtain to pull across so he didn't see the three of them in their unbridled joy. She feels naked and sized up, and she tries to ignore the chill coming from his side of the room, the icy current that smells like cologne and other people's money.

Chapter 15

DESPITE EVIDENCE to the contrary on display at the little meeting, Sian does not feel good about the trio idea. She feels tricked, angry, cranky, maybe hungry, but definitely not right. Why did they want her? And what was with the rental of the whole conference room for just the four of them? The acoustics were shit, and she wants nothing to do with these ladies. Gloria is some '80s has-been who pops up on those rate-a-singer and cooking shows and throws her weight around like she's an industry darling. She's been out of the game for longer than she's been in it, and worse, she's practically a novelty act.

And Honey. Dear lord, where did they dig her up? Sian had been at the awards show where Honey had lost her shit. Girl hauled off and punched one of the biggest producers in the industry, blinding him. He says it was a big misunderstanding, but Sian knows Danny Dire, knows him intimately. No one in the industry says no to Danny Dire. Sian's been in more than one bathroom at more than one venue to find him waiting for her. He demands the terms, it's over when he's finished, and he's paid everyone off ahead of time to make sure no one is about to rescue your ass. That's how it is. That's how it's always been. So if Honey had some misunderstanding about what Danny Dire wanted from Honey, it was because no one had explained these rules.

Fucking Danny Dire. All the Danny Dires and the Van Jurgens and the Seth Allens and the Jacky Joneses. All of those goddamn prima donna producers and their hairy balls and stinky dicks and oniony breath and trays of free coke and speed and drinks and needles and whatever else would keep you on the stage and then on your knees.

And then, when you were all used up and the next bright thing was coming through, ready to be gutted by the machine, the banality of evil rose up and reigned. The whisper campaigns and rumor mills and well-placed hit pieces and memes, and if any one of those former fans who shared images and idly talked or listened could think for a minute, they might understand they were part of the tank running over someone who not long ago was a nineteen-year-old girl with a golden voice and a killer body, and they would maybe stop the tank.

But they never do. They talk and click *share* and laugh and make a joke and move on. And the killing floor churns.

Honey had taken it on and maybe thought she could win. As Gloria might say, *Bless her heart.*

Sian calls Mal, the drummer from the first iteration of the Whirlygirls, and still one of her best friends. Mal was the drummer for Backbend, who'd made it huge back in 2008. Right after Mal quit, they had met up and drank until they both got kicked out of the bar and pissed on the street and spat on passersby who fucked with them, but they both admitted that it wasn't as much fun anymore. Mal's son has just graduated from some college with a degree in animation, and Mal's wife Jackie is looking at beach houses in Delaware. Mal might be available for some advice on this project because Sian has a twist in her gut about it.

Mal answers on the first ring. "I was just thinking about you," she says. She always says that. Sian knows it has never once been true. It's like some weird social tic Mal has.

"Oh, were you masturbating?" Sian jokes.

"Well, I thought of you while I was thinking about masturbating, but then I thought of Jenny Lewis to get me off."

"Nice choice."

"I know, right? I like my fantasies age-appropriate."

"And, apparently straight." Sian is smiling now.

"Damn straight, in fact. So what bad decision do you need me to talk you into now?"

"Funny you should say that…" Sian tells Mal about the warehouse-sized conference room in the hotel off 95 and the three of them harmonizing to one of the Whirlygirls' songs, "The Game."

"It actually sounds like they're fucking with you, babe," says Mal.

Sian considers it. "I don't think they are. I think Gloria's being a manipulative cunt, but I don't think she is fucking with me. And Honoria Conaway? She's sincere for sure, but she's also clearly not all in. She wants this album bad, but I don't know what that's about. My guess is money, but maybe she does want another bite at the apple."

"Maybe she wants to do something real. Maybe she does think she has a shot at, like, a hit."

Sian lights a cigarette and holds it between her thumb and forefinger. She's not supposed to do anything that reminds her of getting high, but it feels good in this moment. "Mal, am I this person?"

"I don't know. Do you feel like a trio person? Do you vibe with them?"

"I don't mean that. I mean, I'm sitting in a tank with some really old lobsters. Is this my last option for making something of myself? If I don't do this, do I just give up and go grandma and fuck it all?"

Mal is smoking too. Sian can hear it on the other end. "Honestly, it sounds like you have a chance here. You have to decide if you're someone who can do this. You've never played well with others as long as I've known you, but there's a first for everything."

Sian grimaces. Mal is not wrong. The Whirlygirls had been a solid act, with all the A&R guys from the top music labels were after them, and it had always been Sian who didn't show up, Sian who threw a drink in a face after someone grabbed her ass, Sian who fucked the wrong A&R guy and got them a crap deal, Sian who signed for their gear and left it on the porch until all of it was stolen, bit by bit. Mal's the only one who still loves her, has forgiven her. But back then, Sian's face was buried in coke so long she didn't notice everyone bailing around her.

She did have a comeback album, but it had come out just after she had Lulu and while her then-husband Jerry was doing the mommy-role thing. He didn't have a job, so it was okay for a while, but soon he got sick of taking shit from his friends, getting called Mr. Sian Star and having nothing to talk about except diapers and playdates. Jerry left and she had to cancel tour dates. Then her mom died, and Jerry moved back in, and Lulu got a master class in administering Narcan and knowing when and when not to call the cops for an OD.

The one thing Sian did right in all of it was to make sure she didn't spend all Lulu's money. Her accountant always put half the royalties into a trust for Lulu, so now her daughter owns her own house and doesn't have to work, though she does at a PR firm. Sian couch surfs when she and Lulu are on the outs.

But that's all right. Sian has exactly what she needs: friends, temporary sobriety, a PO box, and a face that gets her whatever she wants from a restaurant at least once a week. So this trio album might help her back on her feet. The only thing she really worries about is what bad places those feet will want to take her to once she's upright.

"Yeah, I guess I'll give it a try. But can you do me a favor?"

"Protect you from yourself?"

"You know me so well."

Sian steps up to the mic.

This is my swan song...

She reads the poem slowly to the rapt audience, trying not to shake with fear. When she sings, the words become something else and she can feel her body lean into the performance, but here, with just an open notebook in front of her, her voice trembles with emotion.

Once she finishes, she takes a breath. "Thank you."

There is clapping, but she knows the poem isn't done. The words don't mean what she wants them to yet. The first two parts are absurd, body parts cut off from each other, and nothing brings it home. She wants to be called out, to not receive praise, but no one will tell her this poem sucks. She wants to disappear into bad art, into half-baked ideas, into faux intellectualism. Her happiest days had been with the grad school drop-outs who supplied her with ecstasy, heroin, and special K as she floated around the Lower East Side, ripping it up at underground punk clubs and packing rooms to see Nuyoricans read slam poetry, but you really can never go back. Now she's in a room with white-haired suburbanites in pantsuits. It's possible some of these people are the same people she ran amok with, but she hopes to god they aren't.

After the readings, she's rushed by fans. They ask her everything, but she can see the question in their eyes. *Did you really drive into the Rock & Roll Hall of Fame?*

She had. But as with everything, it wasn't that simple.

It had been late, and she'd been in Cleveland for something, maybe a panel for some local singing competition that she blew off but was likely to be canceled anyway. She went out with some guys she met instead of answering her agent's frantic calls and threats. The guys were named Rookie and Jerzy. *Jerzy* not *Jersey*. It was a running joke and she would say, "Hey, what exit?" But he was Jerzy with a *z* and didn't know what she was asking. And she'd laugh her ass off because she was super high and then she'd ask again. And Jerzy was like, "Let's go look at the Rock & Roll Hall of Fame," so they drove there. And it was close to the water, and hard to get your car anywhere near the place, but also it was COVID times, so no one was there. It was gorgeous as shit. Rookie said, "It's like a glass pyramid," and Sian said, "It's exactly a glass pyramid, you idiot." And Jerzy laughed, which made Sian say, "What exit?" and Jerzy had had enough, and he reached over as if to throttle her, but he was driving and when he leaned, his foot hit the gas and they hopped the curb and drove past the LONG LIVE ROCK sign and got close to the entrance, but then Jerzy realized what he had done and stopped. And then they just sat there in the car, across from the dark museum. Sian was feeling overly speedy and terrified and felt like Jerzy was going to kill her, so she kicked him out of the driver's seat and made like she was going to be reasonable and get them out of there. Because there were cops coming at them now because they were sure as fuck not supposed to be close to the museum with their car. But then she thought, *I'm going to drive this car right into that fucking building.* And she did.

So, maybe it wasn't that complicated.

Later, when she was recovering from her wounds in the hospital, she heard that Lulu had delivered a healthy baby girl. So Sian has been clean, mostly, since.

She sits by herself after the people leave with their fresh stories about having met her and listened to her shitty poetry. And she thinks, *Okay, I can do this thing, and I can do it well, and I can make a change. I can be something other than the fucking idiot who drove her car into the Rock & Roll Hall of Fame with two moron drug dealers.*

But at the base of the lofty idea she knows, even if they make it big, when people talk about the trio, there will be the alt country bitch, the gospel psycho, and the one who drove a car into a museum dedicated to rock and roll. And nothing she can ever do will shake that.

Chapter 16

THE INVITATION COMES to Honey in a detailed email from Len's secretary. The gig is for a week in New York, all expenses paid, lodging included, so they can build out a set list of at least twelve demo tracks to shop around to labels. Apparently they'll be staying in a private residence, not a hotel, which makes sense. Honey has never worked this closely with other artists before. Back when she'd been on her own preparing *Staircases*, her manager had bought a bunch of rejected and low-cost songs and the arranger had tweaked them for her range. She poured her heart into that album, and it was great. It was really great. And the industry agreed: She still has her little Grammy on her shelf.

There was talk of collaboration, and then there wasn't. Her reputation had been so smeared and destroyed that even her brother, Barnabas, whom she still called Bunny, questioned her choices and constantly wanted to relitigate what happened between her and Danny Dire.

"You know that's assault. Mama never taught us to hit people. That's assault," he'd say. "I bring jokers in all the time on that charge."

"He tried to touch me," Honey said whenever her brother brought it up. It was as close as she could get to ever saying the words, what Danny had done to her, tried to do. She couldn't get those out of her mouth. She couldn't get them out of her ears.

"So you talk to someone about him. You don't hit him. Assault."

"Who was I gonna talk to, Bunny? Seriously? You think there's some sort of advisory board there that you can just march up to and be like, this producer says he wants to do some things to me that can't be named in front of the Lord?"

"So he didn't even touch you and you hit him? You blinded him."

One would think a little brother would be more protective of his big sister, but Bunny was harder than most. When she was seventeen and he was only seven, he had tried to rent her out to a friend. She'd been getting changed and suddenly there was this skinny boy in a tank undershirt standing at the door of her room. "Get out!" she yelled.

The kid looked confused. "He said… Hey, Barnabas! I want my five bucks back!"

Sure enough, Bunny had set up the deal. Even the kid knew it was messed up. Later, Bunny snatched five dollars from her secret stash to make up for his cut.

But he wasn't a bad guy. The military had shaped him up some, and now he is a cop. He just isn't supportive of her career, and he really doesn't give a shit about Mama. He's hardly pitched in a dime since the accident, and the only person Honey had ever met who is more self-involved than Bunny is his wife, Cassandra. And Honey suspected that if Bunny even ever slipped cash Honey's or Mama's way, Cassandra would kick him onto the couch and he would complain like hell about women until she let him back in to the bedroom, promising to keep their money for their own children.

Honey is more than happy to keep him at an arm's length anyway. She doesn't think he is a good influence on Mama, always insisting that she is, in some way, faking her illness. She doesn't know what the deal was between those two. Barnabas had been a good enough kid before Honey had left for New York, but when she came back, he was changed. Maybe he had needed the influence of a big sister more than she realized.

But Honey was in a bind with Mama those first years after the accident and since Honey's career came to a crashing halt. The money Honey made wasn't enough for a nurse, so she rolled her mother's needs into her own packed schedule. She made sure her mother ate, had bowel movements, was clean, did her exercises during the day, was making sense, and took her medications. She bought her mother treats, like a few ounces of weed and ice cream, but in general, Honey trusted some of the sites she found on the internet to support her mother's treatment rather than medical advice, not that she had money for expensive doctors anyway. And Bunny never believed her mother needed half the treatments Honey provided.

After a while, she and her mother had a rhythm and a dance that felt like an old married couple, so the few strained dates with real-life men that her friends set Honey up on went nowhere. If men didn't leave her when they found out she had no money, they left as soon as they found out about Honey's job as a part-time nurse for her mother. She had not dated any man for more than four months, and the one who lasted that long spent much of it in his car outside her house needing to be talked into staying. Honey had long ago decided she was a package deal with her mother, and the world had long decided that package could stay on the shelf.

It's exhilarating to think of a whole week away, in New York, all expenses paid. But Bunny is going to need to either pay for care for their mother or come down himself and do it. And she knows that his response to either scenario will be no.

She calls him, but after one ring, it goes to voicemail. She knows he pressed the reject-call button or it wouldn't have rung like that. She leaves her first voicemail very politely: "Hi! I hope you're doing well. I need a favor. Can you give me a call back?" Then her second. A third. By the fourth, she's just yelling into the phone, and then she just calls and hangs up, calls and hangs up, until he finally answers.

"Chichi, what the hell are you blowing up my phone for?"

She gets straight to the point. He's in a good mood, even though she knows she's harassing him, because he uses her secret nickname, the one only he uses. "Bunny, I need a favor."

"You don't even say hello. Ain't that something."

"I'm sorry," she says, and she is. "Hello, dear brother. How are you this fine evening?"

"Better now you're treating me like a man. I don't recall owing you a favor though."

"You wouldn't call taking care of your mother for the last eighteen years favor-worthy?"

"She's your mother."

"She's your mother too," she retorts. Then she takes a breath and says the thing before he can get any more childish. "I got a job, and I need to be away for a week."

"So?"

"So Mama cannot take care of herself."

"She's a grown woman. You baby her too much."

"She is disabled and she needs someone to be with her for a week. You can do that. I'll fill up the fridge and you can just be in the house, make sure she's okay. I'll even get Mia to watch Herbie." Honey listens to her own voice, monitoring for that twinge of desperation that had turned Serafina. She doesn't hear anything suspect, but Bunny groans like a child.

"Call what's-her-name, Maria."

"Maria our neighbor? The one who moved away like four years ago?"

"Yeah. You keep in touch?"

"Even if I did, do you think she's going to come here and take care of Mama for free?" She can hear her voice go a little shrill and covers her mouth.

He's shuffling through something. The phone gets scratchy. "What about Mia? Can't she take Mama if she's taking the dog?"

"I'm not going to ask my friend to take care of my mother. Our mother. I'm going to ask someone first who's related to the woman."

"You know I can't do that. I'm working."

"You're always working. I'm telling you, I have to work too."

"What kind of job is it?"

She holds the phone away from her ear and looks at it. She takes a breath before responding. "What difference does that make?"

"I want to know what is so important that you're asking me to take a week off of my life and my responsibilities for. You know what I'm doing with my day. What are you planning to do all week? Or is this some sort of romantic getaway?"

She actually laughs aloud. "You can't be serious. What do you think I do all day?"

"I don't rightly know, and I don't rightly care. All I want to know is what you'll be doing."

She's breathing fiercely through her nose. She's so mad she could scream. She hates that he has so much control over her, that he's perfected his cool, hard logic so anything she could say would seem unreasonable. He made lieutenant last year, and she only knows because of Cassandra's glowing Facebook posts, but she also knows that with each rank he's gotten cooler-headed and meaner. He treats her like a suspect, like she's hiding something, and he does it so well, she almost thinks she may be.

"It's a record deal."

"How did you get a record deal? You've been out of the game a long time. Did Savion set it up for you?"

"Kinda."

"Well, at least it's on the level if he's involved. So are you going to be in a recording studio for the whole week, or can you come home at night and we can switch off?"

"I have to be in New York. I don't think..."

"New York! Why can't you use a studio that's more local?"

"It doesn't work like that."

"Chichi, you have never learned how to negotiate. You set your terms, and you hold something back until you get what you want." Honey bristles now at the nickname he gave her when she was in New York, when he said she was too *chichi* to come home. She knows he's using it to lord over her, tell her she's being selfish again.

"Just like you're doing to me now," she huffs.

"You don't have anything I want," he says, and she gets chills. He's right that she is at his mercy. If she can't make Bunny help her, she doesn't have the money to make it work. "So you need to renegotiate. Tell them that you need to be home at night."

"No," she says. She wraps her hand around the back of a dining room chair. "Bunny, I need this. I need to be in New York. I'm collaborating with other artists, and it's paid. I will lose it if I ask for anything else. I haven't asked for anything from you in eighteen years. This is all I'm asking for. Just one week."

"Correction: You have asked me. You've come to me for rent payments and money for the roof."

"Which you haven't given me."

"No, I haven't. But you have asked."

She doesn't want to cry because she knows he'll hang up. Her desperation has lost her his sympathy before. She steels her face and says, "This is my last chance. Do this week for me, and if this album doesn't come together, I promise, I'll never ask you for anything else again."

"I'll do this, but, win or lose, you don't come to me for anything. Not until it's time to put Mama in the ground, and then, only to show up in a suit."

Honey doesn't understand Bunny's disdain for Mama. Their mother did her best, whatever that was, at trying to raise them both, but something had turned when Honey was away in New York during those years and it was just the two of them. He's never talked to her about it, but she hears something in his voice, something she sensed but never truly heard before. She feels protective all of a sudden, realizing something about her own role in this, that her own rise to fame may have dovetailed with something dark and unnamable, and she wasn't there to safeguard him then.

"I'll make this right, Bunny. It will work. I promise not to ask you for anything again."

He grunts in affirmation and hangs up. She stares at her mother's closed door, dim light seeping out into the dark hallway, wondering at the shadows and silence.

Part II:

What's Love Got to Do with It?

"The word 'iconic' is used too frequently—an icon is a statue carved in wood. It was shocking at first when I got that reference. It was a responsibility, and it's impossible to live up to—you're supposed to be dead, for one thing."
— DEBBIE HARRY

Chapter 17

THEIR SCHEDULES are wide open, and Len has rented them a house in Staten Island with "great acoustics." The acoustics suck. They can hear the neighbors through the walls, which would be okay, except these neighbors seem to be throwing an inordinate number of shoes at each other to punctuate their rants. The house has a view of the bay, but the tide is low and rank in the sunshine, and their few forays to the back deck have given them a full view of a beach, which is chock-full of oily bodies and loud music.

Sian drops her stuff on the floor in the living room and lays herself out on the couch. "I'm good here. Y'all figure out the rest of the house."

Gloria claims the back bedroom, the one that looks out onto the beach. It is noisy and cool, and Gloria says she doesn't mind the low-tide smell, that it reminds her of Galveston after flooding.

The front bedroom is large and sunny. Honey decides to claim that one. There's another room in the center, but if Sian is colonizing the living room, that will remain empty, and it puts a whole open space between herself and Gloria, which suits Honey just fine.

Gloria has brought a banjo and her Rickenbacker semi-hollow and a little amp to plug it into. Honey has brought a travel keyboard she uses for her vocal classes, when demonstrating a note or a tone is more helpful than a voice, or sometimes, to accompany a student who needs it.

It has a piano setting, but it's nothing like a real piano. Sian has brought a tambourine and another guitar lent to her by Mal. It had been her bandmate's before he died, and she tuned it up but hasn't tried it yet. It's a gorgeous seafoam-green Gibson Firebird, and she brought a slightly larger amp but hasn't tried that out either.

All three seem hesitant to get started. Gloria is taking her time unpacking her things into the drawers and then rearranging them. Sian is reading a book called *Cherry*, flipping the pages hungrily.

Honey gets a call from her brother.

"Why is Mom in diapers?" Bunny asks.

"For the regular reason anyone is in diapers, Bunny. She's incontinent."

"Incompetent?"

"No, incontinent. It means she can't control her toileting needs."

Bunny is sighing and huffing and puffing. "She wasn't like this when I left. She was better than this. She was getting better." She hears his heavy tread on the stairs, but she doesn't know if he's moving up or down. "I don't know if I can do this, Hon. I didn't know you were living like this."

"Like what?"

"The roof is rotting. Didn't you see that? You have water damage on the third floor."

"I know, Bunny. That's why we're living on the second floor. And that's why I asked you for a loan to fix it."

"Honey, seriously? You have to have this house looked at. You are so irresponsible, and always have been. You have to fix it up."

This is an old fight, and one her brother who has been living as a cop in the county hasn't paid attention to. "I've been telling you for years that I need to get the tar done."

"Well, you need new beams and a whole new roof now. You should have done it earlier. Why didn't you use some of Mom's government money?"

"You never listen. That money is for her life. For her living. That's her money." Honey can feel her anger rising. He gets under her skin so fast.

"You should never have bought this house. I can tell these stairs are going too."

"Then replace them! Or find somewhere for Mama and me to live. I'm doing my best. I've *been* doing my best. You haven't come around in years. I always have to come up to you to see Cass and the kids, and you are always rushing us out the house because you have dance lessons and gymnastics and lacrosse to take them to." She's mad now, yelling. "I've been doing my very best. It's not easy. And I'm asking you for one week..."

"I hate this goddamn house," he says gruffly.

Before Honey can respond, she hears her mother's voice. "Is that Honey?"

Honey holds her breath. Then she asks, using his given name, "Barnabas, am I on speaker?"

"Uh huh," he says.

"Take me off speaker," she says, as calmly as she can.

"Nuh uh," he says.

She closes her eyes and silently screams into her fist. Then she puts the phone back to her ear. "Hi Mama! You doing okay?"

"Yeah, Bunny's taking real good care of me. He got some steaks."

"Did you tell him about your special diet, Mama? The one prescribed by your doctor?"

"Oh, that's all over now," her mother says. "I did the diet, and it didn't change nothing."

"Yeah, if she wants steaks, I'll get her some steaks."

Honey is so angry she can barely keep her mind straight. "I will be home in one week, Mama, if he keeps you alive that long. One week."

"Have fun, baby!" her mother calls.

"Yeah, have fun, baby," says Barnabas, just before he ends the call. She knows he's laughing at her, at least on the inside.

The dull pain in Sian's groin is spicy today. She wants to take her mind off it. Honey seems to be upstairs on the phone on some call, yelling and hissing. It's good to hear Honey is a real person, someone who gets mad and doesn't just act like a doormat all the time. Gloria is out on a mission to get golabki and kielbasa from some place in Newark she swears by, and then swing by Bay Ridge and grab Italian. Sian would have gone with her, but she can't go to Newark or Bay Ridge. She can't even really go to Jersey at all. Too many ghosts, too many phone numbers, too many streets she'll ache to drive by. But she doesn't know a damn soul in Staten Island, so she's safe. Safe and bored out of her mind. Her new manager, Orla, has set it up that way, she's sure. Orla has been mama-birding her, probably because Orla is pregnant. And Sian hates to be nested, but at least she's out of Lulu's grasp for a week.

Sian finds a tennis ball, throws it up in the air, and catches it, then challenges herself by trading hands, and finally, by bouncing it against the wall, trying to peg herself harder and harder, but also to squinch out of the ball's path just in time. The thwack of the ball when it hits her skin is delicious, and it takes her mind off the groin pain. Honey appears in the doorframe.

"What are you doing?" Honey asks, perhaps sincerely, perhaps in an attempt to get Sian to cut it out.

"Suicide," Sian says. Honey's eyes widen. "The game. Not, like, suicide. I used to play it as a kid. You throw the ball at the wall hard, and the goal is to hit the other players. But I'm both the person who is throwing the ball and the one trying to get away, so it's like I'm fighting with myself. Which is, actually, a whole lot more like actual suicide, now that I think about it."

"Right. We called that *wall ball* where I grew up. Your term is so grisly." Honey does a little dramatic shiver as she sits next to Sian on the couch.

"I guess," says Sian.

She doesn't want to hit Honey and gets the sense this is not a game Honey would enjoy, so she just bounces the ball in a rhythmic hit-bounce-return, aiming at a small spot on the wall where the paint appears to be wearing down. The thump of the ball against the wall is equal parts maddening and comfortingly repetitive. Sian considers whether she is falling into a trance due to the rhythm but assumes if she's thinking about being in a trance, she probably isn't.

"I had your albums," says Honey, rubbing her hands on her thighs. "I had the Whirlygirls, but I also had your later albums. I really liked them."

"Thanks," Sian mutters. She has never known how to take a sincere compliment. In fact, she's never known how to deal with sincerity at all. Her whole life has been sarcasm and ridicule. Her mom had been the queen of the backhanded compliment, and Sian had to learn early to twist the meanings in her father's sentences to find the truth.

What a smarty you are! meant "You're an idiot."
How charming… meant "Your manners are fucked."
Thank you so much meant "You selfish cunt."
I love you meant "I just did something so shitty to you right now, and I want you to know that I can't wait to taste your pain."

Honey seems to be waiting for something. Sian can feel Honey's big eyes traveling across Sian's body, across the ball spinning in Sian's hand, the room, not finding purchase within Sian's discomfort. Sian is having a hard time deciphering *I really liked your music.* She's afraid to take the statement at face value, and Honey really does seem like she's on the level. Still, Sian has to press. "Cool. What was your favorite song?"

Honey seems to consider for a long time. So long, in fact, that Sian gives up and starts tossing the ball again. Just as she's about to bounce it for the third time, Honey reaches out and puts her hand on Sian's to stop her.

"'Lucifer.'" Honey nods knowingly, like she gets something about it that only Sian would know.

It's a deep cut, and Sian wonders about it for a minute. On the surface, it's a response to the Stones' "Sympathy for the Devil," including clear callouts to the song. The persona is a girlfriend of the Stones' devil, now disenchanted with the bad boy, and though it's a different tune, it's written in the same meter.

When we met, your ancient eyes
Betrayed a lifetime of fated hate
And I was pleased by all your lies
I went through that gate

I've been around for long years too
All my friends are dead and gone
If misery is your only mission
Baby, I'm not the one.

Her collaborator, Tim, thought it was dead clever, but her producer put it on the album begrudgingly. That asshole only wanted pure pop, catchy songs that stood alone, got stuck in your head, made you happy. This one was too cerebral for his dumb ass.

"Why that one?" Sian asks.

"It's really smart. It doesn't capitulate to the Stones' hit, and it puts a woman at the center, a woman who makes better choices. Plus the melody is really good. It's sultry, and that's different than the other songs on the album. It's not dark, though it seems to be. The other songs, although they're happy and peppy, they're the dark ones. They're self-destructive. I understand them; I mean, I came up singing opera!" she says and smiles, as if that explains anything to Sian. "But the dark songs are just performative, and I never really believed you were someone who hated yourself. I always believed that you were fun, that all you wanted was freedom."

Sian crushes the ball in her hand, and her knuckles are turning white. She feels very visible, more visible than she's been in a long time. In most therapy sessions, she doesn't let herself get this exposed.

"Your professional persona, that is," Honey corrects. "I mean, I don't know you personally at all. Just the person you share with the world."

"Opera?" Sian asks, redirecting.

"Yes, in high school and then for a year, before I started the career that you know, if you know my work at all!" She laughs, self-deprecating. "I was headed to apprentice with the London Opera House. But I chickened out and just followed some friends to New York."

"I know how that is."

"Do you?" Honey asks, leaning back a little.

"Yeah. Just, my career came first. Then I chickened out. And I haven't really been brave enough to do anything else."

"Well, you do seem like you have a lot of freedom now. You could go in any direction with your talent."

"Freedom is a lot," Sian says. She stands up and throws the ball into another room, just to get it out of her own hands. "Where is Gloria? I'm ready to start."

The sunset on the beach is gorgeous. They're on the back deck with a view of what must be New Jersey, but it is the whole bay away. They've just finished the Polish and Italian takeout Gloria picked up, and the plates are smeared with red sauce and crusts of bread. Sian furiously smokes. Gloria picks around on her guitar.

"Why do we have to write any songs?" Honey asks. "Can't we pick some standards or old folk songs?"

Gloria huffs. "Do you have money for royalties? And standards are donezo. I can't do a standard."

"Fine," Sian says and crushes her cigarette into the bottom of her boot. "We can start with some poetry. I've been working on some."

"Do you have music in mind?" Gloria asks.

"No." Sian pulls out a notebook and starts flipping through it, turning pages quickly, rejecting everything. They wait for her to hit upon an idea. "Forget it," she decides, stuffing the notebook deep in her backpack. "It was stupid."

Honey speaks carefully. "If we're going to harmonize, we have to believe in what we're singing. I do a lot of singing with my church, and that's why gospel works. You can hear it in the singers when they don't have faith or when they aren't giving it up in praise. They sound more prideful, more out of sync with the other people."

"Baby, we are not doing gospel," says Sian. She lights another cigarette.

Honey waves the smoke from her face. "I didn't say we were going to make a gospel record. According to Gloria, we have to find a subject that's lonely, pissed off, and prayerful. Did I get that right? What fits that description?"

The sounds of screeching seagulls, cars, and watercraft surround them as they plumb their brains for possible topics. Honey thinks about her mother's care, how lonely she feels sometimes on those bad days. How she really would love to have someone who would help her with the burden. Not that her mother is a burden. Life is the burden, but her mother's care, that does bring her low in her dark moments.

Sian's mind goes to the scraped-out lows of her deepest misery, those moments when she can't imagine the feeling of living another minute in her skin, whether it's because her body is jonesing for drink or speed, or because she can't feel without pain, or because she doesn't see any coming back from the shit she's done over time. This pain is personal and tender, but it is the only thing that fits the bill. She waits for someone else to say something.

Gloria thinks about Len's infidelity, how he scheduled her tours to dovetail with his affairs, brokered deals to finance the demands of his lovers. It's amazing she even talks to him still, but the fact is, she probably still does love him. He's damn lovable. He makes you feel seen and can thrill her in bed, knowing all the secret ways she likes to be pleasured. And he probably does love her. His problem is he has too much love to go around. But she doesn't even know these two blank-faced losers and can't imagine sharing this personal pain with them.

"I got nothing," she says. Sian and Honey shrug and wait.

Gloria picks up her guitar and strums. She finds a little run of notes that feels new and fresh and hums a melody she picks out of the air. The other two hum a little as well, each stretching their voices in and through their ranges. They give each other turns with the melody and then with a harmony. Sian hears a space open up that could be a verse, and she picks it up.

"*I took my man to Target and he called it Tar-jay.*"

Honey smiles. "Good one! Let's try that out."

Gloria sings, "That's just about the time I knew he was gay."

Sian frowns. "Too easy. Let's try something else… *play, pray, gray, stay, bidet, Tanqueray?*"

Honey adds, "How about *all day*, or *in a day?*"

Gloria snaps her fingers. "Old Bay—down where you're from, Honey! *I asked him for some salt and he brought me Old Bay?* Maybe it's a song about a lover with bad taste?"

"What's wrong with Old Bay?" Honey laughs. "Actually, I don't even eat crabs. Don't know what it tastes like!"

"What kind of guy pronounces it *Tar-jay* anyway?" Sian asks. "Oh, maybe that's the next line. "*What kind of asshole would say that anyway?*" She wrinkles her nose. "What's in a Target?"

"Housewares," says Honey. "And I sometimes pick up my groceries there. But Walmart is cheaper."

Gloria asks, "What about a date at Walmart? Or Target? Like it's a place to hook up?"

They brainstorm different lyrics and toodle out a few ridiculous verses, and Honey laughs so hard her stomach aches. Gloria and Sian are so clever, and they try to one-up each other with their witty banter. As the song develops, it sounds very campy, and Honey can't remember the last time she had so much fun. Possibly back at the School for the Arts when she and her girlfriends would make up silly opera songs and stand at the top of the main stairway, singing songs like "I Left My Wallet in El Segundo" or "U.N.I.T.Y." accentuated with expressive coloratura, letting the sound echo in the beautiful marble entryway, until an administrator or teacher would yell up at them to quit it.

As the sun slips below the horizon, their faces are lit mostly by the indoor lamps and a citronella tea light on the table. A wave of sadness, or homesickness, passes through Honey, and she wonders at herself, at her carelessness at leaving her mother in her brother's incompetent hands. The song suddenly doesn't seem so funny.

"Is this a novelty album?" Honey asks, pointedly.

Sian and Gloria turn to her, taken aback. Sian raises her eyebrows skeptically. Gloria zips a Spanish-style flair across the guitar. "Just having some fun, kiddo."

"I think..." Honey begins, but she realizes she's unsure how to put her thought into words. She's so far from home, and this can't turn out to be pointless. This is her last chance to make something good, something that will set her and her mother up for life. Bunny will leave, and he won't come back. She has a dark feeling about his time in the house, and she has sudden and powerful visions of him burning it down with her mother inside it or pushing her mother down the stairs. She has no evidence Bunny would do such a thing, so she shakes her head to clear the visions, but she is certain that what happens next must have import. It can't be stupid. It must be good.

"I think," she says with renewed purpose, "that this album can't be a joke. It has to be real. We have to believe in it. *I* have to believe in it."

"It's getting cold. I'm going in." Gloria puts her guitar back into the case and blows out the candle. She sweeps back into the house, leaving Honey and Sian in the dark.

Sian, however, seems to see Honey clearly for the first time. This isn't just sincerity; it's forthrightness. Sian has perhaps never seen it up close, except maybe in a session musician or two, but it just seemed like weakness to her at the time, an inability to adapt, a childish stubbornness. She hasn't seen forthrightness otherwise in music-making in a long time, if ever. She's not sure what to do with it.

Honey puts her hands on the table, fingers interlaced as if in prayer. "Do you know what I'm saying, Sian? Isn't this a serious project?"

"I think so," Sian admits. Her agent, Orla, was insistent on Sian's working with Gloria. Sian wasn't sure why, but Sian didn't have a house, so at the very least, it was a place to crash for the week. But Sian really hasn't thought past the week yet.

And in fact, it hadn't occurred to Sian to say no to the offer. Checks for gigs and appearances descend like little snowstorms on unwitting school mornings, the promise of temporary respite from responsibility. The offer of another day in bed, warm cocoa, and as many cartoons as you could take until the plows come through. Except, in Sian's case, the bed was shared with some dirtbag, and the hot cocoa was swapped for drugs or Mezcal, and the cartoons were still the cartoons, or maybe a Kerouac novel if she was in a reading mood. And the plows are both the harsh reality of no new next thing and the beginning of the hustle of finding more work.

A serious project? A thing that isn't just for cash, but for, what, posterity? Legacy? Sian has just enough fame to allow her to coast through and ride on others' goodwill, or sometimes less than goodwill. It is definitely the case, according to her sometime therapist and sometime spiritual advisor, that she can't handle her own freedom, that with too much success, she is at risk of falling into all her old habits. In short, real success would probably kill her.

But look at this woman: Even in the dark, Honey's eyes well up with so much hope and trust. Sian wants to hold her, almost. And while Honey would be fuckable in her way, and Sian could be convincing enough to turn a straight girl for a night or two, it isn't sexual. She wants to please Honey, or more like, she wants to satisfy some hunger. Honey's yearning is a flavor in Sian's mouth. And as with all the shitty promises she has made over so many shitty years, it sounds stupid and patronizing when she says it, even if it feels true.

"It will be important, Honey. Let's make it important."

Chapter 18

GLORIA IS NOT PLEASED to see Tim Karman standing in the rented living room. He's soft and graying, and the last time she'd been paired with him, she'd thrown a flowerpot at him. And she'd liked that flowerpot.

"Who invited this joker?" she asks, coming in from a brisk walk in the foggy morning.

"I did." Sian raises her hand. She's wearing the same clothes as yesterday and has a little red mark where her nose ring usually is. But she looks freshly scrubbed and smells like bath soap, so maybe she cares about what Tim thinks of her. "We were having some difficulty cracking the code on songwriting, so I asked Tim to come. We can pay him out of my share."

"Damn straight, 'cause I'm not splitting a crooked nickel with this man," Gloria huffs. "And who said we were having trouble? I don't remember any trouble last night."

"It's just that Honey wants to do something real. Like a serious album," Sian says, and Gloria looks to where Honey isn't and then points upstairs, accusingly.

"'Date in Walmart' is serious. People do have dates in Walmart. And Target. And they call it *Tar-jay*." Gloria is getting angry. It may be unreasonable because she doesn't believe for a minute that the song had any import. It was stupid, but it was a start. They would get somewhere with it eventually.

"Yeah, but who cares?" says Sian. "We are grown-ass women. We must have more to say, right? I know I do." She looks away though, like she doesn't want to say whatever that is.

"And you think this outhouse breeze is the right air freshener for this project?"

Sian looks to the back of the house and sniffs the air. "Didn't your ex choose this bay location?"

Gloria jabs her finger at Tim to clarify. As the realization dawns on Sian, Gloria notices the hurt in her face. This man means something to Sian. Gloria's not sure what it is, why this hair-metal reject is the right prescription for their precious album, but she recognizes a crutch can be critical, especially when you're not currently walking all that well.

Gloria can turn on a dime, be the professional bitch people expect. She has always been able to be the bigger person, as long as she's clear the other person is, indeed, smaller. She holds out her hand pleasantly, as if Tim is an expected guest. "So glad you can make it, Tim. Good to see you again."

He shakes it. "Gloria," he says and nods.

"You still owe me a flowerpot."

"You still owe me the medical bill for five stitches."

Gloria smiles. "Let's call it even."

Once upon a time, Tim had saved Sian's life, so of course Sian called him. When Honey was having that meltdown last night about making something real, Sian saw Honey's need, and she knew the fix. Gloria wasn't going to let anyone in on the songwriting, and in time, Sian could see that it was going to be the same sort of goofy T-shirt and bumper sticker hooks that Gloria has always been known for. "The Five Items" is good, but "Landslide" is legendary, and they needed a "Landslide." No hand-clapping game music on this album.

When Sian's last manager, Ursula, had organized Sian's comeback album, all Sian had wanted to write about was partying and still being sexy. She'd worked first with her drug-buddy-songwriter Pokey, who was also in Ursula's portfolio. Being Colombian, Pokey would add some flair and Latin rhythms that always made the songs a bit more jamming. He also negotiated great deals for cocaine on the street. Sian didn't speak Spanish well back then and didn't want to be perceived as appropriating, so she was always unthreading those fun Latin aspects of the music to maintain any modicum of authenticity, but she did do all the blow he had on his person. In short, she let her addictions drive the bus.

Ursula, who was a solid manager, was onto him, and onto Sian. She pulled Pokey away from Sian and hooked him up with a Latin Christian band, which actually elevated his game because he understood how to make songs work both for true believers who wanted to party on Saturdays and pray on Sundays, and for guilty reformed sex addicts who wanted desperately to believe that they could be saved someday when they got around to it. Having solved Pokey's issue, Ursula paired Sian with Tim.

Tim was a southern rock, ex-metal, self-taught musician with an ear of gold and a heart of sugar. Sian rejected him hard. She was cruel, snorting in the studio, prowling around him like a tiger. In time, his patience and corniness wore her down, warming her up and scratching her belly. Soon, she was pouring out her real emotions to him, and he was spinning them into aural treasure. "Lucifer" was their first collaboration. It was Sian's basic and stupid idea, but Tim was the alchemist. They listened to the Stones song over and over, analyzing the lyrics, picking apart problems with what "the devil" was saying and imagining truly being with him, accompanying him on his little petty victories.

The line they got deep and dark with equated cops and criminals and then sinners and saints. At first, Tim just philosophized about the darkness and light in each person, but something in Sian broke apart. She had always thought of her dueling selves as a separate angel and devil pulling her in one direction or another, but if they were the same, could she trust anyone? The line between righteousness and self-interest is so unclear.

She spiraled into a place where she could find nothing good inside herself. He let her cry, waited until she found some small purchase in her soul; he didn't carry her up those rocks back to purpose, but he did see her at her worst, and he still loves her. She is certain without him, she wouldn't have survived the night. And then he helped her make a fantastic album. He's more than a songwriter. He's a miracle worker.

As Tim and Sian embrace, he whispers, "I'm not sure I can do this. Gloria is a rare beast."

Sian smiles. "So was I when you met me. And besides, it's Honey and me you'll be working with mostly."

He searches her eyes and Sian hopes he doesn't see the faithlessness there. Whether he finds it or not, he seems eager to jump in. "Where do we start?" he asks the room.

Honey looks tired when she finally emerges. She drinks back-to-back coffees and checks her phone nearly constantly.

"What's on your mind?" asks Sian.

"I'm sorry. It's unprofessional," she says. She slips her phone into her pocket and adjusts herself on the couch. "It's nothing."

"It's not nothing. If you have to attend to something, it's okay," says Sian.

Gloria rolls her eyes. "We're here to work. I *will* thank you for putting that damned thing away and focusing," she says as she nods to Honey and casts her gaze to the pocket holding the phone. Honey brightens her smile and holds her hands together, ready for a productive day. Sian shakes her head. Already playing nice and not meaning it. This is how it gets ugly with women.

"So what kind of songwriters are we?" asks Tim. "Like, do you generally start with a lyric or an aspect or a melody? What gets you going?"

"We are great songwriters," says Gloria. "Ones who don't need help from baby dicks like you."

Sian clears her throat. "I don't think we know where to start with each other. We can make each other laugh, but we don't have much in common, right?"

Honey shrugs and Gloria cracks her neck.

Sian realizes she'll have to model Tim's method for the group. "As you know, I tend to take inspiration from other, new work. I listen to everything, and I try to grab what I can from what I hear."

"That's a perfect beginning. So what has inspired you recently?" Tim asks, eager for a volunteer to play along.

Sian flips in her head through the recent music she's exposed herself to. It's a lot of kids' songs Lulu plays for Carly, but she also listened to a podcast about reggaeton. Then she remembers the last project Honey and Gloria were working on. "When I heard about the duets album, I was listening to Serafina's music. I kind of like her dark vibe, that killer bitch thing she's got going on."

Honey shivers. "Yes, I wasn't at all certain how Serafina and I would find any points of reference. When we met, she did suggest just putting my part on the harmony, and she would take lead on the song that she picked out. But to be honest, I don't think it would have worked."

"So she was giving you backup vocals to do?" Gloria asks.

"Pretty much," Honey shrugs. "I'm comfortable in that space."

"She's a cherrystone bellyache," says Gloria. "And you, Honey, you are the cherry." Honey smiles, but Sian catches its fleetingness, and Honey's distraction.

Sian recognizes Gloria's move to direct the songwriting by throwing in a little resonant phrase and a clever rejoinder. She didn't come here to make a Gloria song though. She redirects them. "I like the intensity of Serafina's music, like how she whispers in her songs."

"Oh, that's a great prompt. Let's try it. What would you whisper about if you whispered in a song?" asks Tim.

"*Get out of my fucking house,*" Gloria stage-whispers. She puts on her cute face, but no one finds it funny.

"I haven't eaten a vegetable in a month," Sian whispers, twirling her hair in her finger.

"I'm terrified of Gloria," Tim whispers. Gloria makes big *Who me?* eyes at him.

"I think my daughter hates me," Sian whispers.

"My girlfriend left me, and I gave myself alcohol poisoning earlier this week," says Tim. Sian leans back to take in Tim's confession. She puts her hand on his back and he gives a pursed smile.

"I'm scared my brother will kill my mother," Honey whispers.

They stop and look at Honey.

"Seriously?" Sian asks. Honey nods. She checks her phone again and drops her eyes to the screen.

"Let's put that one on ice for a minute," says Tim. "We'll start with your daughter, Sian."

They work through the morning on the heart of the song. Sian knows Lulu is embarrassed of her, mostly because of Sian's choices. But the song can't just be about a mother failing a child, even though "Cat's in the Cradle" is pretty much about a father failing his son. It's got to be about more, maybe some looking forward, some promise that carries into the song.

Tim has given them license to externalize the character in the song so it's not like it's all about Sian. Instead, they can all find themselves in the story of the central persona and try to listen to it not as the daughter in the song, but as the daughters they are, and to hear it from their own mothers.

By midday, they have a refrain that they feel good about:

The child is a woman – She's a mirror of myself

And she don't need me now, she don't need any help
But when you look in that mirror I'm always there in you...
It's true.... I'm your tattoo.

"What kind of song is this?" Gloria asks. She's not wrong to ask. They've got the lyrics, but in each of their mouths, it has sounded a little country, a little bluesy, a dash of rock and roll, but really without the home of a genre.

Tim rubs his hands together. "We started with the intensity of Serafina's new work, but I'm not feeling that anymore. This song is an apology. I think we can start with maybe a little riff that feels nostalgic."

"Like this?" Gloria strums a few chords, and Sian can hear it. She picks up in a space Gloria leaves for her, and as she claps on the beat, she jumps into the rhythm. This part always feels to her like double Dutch, finding the little platforms for the words in the song.

Sian, Tim, and Gloria are bobbing their heads, also looking for a way to weave their voices into the rhythm. Honey is outside of it.

"I'm hearing it slowed down a lot." She claps a 4/4 beat and Tim slows it. In Honey's voice, the song is dirge-like, heavy, and Sian feels weighted. Honey pushes out the word *true*, holding it for the whole measure, and then closing up with a whisper, *I'm your tattoo.*

She crinkles her face. "*I'm* her *tattoo? I'm* your *tattoo?* Is it to her or about her?"

They mess around with the lyrics, holding on to Honey's tempo and low register, but it starts to morph into a different piece, almost a blues song. Gloria picks it up in her soprano and scrapes the lyrics with a little fry. It sounds good, and Honey finds herself put out of the space she had claimed originally. She isn't sure how to get back into the song.

"Where do I fit now?" Honey asks, helpless.

"Just do some backup, like *true, true*, after me," Gloria suggests.

"No," says Sian. "Honey is not a backup singer here. I think... I think we can do it with two voices. You both try it together."

Gloria and Honey each take a breath and pull together, looking at the scrawled lyrics. *Slap, slap-slap* on the guitar, and the notes lift and offer a framework, ready for their voices. Just as in that crazy Swan Room in the hotel, they meld perfectly, Honey's power in her low register holding her own within the personality of Gloria's own force. It's hard to tell which one to listen to, so the ear mixes them together, finding a new sound, one that really does entwine them. When they finish, they're both breathless and stunned.

Sian and Tim clap. "That's it! That was beautiful!" Sian says.

"But what about your part?" Honey asks Sian. "It's your song, your story. Can you find some room?"

"I don't know," she says. "Maybe I'll do the backup harmony. I don't need this one to be mine. It started with me, but I'm glad you two took it on." Her eyes are dry, but she looks like she's holding something back.

Tim puts the guitar down and holds out his arms to offer a hug, but Sian isn't ready for touch. Not all the songs can be this way, or she'll never make it through the week. She rubs her eyes with the heels of her hands and stands up to expel some extra energy.

"Damn, okay. Okay! We're doing this. One down. What, twelve to go?"

Honey shares what she knows with them, her brother's rejection of their mother's diet, his refusal to visit, the stakes of this particular recording session. They all listen intently.

"What an asshole," Gloria says. "Did she abuse him or something? Sounds like abuse."

"Why? What makes you think that?" Honey is alarmed. She isn't sure how her mother could have possibly abused him.

Honey retraces her memories, searching for clues or warnings. Her mother has never been like that. She was loving, but he just rejected her love. Honey still isn't sure why, but something must have broken when she left after high school. It was before cell phones and when Honey wasn't all that reachable in New York. She got a message from him every so often back then, but she just thought he missed her, not that he needed her to protect him from their mother. Maybe her mother had a boyfriend. She had some woman living at the house for a time, and maybe that woman brought someone over who beat him? Or maybe that lady did? Even Mama doesn't talk much about that lady or that time, but she always blames it on how Bunny grew wild, how he started running around with boys in the neighborhood, out of control. She seemed glad that he joined the military. Maybe she was happy that he got out of Baltimore, or away from something bad happening to him in their neighborhood.

A wave of shame crashes over Honey as she considers what could have happened in her absence, and she loses her balance on the couch, putting her hand down to hold herself fast to her seat.

"So you feel guilty not being there for him?" asks Sian, through the roar in Honey's head. Honey wonders at the question. She does. She has also resented Bunny for so long, but that question was always out of reach. It's like she's accepted that pursuing something she dreamed of was selfish, and the stress, the exhaustion, the barely making ends meet is all payback for that. Sian adds, gently, "You know you couldn't have done anything differently."

Honey turns her eyes to Sian, pleading. How could this not be all her fault? Her need to chase down some stupid dream, abandoning her brother to whatever.

"Art is hard, right?" says Sian. "Being an artist is like this constant game of trust and confidence and you always feel like you're losing. There's no way you can live up to what people want you to be."

Tim grimaces, and then says, "Whatever happened, it's not because of art. It's because of life. Life is suffering." He smiles wanly, as if everyone can't help but agree with him.

The violent ocean in Honey's head is rocking her. She remembers a hint of a story, something about the lady getting fired from the school. Her mother might not have known. Or maybe she knew and just felt like she had no choice, that the woman wouldn't possibly hurt Bunny if Dottie were kind to her, and that Honey needed to get to London. Was this the sacrifice? Was Bunny hurt to pay for Honey's dream? And that phone call earlier, what was Bunny doing on the third floor anyway? Looking for clues to his own past? Trying to confront something he couldn't make sense of? "My brother is watching my mother this week. And I just don't feel right about it," Honey admits.

"You shouldn't feel right about it," whispers Sian. "Maybe you should go home. I mean, is there someone who can do a welfare check?"

Honey goggles her eyes. "I'm sorry, but do you read the newspaper? Do you really think I'm going to sic Baltimore City Police to do a welfare check on my brother?"

"But he's a police officer too, right?" Gloria asks. "They won't shoot him."

"That's even worse. If they don't kill him, they'll protect him. I mean, I don't have any evidence that anything is really wrong."

Tim leans in and asks, "What's the best way we can support you right now, Honey?"

"Let's write these songs and get them ready for the studio. I have one week to focus on you, and then, whatever happens after that, I can go home and take care of it."

Tim searches her with his eyes. Honey feels visible, uncomfortably so. She can sense he is trying to be kind, but she doesn't like this look. She's already shared too much with these strangers.

"Okay, let's do it." He claps his hands and rubs them together. "How about some standards? Or folk songs? Any that stand out to you?"

The three women look at one another. Standards are outside of their interest.

"Like, 'Fly Me to the Moon'?" Sian asks, spinning her finger in the air and rolling her eyes.

Tim roots around in his satchel and extracts some sheet music. "Well, I like to poke around for old blues standards, and I came across this one by the Mississippi Sheiks. Let's see what we can do with it. First, let's all try the beginning. It goes,

Please, baby
Pleee-ase, baby
Won't you come back to your daddy
One more time?

They practice it, first in a round, and then as a three-part harmony, which sounds terrific.

"Let's try that run as *Won't you come back to your mama?*"

They practice the first few bars until they find a harmony that suits them. Gloria is kicking back, shaking her head while she sings the smoky old blues song. Honey's voice takes shape inside the riff, becoming another instrument that trembles along with the strumming strings.

"I'm loving this, loving it!" Tim slaps his guitar to keep rhythm. Sian's voice is thin and clear, not really getting the juice out of the lyrics like she could.

"Sian, where are you?"

She shrugs. "I guess I don't want anyone to come back to me that badly."

He laughs, but Honey takes her up on the comment, reiterating her trust in belief. "I had a teacher back in high school who would remind us that if we didn't believe in our soul what we were singing, even if it was in a different language or about a subject we didn't care about, the audience wasn't going there with you. A song like this, it doesn't have to be about any old man coming home. It could be about that brass ring. What could you look at and say, *That, that right there is what would set my heart right?*"

To Sian, it sounds so simple. Why hasn't anyone ever told her this before? She flips through her own songs in her head and realizes she had always been able to just make herself believe in the thing, that maybe the joy of singing is what carried the song for her. She loved performing, so when she sang, "We Were Made for Dancing," she really believed her body was made for dancing. She remembers that, believing in the lyrics, moving her body to the bouncy little number, having loads of fun, and trusting the brightness of her voice to hit those notes on happiness and rainbows alone. And it did, for a while. But she couldn't carry a song like that forever. No one can stay that happy. And certainly no one could fake it.

But why didn't anyone ask her to plumb her life for those happy moments, to turn it into something else, just to get her through? She remembers exactly when she stopped believing, when standing on the stage was a chore, a means to an end. She fears she may have lost those pure, unadulterated times and turned them to shit as she burned through them on stage. If she still had access to them, she would have snorted them to stay happy the way she used cocaine. Still, she might be healthy today, if devoid of anything that was her own.

"I don't know what I want," says Sian. "I lost that a long time ago."

Honey looks down, and Sian feels a thread pulling at her. She's not alone. Honey is working at this too. It's not as easy as she's making it seem. It's work, but she's damn good at it. So good, it seems effortless. In fact, it's work for Gloria too. Sian sees a bright line of sweat shining on Gloria's face, a little darkening of the pancake makeup she wears right up to her thinning scalp. She's working. None of them has gotten here for free.

Gloria says, "When I sing *please*, I'm thinking about my last scrap of freedom. Someone walking away and leaving me in a jail cell. I'm seriously claustrophobic, so I'm thinking like a tiny little cell. Just *please, baby. Please let me out!*"

Sian sees it. She can imagine herself caught in a cell, but there's something comforting about a box, a place with few choices, only so many ways she could cause more pain or do more wrong. *Please lock me in.* Better yet, *Please, please keep me from myself.* She draws in so much breath it hitches as she's overfilling her lungs. "Please, baby. Pleeee-ase, baby." She pulls down and presses out the lyrics, but *baby* comes out like *beh-bay* and sounds stupid.

"Can we change that to another word? I'm not going to call him baby if he's taking something from me," she asks.

"What do you want to call him?" Gloria asks.

"Sugar?" Tim volunteers.

"No." Sian and Honey both shake their heads.

Tim offers, "Honey? Darling? Lover?" They raise their eyebrows at *lover*. It could work.

"Bunny," Gloria says, pointing and shaking her manicured finger at Honey. "I think we should use his name. No one else will know we're singing about him, but it might could send a message."

Honey is horrified at first, but the more she thinks about it, the more brilliant it is. She's in this desperate situation because of him. *Please, Bunny* sounds great. She tries it out, and Sian harmonizes. They adjust the lyrics to align to the situation, coding the message in the existing words. Gloria jumps in on the third run.

Please, bunny
Ple-eease, bunny
Won't you come back to your mama
One more time?

Please, bunny
Ple-eease, bunny
When I get my money, I will
Give you my last dime

I'm so blue, bunny
I'm so blue, bunny
I can't sleep at night
I can't hardly talk for cryin'

You know, bunny
You know, bunny
You always fore-'rever on my mind

As they finish the verses, Honey uses her fingers to draw the wetness away from her cheeks. It's intense, but she knows it's the right move. Sian's dug-in tones sound perfect in the harmony. The three of their voices braid elegantly on the song, each contributing the right color and depth. Gloria sounds almost angry and petulant, demanding what's hers, and Honey channels her desperation. Sian, though, has found a new way. A thin, vibrant hope runs through Sian's contribution, something that flutters around and you want to capture, but it's just out of reach, and dancing with the other two steady and power-laden voices, it's exactly the right fit.

As Honey brushes her teeth later, preparing for bed, she finds the tune lodged in her consciousness, and she hums it. Even if this album comes to nothing else, they have this.

Chapter 19

BY THE FIFTH DAY, they are all sick of Staten Island, sick of writing, and sick of each other. Tim returns bright-faced each morning with a tray of Starbucks. Gloria always refuses hers, dropping a hint for a slightly different variation each time. Sian has been drinking the rejected grandes, skyrocketing her blood sugar and perking her up at the ungodly hour of ten a.m. By the time Tim arrives, Gloria has usually been messing with the songs, changing the registers or keys or some run of notes in the middle. She always has improvements, and Tim is usually cheery about the changes. Which continues to piss Gloria off.

Though there is precious little street noise for a highly populated area, a young woman staggers to the front of the house sometime after the bars close each night. She stands on the sidewalk, and yells for someone named Wayne. Other neighbors scream back, lobbing obscenities or sometimes beer bottles at her, but she persists in her wail for hours, disappearing and reappearing with new laments, each time breaking down in tears.

The condo is non-descript, with powder-blue aluminum siding and a single allotted parking space, a white balcony on the upper back deck, and no shutters adorning the three front-facing windows. The listing included no details about this particular street haunting, so Honey assumes that either the woman is confused about Wayne's whereabouts, or Wayne was one of the place's last residents.

The first night, Honey had put in her earplugs and tried to sleep. There could be some rowdy and noisy nights in Baltimore for sure, and she was no stranger to sleeping while a police helicopter streaked lights through her bedroom window, or trying to settle while a party spilled into the wee hours, but these sounds were different, soul-penetrating. Whatever Wayne did to this woman is unforgivable. But he is also not in this particular house, so it's unclear what will bring this wailing to an end. She sat by the window and watched in the dim streetlight, this waif with wild hair and a glittery dress. The woman glimmered, giving sparks caught by the light, like electricity from an underwater eel. Other pedestrians crossed to the other side of the street to avoid her. The woman would cry out, adjust her plea, wander to the end of the street, and return. There was some Greek tragedy in this, and Honey considered how she could capture this woman's despair in a song, but as quickly as she considered it, Honey shook at her own dearth of empathy. She watched for as long as she could stand, hiding behind the slats of the blinds, and eventually, she went to bed and waited for the woman to give up.

The second night, Honey had tugged on her bathrobe and tiptoed by Sian, snoring on the living room couch. She ducked down the stairs and stood in the darkness, watching the small woman execute her faithful tirade. Honey peered through the edge of the frosted window, getting a much clearer view. Honey could see now that the woman was young, no older than thirty, with mussed hair and unseeing eyes, and when she wailed, the tendons on her neck stood out like spines, her mouth widening like a portal to another dimension. She wasn't wearing a fancy dress this night, just a white cotton sundress and cork wedge heels. Her skinny arms were full of glistening things that flashed gold under the streetlamp.

"Wayne! Come get your shit!" Then *crash, smash* against the aluminum siding on the front of the house. "Come get your shit! Wayne! Come down now!" *Smash, smash!*

She was hurling things at the house. Each was about the size of her hand and caught the light, just for a bit, as it flew. Honey ducked back into the house when one flew directly at the front door, bouncing off the frosted glass block Honey had just been peering around. Honey's heart started to race with concern, both about being the mistaken target of this woman's wrath, and about having to pay for whatever damage she caused to the house. At home, Honey would just run off someone like this without fanfare. The minute she opened her door, the local miscreants would run, cowed by her celebrity and grand-dame presence, and they were never white boys who bothered her, white boys who could get her into trouble. Here in Staten Island, if she came outside and all these white people saw her trying to shoo off this banshee, who knows what they would do to someone like her?

Honey dashed into the kitchen to get a knife, just in case, and opened the front door. The woman was gone, but about six glass containers were broken like shells on the sidewalk, with bright red and orangey smears all across the concrete. The jars didn't appear to have smashed when they hit the siding but bounced and shattered on the sidewalk. The gold flashes were the Mason jar lids, which had spun off like small suns and rolled as far as six houses away.

Mercifully, that morning, a heavy thunderstorm rolled through and washed the smeared jam away, along with much of the splintered glass. Honey swept up the rest during a mid-morning break. She hadn't told anyone else about the woman, except to ask innocently if anyone had difficulty sleeping.

But last night, the woman had come again, and this time she'd been tossing large pickle jars. "Wayne! Wayne! Come down here 'fore I break every damn jar! I can't live with these things in my house! Come down here now!"

Honey had been keeping vigil and, steeling herself, she prepared to meet the forlorn woman. She flung open the door, which sent the woman scrambling backward. The woman hunched back into the darkness, away from the light cast by the streetlamp. The night was misty; it was not raining, but the clouds sunk low enough that Honey's skin attracted a sheen of moisture as she stepped onto the concrete stoop.

"You all right, miss?" Honey asked, softening her voice. "You been left by someone?"

The woman looked up, narrowed her eyes, and emitted a vibrant and unsteady scream. Honey blinked and took in the sound, automatically assessing its timbre and collecting notes, as she had with arias for nearly two decades. Then the woman threw a quart pickle jar at Honey on the stairs, barely missing Honey's feet, but smashing glass and vinegar all up Honey's leg and into her bathrobe. Honey shook her assessment of the woman's noise out of her head and leapt onto a different stair, pulling as far back to the railing as she could.

The woman ran. When she was at the end of the block, she turned around, a tiny dark figure under the streetlamp. Honey could see the doll-like thing ball her fists and bend forward to yell, "You can keep him, bitch!" Then she disappeared into the dark.

Honey, in house shoes, kicked some of the glass to the sides of each riser and off the stoop. Then she shook out her bathrobe and took stock of the lights of the other houses around her and heads peeking out the windows.

In one, not directly across the street but just off-center, a house with a cheerful green door, a woman's figure was backlit on the first floor. The woman was smoking a cigarette through the window screen. She caught Honey's eye. "Wayne can suck my dick," shouted the woman, crushed her cigarette, and with some difficulty, slammed the window shut.

"Charming city," said Honey, shaking her head, and she returned to bed.

She couldn't sleep though, even after she rinsed the pickle juice from her leg. What was the story there? Was Wayne some sort of cook? Were preserves and canning their love language? Why had she come so often? To this house? Honey found herself drafting several versions of the story, and in the morning, she shared the first few lyrics and a little keyboard trill of her song, "Yelling Wayne."

On Thursday, the night before they're set to leave, only one more writing session before them, Tim suggests they hit a karaoke bar. Sian thinks it's brilliant. But she can't find anything to wear, so she puts on her best long blue jeans and Tim lends her a Go-Gos T-shirt. Gloria appears wearing an A-line dress with music notes on it, red shoes and a shiny red scarf in her hair. Honey is in a smart kelly-green suit with a white blouse, large earrings in the shape of Africa under her high bun.

At dusk, they head into Manhattan on the ferry. One of Honey's old boyfriends had been a Marine Unit police officer who took her out on boats around the Baltimore Harbor down to Annapolis, and Sian had grown up near the water in Delaware, surfing and sailing. Gloria too had grown up around boats in Galveston, so of the four of them, Tim is the only one hiding in the air-conditioned commuter space. With wind whipping their hair around, they stand together at the bow of the ferry, the southern New York skyline behind them. Gloria hands another passenger her phone to snap a photo, which will become the album cover.

Once they dock, Sian vibrates with the energy of the city. It holds a trash bag of slimy memories of her worst selves, pissing into the street off a balcony above Tower Records, having months of anonymous sex, racking up more than a dozen arrests for disorderly conduct. Here she is, a grandmother in blue jeans, striding in as if it doesn't hold her secrets, as if it didn't incubate that darkness. All her old connections on Houston, Avenue A, 4th and Bleecker, then up in Murray Hill, Hell's Kitchen, Sheepshead Bay, Astoria. She knows people everywhere who can get her whatever she wants. Everywhere except Staten Island, and there, it's just a courier away if she has enough cash or a cash app, which Lulu deleted from her phone. These selves are clawing inside Sian, stabbing her on the inside with shame, desire, hunger, rage, louder than the twisting pain just below her stomach, which is insistent now, held at bay by a steady regimen of over-the-counter NSAIDs. She takes Tim's hand, and he squeezes hers back, sensing her vibe and mistaking it for thrill.

Honey is uniquely unaffected by her environment. Everywhere they've been, Honey walks purposefully and without gawking. Sian wonders if

Honey doesn't want to be caught as the outsider, if she's afraid to be taken for a ride. Smart cookie. Gloria is all business too, but this is her city. She can sense the cocked heads and discerning eyes blocks away, and she has little moves to acknowledge these fans. *Oh yes I am*, she seems to say with her eyes. *In the flesh.*

They take a cab to the West Village and find the karaoke club. It's filled with hipsters and drunk poets and the greasy smell of unwashed scalp. Sian scans the room, sizing up the young, nubile bodies. She idly wonders how sexy of a partner she can attract at this age, what young hot thing in here wouldn't mind eating her grisly and threadbare pussy, sucking on her droopy tits. She still gets plenty of sex, but it would be different. She wouldn't have to settle for redneck ass. She also wouldn't be high if it happened tonight and might remember it, and that raises the stakes a smidge.

They get a table and some drinks, mulling over their progress. They talk shop, considering additions to songs and discussing instrumentation, and Sian is distracted for a bit from the scene. They won't get studio time for a few more weeks, but they have ideas of session musicians they would like to book, slotting in cheaper and more available ones, cutting out expensive ones or people who turn out to be dead. As they compile a list and the faces of old friends and collaborators turn up in her mind, Sian remembers how much she likes rolling around in the process of music-making.

The karaoke deejay is setting up in front of a glittery stage that likely features comedians on other nights. He has a trim setup, a laptop and a couple mics. The house PA system is currently playing some automated playlist; if Sian had to guess, it would be "Upbeat Indie Jams" or some other facile title. A trio of women in tight dresses and different-colored wigs trip their way up to the sign-up sheet, which triggers a hustle forward and the formation of a line.

Gloria leans forward. "Let's do a song from the *Trio* album. Wouldn't that be cool?"

"The one by Linda Ronstadt and the other two?" asks Sian.

"'The other two.' You are such a horrible person, Sian. Seriously." Gloria shakes her head. "Yes, Dolly Parton and Emmylou Harris. Do you remember any from that album?"

"Play it for me," says Honey, and Gloria finds it on her music app and holds her phone to Honey's ear.

"Ooh, it's real country," says Honey after a beat. "I don't think I could do that. Let's try something we could all do." She queues up a few options, including the Supremes' "You Keep Me Hangin' On" and TLC's "Waterfalls."

Gloria points at the phone. "I don't listen to that shit."

"What did you say?" Honey deadpans.

Gloria looks away. "Never mind." She has finished two drinks already and she lines up the empties, snapping her finger at a waiter to bring her a third.

Sian grabs at Honey's phone. "How about this?" She pulls up "We Are Family" by Sister Sledge.

Honey rolls her eyes, and Gloria takes in a big gulp of air before slapping the table and relenting. "Let's do it!"

Sian cocks her head. "You think we should do it together?"

Gloria shrugs. "Yes, sugar! I mean, it would be a great PR stunt, don't you think?"

Honey smiles. "Oh, we could get into such trouble... Good trouble!"

"What name should we use to sign up?" Sian asks. "So they don't recognize us at first."

"Don't worry, I got one," says Gloria. She stands and marches to the back of the line, carrying her fresh mai tai. She queues up like everyone else, which doesn't look terribly natural on her. She keeps tossing her hair and peeking around as if she's curious about the stage, but Sian thinks she's probably looking for a way to cut the line.

Sian thought she would feel great getting out, but she feels exposed and raw, like everyone can already see the loser she is. An older man with dappled skin and close-cropped natural hair has been side-eyeing her, and she's not sure if he's a fan or if he likes her look. Sian doesn't feel like anything. Her roots are growing out, and she puts her fingertips to the line of gray at her scalp. Why should she care? He licks his lips as he looks at her now, but she looks away. *Too much, sleazebag.*

Sian takes out her phone to look up the lyrics to the song. She puts the phone to her ear to hear it under the Lana Del Rey song blasting on the PA. It's very jangly and enthusiastic, but she loves that little harmony part in the middle. She sings it to herself. Honey scooches her chair close, and they share the phone with their heads together, practicing. They're giggling as they try to catch onto the lyrics.

When Gloria comes back, she smacks the table. "Slim pickins tonight, gals."

"They didn't have the song?" asks Honey.

"No, they had the song. I mean the men in here! I guess if I wanted a man who is short on hair and long on opinions, I could take my pick. But I don't have much interest in a man who thinks he's smarter than I am. Unless he is, of course."

"Was Len smarter than you, Gloria?" asks Sian. As soon as she says it, she wants to take it back, but she doesn't. Instead, she downs the dregs of her beer.

"Nooo, but I'll tell you who was: my second husband, Charlie. He was a genius. Ex-military. He could just fix any old thing without much trouble. He couldn't read much, but I don't put stock into being a reading sort. Give him a bunch of numbers to add or multiply in his head and he'd be right every time."

"Sounds romantic," says Honey. She seems to have surprised herself with sarcasm and covers her mouth. "Oh, I didn't mean that. I didn't mean it!"

"It wasn't romantic at all. He would sit up nights and just figure out funny patterns with math. He couldn't get into college, but he just had that gift. But never a romantic."

"The sex was good?" Sian asks.

Gloria swirls her drink and shrugs. "It was second-husband sex. He could surprise me, but he didn't feel like he had to work too hard to hold on to me."

"Why did you get divorced?" asks Honey.

"We fought all the time. And he could get real mean when he was drunk. Real mean." Gloria slides her empty glass over to Tim and nods at the bar. He goes off to get a fresh drink.

The table is quiet for a moment. Sian has her own share of mean-drunk stories, some in which she was the mean drunk, but many when she was on the other end of the wrath. Honey looks into her drink, put out of sorts by the statement.

"Oh, but we stayed in touch. He bought me these," Gloria says and sticks out her fulsome chest.

"I guess you got a good deal then, huh?" says Sian, laughing. Tim delivers her a third beer, and Sian is feeling a little more open, surly even. It's a dangerous place to let herself go deeper. She can still feel the pain in her groin, which has, of late, stretched like a band across her midsection, and she worries that with too much drink, she won't be able to lean into it or might lose track of it. She might start making calls, looking for a little partying. Honey is still close, and Sian whispers to her. "Don't let me drink any more, okay?"

Honey nods earnestly and slides Sian's glass to the other side of the table.

"Good woman," Sian says and slops a kiss on Honey's cheek. Honey smiles primly, but Sian catches Honey blotting the wetness with a bar napkin. It makes Sian grin.

The music on the PA dies down and the deejay calls the first act, the three women in tight dresses. They perform "Woman" by Doja Cat, but they're falling all over each other and barely keeping up with the words. Two of them push their voices out, but they are alternately heavy and squeaky, played off in fits of giggles and flat-handed facepalms. Only one of them can sing, and as she thrusts her pelvis forward, Sian catches the slight bulge. Sian squints and sees the telltale signs in each of the three. "Good for them," she says and wolf-whistles when they finish.

The next performer is an earnest man with long hair who belts out some showtune. An older woman with bowed legs who must be his girlfriend takes pictures of him as he sings, and he hams it up for the camera. The next is a pair of young men who sing some country song about liking girls in short shorts. Gloria stands and ostentatiously takes pictures of them with her phone, getting close to the stage and standing in front of other people as if she's their grandmother. When they finish, she totters back to the table, definitely a little more than buzzed.

"What were you doing?" Tim asks.

"Embassarring the shit out of those little shits. Hate that fucking song." She puts her phone away and takes another sip of her drink through the straw. "Gotta slow down on this," she says and drains the glass.

The signups are called, and a few have aspects of impressive voices. One young woman has moments of great power on the chorus but flubs the verses and can't get the tempo right. Sian notices it's not as divey an establishment as she initially thought. There could be scouts in the seats, or someone could be here practicing for a Broadway audition. Everything in New York is just a little fake, just enough for self-protection.

"'Three fat sluts in heels'?" the deejay says as he squints at the card. "Come on down!"

"Thass us," says Gloria and drops her drink. It slops onto the table sideways, and Sian pushes back to protect her lap from the approaching pink spill. Gloria is up and moving to the stage, waving her arms and hooting.

"I've about had enough of this one," says Honey, jabbing her thumb at Gloria's back. Sian too stands and readies herself for the stage. Tim straightens the glass and starts mopping up the table with their extra bar napkins, placing their cell phones and purses into his lap for safe keeping. Sian thinks that if she were a reasonable person, she'd marry Tim and let him babysit her for the rest of her life. But there is not one reasonable bone in her body.

Gloria is ready to rock and roll. She throws her head back, and as soon as Sian and Honey arrange themselves near the microphone, Gloria yowls.

The song starts out with a disco rhythm, a little funk guitar, and Sian, surprisingly, is jumping up and down right away, grooving along, waving at people in the audience to get up and dance. Gloria also launches right in, hogging the mic. After the introduction, they harmonize, and Gloria, closing her eyes, gets brighter and clearer and takes on the first verse. Sian picks up the second, and the heat of the lights is feeling great on her body; her exposed neck and arms are cocooned by the audience's rapture. They sound amazing together.

Honey is doing a thing too. She's not keeping pace with the bounce of the song, but she takes the third verse, the one that drops a little in register, and something about the notes she's hitting is operatic, especially as she sings about her sisters, and it sounds almost mournful. *Damn*, thinks Sian. *Does this woman ever sing anything with joy?*

Sian sees in the audience that the two boys who were singing before are now holding up a cell phone and videoing them. She doesn't like being recorded without permission, but Gloria's stupid stunt probably puffed up their balls. She figures her face will be on the socials later somewhere on an account with twelve followers and some gritty, asinine comment about Gloria.

They finish the song with a sweet, sisterly flourish, and a few people in the audience clap wildly, one yelling *That's Gloria!* Sian realizes that they are no longer incognito. Honey may be, but they'll all be identified soon enough.

Suddenly, Honey looks horrified by the crowd, as if she's just seen them for the first time, her eyes wild with panic. Sian grabs her hand and pulls her close. In the dark of the room, all eyes trail the stumbling Gloria as she makes her way back to her seat, so Honey and Sian are able to take a longer route to the table.

It's obvious Gloria knows people are watching her, and she's loving it, toying with them. The minx trips purposefully across a table, landing her cleavage in front of a college-age white kid in a flannel. She's chosen well, Sian thinks, assuming she wants to terrorize a very pretty child. The boy has reddish lips and large white teeth to match a long face and credulous eyes. He leans back in his seat, not sure where to put his gaze or his drink, but he is smiling wildly, releasing a pair of dimples in each cheek. "Whoa," he says, because of course he does.

"Whoa you," says Gloria. She leans down and licks his hand, but then seems to catch herself. "Msorry." She pushes herself off the table, and expertly, Sian swings by to ease her arm under Gloria's and hustle her back to their table.

"Let's leave the littles alone, shall we?" Sian hisses.

Tim looks up from his phone as Gloria lands in the seat. "What'd I miss?" he asks.

Honey sits stiffly at the table, arms over her chest. "I don't think that was a good idea. I have a bad feeling about it."

"Little late for a bad feeling, Honey," Sian says as she deposits Gloria into a chair. "The shitshow is already underway."

"No, I mean, I think something bad is going to happen to them." She indicates the girls in the matching dresses from the first performance, and Sian sees exactly what she means. They are just outside the plate-glass window, and a ponytailed white woman is yelling at them and pointing, shoving her face into their space. Two of them are trying to look bored, but the eyes of the third keep flicking to the inside of the club. Sian wonders if the window outside is mirrored and whether the girl is looking at herself or can see all the people in the club just watching them get harassed. Sian can almost hear the woman's screams over the karaoke onstage now.

Sian smacks Tim on the shoulder and points. He shoves his phone into his back pocket, and they step outside, leaving Gloria staring into space and Honey rubbing her arms at the table.

When they enter the cool night on the street, Sian's forehead stings with tension and bottled rage. The woman is screaming now about freaks and pedophiles, and a small crowd has gathered. This being New York, most people are glassy-eyed and waiting to find out what will happen. The bright righteousness on the blond woman's face is all Sian needs, but really, the T-slur and the savage finger pointing at one of the girl's skirts, a gesture which Sian wouldn't have tolerated for any woman, shoved the boulder over the edge of Sian's patience.

In retrospect, Sian didn't have to throw the first punch. She didn't have to cause her daughter and granddaughter any more stress or pain or trauma or disappointment. She didn't have to scream at the police officer who came to break up the fight, and she didn't have to resist arrest, kicking at the police car and managing to get one good kick into the upper thigh of one of the cops, she's sure, leaving a bruise if not striking the motherlode. She wasn't even drunk, wasn't even on her old beat, wasn't even having fun. It wasn't necessary for her to mouth off to the cops, for her to give only her stage name at the police precinct, and for her to kick the desk of the cop who was booking her. At any point, she could have calmed down. But the city got into her. It coursed through her like a drug, like pure adrenaline, and it buzzed through her limbs and made noise in her head so loud she couldn't hear reason.

Tim talked the bitch out of pressing charges. And before coming to get Sian, he waited with the trans girls to make sure their rideshare wasn't an asshole. And he found a nice diner where he deposited a shellshocked Honey and a sobering Gloria before he came up to negotiate for Sian's release. He didn't have to do any of these things either, but Sian knew, this is why the man is a miracle and she couldn't make an album without him.

Chapter 20

ON FRIDAY morning, Honey packs her suitcase at dawn. She is ready to get out of this house, ready to go home. Gloria is too old to be sousing herself and spent nearly the whole night retching in the bathroom. Honey would rather have had the forlorn Wayne-yeller than listen to a grown-ass woman hurl all night. And Tim and Sian returned loudly at nearly three a.m. Honey never thought she'd say she'd be happy to get back to Baltimore and to her mother for a good night's sleep.

Her mother. Bunny hasn't once put her on the phone, and in fact, has stopped returning Honey's calls altogether. He answered the phone once on Wednesday night, but his responses were monosyllabic at best and barely helpful. Mia has been able to make some quick jogs by the house, and although Patsy from work can't find the key she once carried, she has driven by twice just to make sure the dang house hasn't burned down. Gloria gave her some recommendations on an expensive security system she could buy, but the monthly fee was more than the remaining payments of Honey's mortgage.

The more Honey is stuck in this house, the more anxious she gets. She is no stranger to sharing close quarters with unusual people, but she's had enough of desperate women wailing at the door, people screaming through the wall and throwing plates at each other, and grandmothers who can't hold their liquor. Packed and ready to go, she busies herself wiping down surfaces in her room and tidying up. She peeks into the bathroom, which Gloria has fully rearranged with her nighttime illness. The sour smell is powerful, but no worse than changing Mama's diapers at home. She holds her breath and fumbles under the cabinet for the cleaning products and a scrub brush.

She is in the middle of spraying and washing down the sink when Gloria, completely drug out, appears at the door in silk pajamas. "Leave it," she croaks and pushes Honey out of the bathroom. Honey, gloved and with a wet sponge in her hand, finds herself stranded in the hallway. She hears more retching, so she heads down to the kitchen to deposit the cleaning stuff in the sink.

Tim is crashed out on an armchair across from Sian on the couch. He can't be comfortable. His legs are splayed out in front of him, and the only thing holding him off the floor is the weight of his head draped over the back of the chair. He looks a little like a sculpture, and Honey fears waking him up, lest he lift his head and fall. Sian has a swollen lip and a crust of blood near her ear. It looks like her earring was torn clean out of the lobe, and Honey wants to blot it down with peroxide, heal it somehow. Sian's arm is slung over her belly, and she winces in her sleep. No doubt she took some punches last night to the gut. If she'd known Sian would go after that white woman yelling at those young women, Honey wouldn't have said anything. She feels bad that she got them involved at all and hopes to say so as soon as they wake up. Honey perches on the unoccupied loveseat and listens for Gloria to finish in the bathroom; at this point, Honey is willing to let her clean her own damn mess up.

Honey needn't have worried about disturbing the scene. Out of nowhere, Sian bolts upright and screams into the room, nearly stopping Honey's heart. Tim jostles off the chair but catches himself. Gloria yells through the bathroom door something about *noise* and *mule* and maybe *tin barn*.

Then everyone is awake and looking at Honey, hands folded on her lap, fully awake and waiting over their sleeping bodies like a wraith.

"It's Friday," she says brightly, though still unsettled by the scream and her own nerves. She tries to dispel their disorientation. "Who wants coffee?"

Gloria doesn't come out of the bathroom until nearly noon. She looks exploded from the inside, her mascara splattered on her face and her lips a bright purple from purging all morning. "I look like shit. No, I look like a bag of crap that's been lit on fire and stamped out and then drug across the street on someone's shoe. Don't tell me I don't."

"You do look like shit," says Sian. "I think we all do." She can feel she's being side-eyed, and she pays props. "Except Honey over here. She looks and smells like fresh spring rain." Honey smiles and gives a gracious nod.

"I don't think I can write anything today," says Gloria. She puts a throw pillow over her face.

"Nope! It's your turn." Tim points at her with his full arm without opening his eyes. He, too, is feeling the effects of their late night.

"What do you mean, 'turn'?" Gloria drops the pillow and pouts.

"I mean, everyone else has come clean. We got the Bunny song, which is fan-fucking-tastic. And Honey also gave us 'Not the Same,' and 'Yelling Wayne' about our mysterious nighttime visitor. And Sian was beautifully vulnerable on the first day, and we have two other tracks inspired by her stories. It's your turn. What is so wrong about your life that you just have to sing about it?"

"Ah, this crap again. Now I remember why I threw a flowerpot at you."

He opens one eye and looks at Honey. "She's not holding anything heavy or solid in her hands right now, is she?"

"Not at the moment," says Honey, but she gently slides a sandstone coffee-table sculpture out of Gloria's reach.

"Fine! I want to sing about having the best garden in New York."

"Ennh!" cries Tim, emulating a buzzer. "Wrong answer."

Gloria fishes a makeup wipe out of her purse. Then she lies down on the floor, kicks her legs over the edge of the coffee table, and starts working on removing the mascara from her eyes. "I wish I had a man when I came home at night."

"Why?" asks Tim.

"The usual reason," she says.

Sian picks up the interview. "Would you say you're lonely?"

Cleaned up, Gloria yawns and tucks the stained wipe into her pocket. "I don't know. I have Fred, and Dory the raccoon. And people come around. I don't think I'm lonely."

"Are you happy?" asks Honey, honestly. "Are you fulfilled?"

Gloria thinks for a minute. "Happy is a tall order, I think. I like my life. I like most of it." She picks at her nails a little. "I've been thinking about my grandmother recently. She was a hard woman. She wasn't the kind to fawn over you and tell you were a good little girl or anything. If she said anything nice, you knew you'd earned it."

"That sounds familiar," says Sian. "My mom was like that."

Gloria continues. "The thing was with my grandmother, she raised my mom all on her own. There was a traveling preacher down in Galveston, and she was just sixteen years old and an acolyte in the church, I think that's the term, and he had his way with her the whole week he was in residence. He'd collect her from her home like he was gonna turn her into a high priestess in his church, and I guess he talked so well that my great-grandma thought it would come to something. And he'd drop her off in the morning ragged and sad, and then he'd preach all day about the sins of man. Nine months later, there was my mama. She didn't want for nothing because folks in the church felt so bad for her, but she never could get married, not with her not even knowing what the traveling preacher's game was. She was all used up and barely a woman."

"That's really sad," says Honey. "Men can be real rotten."

"Tell me how this is about you," Tim prods. "Why has this been on your mind?"

"Well, I guess I'm the bastard grandchild of an itinerant preacher. And my father left, and then my sister died, so I just got left behind in the company of strange women, and then I went and grew into a strange woman. There's something in this legacy I don't know what to make of."

"And Len left you," says Sian quietly.

"And Len left me too." Gloria's face gets stormy. "I think he's got someone else. I think she's young, and I think he's got her pregnant."

"Do you know who it is?"

"No, but she better watch out when I do. We had a good marriage. And I worked my ass off to make him stay. My mama couldn't make my daddy stay, and my grandma couldn't make that preacher stay..."

"What on earth makes you think your grandmother ought to have married that preacher. He raped her, right?" Honey is horrified by the mere suggestion.

Gloria shrugs. "Life is easier with a man around, even a garbage one."

"I firmly disagree," opines Sian. "Present company excluded," she adds and nods to Tim.

Tim sits up. "I think we've got a theme here, but it's not really holding together yet. Maybe something like, 'Can't live with 'em, can't live without 'em'?"

"But you *can* live with 'em and without 'em," says Sian. "It's like you have to tie yourself to a train that might be going in the wrong direction, just because, without the train, you won't get enough speed."

"Or like, you can drive the train, but you're just given a teeny little engine because you're a woman," says Gloria.

"I'm not following this metaphor at all," says Honey and covers her face with her hands. "Are you all saying the point of getting married or being with a man is just to be more fiscally safe or have more success in life? We're all examples that disprove that theory!"

"No, the point of a man is to give you babies," says Gloria. "And to make you feel like you're valuable."

"I don't think I've ever felt valuable in the hands of a man," says Sian. "I've always felt exactly the opposite."

"You're probably a lesbian," says Gloria. "I mean, you are, aren't you?"

"The term is pansexual, but whatever," says Sian.

"What, you boink pans? I'd imagine the handles are easier." Gloria laughs at her own joke. "And you're—what's the PC term—something like androgynous? No, asexual? Ace, or something?" Gloria says to Honey.

"I have no idea what on God's green earth you are even talking about, Gloria." Honey looks at the front door, longingly.

"When was the last time you buttered someone's corn?" Gloria asks. "You don't look like you've had sex in years!"

Honey is mortified. "I do not want to talk about my personal life with any of you."

"Yeah, she's hard up for it," mutters Gloria, jabbing her thumb at Honey, who picks up her purse and makes to leave.

Tim stands. "Okay, okay. Let's calm down. We're still working on this." He addresses Gloria. "Let's go back to that theme. Do you think you're a failure for not being able to hold onto Len?"

Gloria stares at him and Sian and Honey can both feel the rage radiating off Gloria's body. Tim has definitely struck a nerve. The tension is a roused snake, coiled and threatening. Gloria vibrates, her face going red with a pent-up scream. Honey clutches her purse and Sian sits up, winces, and leans forward, curious.

Suddenly, a calm settles across Gloria and she eases back in her chair and stretches out her arms. "*Oooh, those ones were just target practice,*" she sings. "*But I am the mark.*" She waits for the reaction. "Like, I'm the mark that he's trying to hit, but also, I'm like the mark of the con man? Double entendre?"

Tim smiles. "I think we have a new start."

"So what happens next?" asks Honey. Her question is multifaceted and vague. She wants to know when she's getting paid, when they record, when the album will come out, whether they should plan a tour, all of it. Today is the first day of her renewed hope for an end to the raging storm that has been a career. She wants to hear about the rainbows and sunshine, or at least the furious rowing that will get them to shore.

"Well, we wait," says Gloria.

"Wait for what?"

"For Len. He'll shop around the demos, and then we wait to find out if there's a market for this. If they can't predict sales with their algorithms, the project gets canned. We just have to hope that what we've pulled together passes muster."

Honey is devastated. It sounds completely backwards. The first and last time she put together an album, the contract had already been negotiated, the songs were already done, and she just had to sing. She had done the harmony on that Elton John album as a session musician, and the A&R guys had come knocking on her door after that. She'd garnered a ton of press, and she hadn't known whom to choose. She went with Danny Dire, but she didn't even have a manager to warn her about what would happen, about the steps. Of course, she'd heard some stuff about him, but he was nothing but a gentleman at first, and he really knew what her voice could do, better than she did. The songs were perfect, rich R&B tunes that sounded like silk sheets and dark wine. And her voice, her baby voice, as she thinks of it now, could handle pretty much anything. In high school, her teachers had pushed her into sultry ranges, just to stretch her and see if she could carry the attitude of it. A fifteen-year-old voice can do sultry, but on a Black girl, it can look older. She remembers singing a rich, buttery Roberta Flack tune and the little inhale of breath and slow blink of her teacher, Mr. Lunes. She loved that effect she could have on men with her voice.

On that album, her sex appeal was maxed out. She appeared on the cover of *Dervish* in a gorgeous lilac silk gown, angled toward the camera to maximize her minimum backside, her head thrown back as if falling into invisible arms. In the raw image, her nipple, stimulated by the silk, had stuck out like a tiny arrow, but they'd rounded it off using editing software. She had noticed they'd also plumped up her bottom. The overall effect was that her twenty-two-year-old body looked like a set of twisted-up bedsheets. Her girlfriends called and toasted to her fame and fortune. The money in her checking account swelled. She didn't need to tour, but she did appearances on talk shows, singing a song or two on late night and smiling through the swoons and bedroom references the old white men made. For a year, she watched three songs taking turns on the Hot 100 and finally, near the end of the year, she was handed the Grammy that was the cherry on top of the luscious sundae of her life.

It wasn't perfect. She got howls and catcalls, but she had withstood those all her life, and then there were the industry come-ons. Men put their hands on her back, their fingers grazing those spaces she hadn't herself explored with her intimate partners. Their touches were sometimes so self-assured, she wasn't sure whether to question that lingering touch on her hip or even around her ass. And then there were the pushier ones, the bored-looking sound engineer at a public radio station who cornered her in a booth and confessed his love while breathing on her neck, and the radio deejay who hounded her to take off her shirt on his radio program, insisting it was Whip 'Em Out Wednesday, whatever that was. She demurred the whole time, and he wouldn't speak to her after, muttering *prude* as he banged out of the studio.

Of course, she wasn't chaste. She had lovers, some kind and some money-grubbers, some hangers-on and some true romantics. She managed to get her mother and brother a house in Baltimore and took out a mortgage. It wasn't much—a derelict rowhome in the neighborhood where she grew up—but she was hoping to fix the place up when she came back home for good. She got her mother a nurse and set up a fund for Bunny to go to the University of Maryland to study pre-law. She never met a man she thought would be a good fit for her family, no matter what fun they were having. She couldn't bring home a partier or an industry rat. The closest she came to a good fit was Michael, a loving dancer and actor who validated her and encouraged Honey's artistic side. He was a faithful man too, attending church services twice a week, or so she thought, until she realized he was going to Narcotics Anonymous. She understood that and prayed on it. When she followed him one night, she saw him stop short of the doors of the church and turn a corner with a slinger. She changed her locks that night.

So Honey was living a full life, holding her own, and Danny decided to crush her flame under his bootheel.

She wasn't even up for an award, but she was invited to the Music In Color Awards show in Detroit. Danny had set it up. He was cool about her next album, pressing her to wait on songwriting, insisting she had to let her first album run its course. She was hungry to work with other artists and had taken a call from David Byrne's people about a collaboration.

She remembers being on alert that night. Few people made small talk with her, and she was searching for friends in the crowd. It seemed tight and turned against her, but maybe that was just in retrospect, the night having soured with her fate. Her nails were sharp, filed to keen points that were in fashion that year, and she snagged them on her dress constantly, creating little nicks and tears across her bodice. She got a drink from the bar, and it was a long time coming. She remembers some sort of heated discussion at the end of the bar before the barback delivered her drink. "No charge," he said, but he wouldn't meet her eye.

She found her seat, and the lights of the room seemed to smear. People didn't seem to have a purpose, wandering and laughing like horses, big teeth and wild manes. She pressed her fingertips to the white cloth of the table, when she found Shine, one of Danny's bodyguards, helping her up. "Let's get you to the powder room," he said, not without compassion, not without care.

Eyes flickered around her as she stumbled. She dug her nails into Shine's hand, more for stability than anything else, but he adjusted her hand, moving her pointy nails to the side and gripping her knuckles. His suggestion of the bathroom made sense. She needed to be away from all these people, all these stares. He had seen the wrongness creeping up in her. She'd smoked pot, she'd done cocaine, she had even tried acid once, but this was all different. She felt sick, nauseated, out of place. She was worried that she was having an allergic reaction to something she'd eaten. It was like a sudden flu, and she was cold and too warm at the same time. The hallway seemed endless, and the door of the bathroom plunged open into a bright light that felt surgical.

Danny was there. And he looked mean. Honey looked back at the door, but it had closed, and she was alone with him. He said no words, just threw her body to the floor. He tossed the folds of her dress over her head and twisted them around so her arms and face were trapped in fabric. She screamed.

He flipped her over and covered her mouth. "You are nothing. I am the king. You don't get to scream. Whatever comes out of your pretty mouth belongs to me."

With a practiced skill, he flipped her over again and sat astride her waist. He placed one hand on the fabric over her face, so she inhaled silk into her mouth and nose when she breathed. He slid down to sit on her thighs, and with the other hand, he pulled down her tights and panties. The waistband on the panties snapped with the force of it, and he jammed his hand into her. She was mortified to find herself wet.

"You were waiting for me, weren't you, little bitch?" he teased.

She pulled her knees up through his legs and flipped herself over, scrabbling on the ground, fighting inside the bag of her dress. There was no time for her to think about anything other than escape, and the police later made a joke of it. *So he trapped you in your own dress?* They laughed behind their hands.

She twisted and bucked, keeping his hand from hers. She jerked back her rump, which hit him in the stomach. He let go of the dress and she shoved it down, freeing her face and gulping for air. His hands were on his stomach and she had a split-second advantage.

She swiped at him with her fingers as he leaned back. One nail cut into the white of his eye. She remembers feeling the sharpened tip of it snag, the way his tongue lolled out in a no-noise scream, the blood that spattered onto her face and then the guttural surge of noise. She would later learn, through reports and articles, that she had perforated his cornea, effectively blinding him. It was a freak accident, she said. She had simply meant to escape. But that defense couldn't stand against the testimony of twenty of his co-conspirators, including the bartender and Shine. The case drained her bank account and destroyed her career.

The photo of her emerging from the men's bathroom was the most damning evidence. Her eyes, wild with the drug, her hands with the jagged nails covering her face, a stripe of blood from her shoulder to her hairline, a tuft of hair sprung out of its neat bun, one shoe on. She looked like Medea, like Lady Macbeth, some other haggard villainess who stumbles out of her murderous spree. And the vicious, cool Danny Dire, rolling around on the bathroom floor covering his eyes, looked like a baby.

She can't believe she's sitting in this room with this second chance at fame, but she also wants to scream. How could she have been so naïve? She's heard stories from her own struggling friends. She'd gotten lucky with her first bout with stardom, and then profoundly unlucky. But now, she has to work. She has to have patience. And she is so tired of patient work, so tired.

Sian reaches over and puts a hand on Honey's shoulder. "It's gonna be a great record. We sound amazing. I know it, and I can tell how much you need this."

The hot tears spring before Honey can hold them back. Gloria and Sian sit helpless in their exhaustion, weathered and soul-scarred. This should have been their album cover, thinks Honey, a bit petulantly. Three weary, last-ditch women, toughened and graying, trying again. This is who they all really are.

Chapter 21

THE ALARM doesn't sound when Honey comes into her house that evening, and all the lights are blazing. Herbie, tucked under her arm, is vibrating with excitement as he senses he is back home from his stay at Mia's. Honey places him on the wood floor and he scampers into the kitchen to look at his empty food bowl.

"Mama," she calls, deeply worried. No one responds.

The smell as Honey mounts the stairs is overpowering. It smells like rot from inside a body, decaying and smoky. The house feels eerily unfamiliar, and she's unsure what's waiting for her. She moves faster up the stairs and into her mother's room. Her mother is curled up on her bed, staring at the wall, awake.

"Mama, you all right?"

Her mother's voice is froggy, thick with the phlegm of disuse. "He's gone." A crust of yellow around her mother's lips is disturbed by her speech. The breath from her mouth is acidic and pungent. Honey's iron stomach falters. She can't be sick in front of her mother, because of her mother. It wouldn't be right, so she holds her breath to keep from inhaling.

She softens her voice. "You all right?"

Her mother turns. "He is all right now," she says. Honey's mind races with what she could mean.

"When did he leave?" Honey asks.

"Day or two," her mother croaks again and leans back. She grimaces. "Made a ruckus yesterday. But he's all right. He's better."

Honey tries not to wrinkle her nose, but when her mother moves, the smell finds a new opening to her nostrils. "Mama, can I start you a bath?"

Her mother hums assent and turns back to the wall. Honey assesses the room. The walker is nowhere in sight. The computer is off, unplugged. Her mother is definitely lying in her own filth.

Bunny was supposed to sleep in Honey's bed, so Honey goes to her own room and finds it completely torn apart. The sheets have been stripped from the bed and tossed on the floor, and her orderly bookshelf has been rifled through. Her clothes have been torn out of the closet and bureau, and dirty bootprints trail across the fabric. What had her brother done? Why would he do this to her?

She didn't have much. She had only a few important things, but one of them is gone: the shelf where she kept the Grammy award is dusty but for the little rectangle where it had stood. And her gold record is gone from the wall too. A hole opens up inside her and she holds onto the wall to avoid falling in. She feels the power of it, the cruelty. Her whole identity erased.

"What happened here?" she mutters. It occurs to her that perhaps Bunny didn't do this, that maybe it was someone who came in after. The alarm was off, so it could be anyone. She drops the clothes she picked up, now thinking of a stranger's hands on her things. Everything will need to be cleaned. Everything is suspect.

"Mama, what happened?" she pleads, calling down the hall. She flicks on the overhead light, but the bulb has been smashed.

But her mother calls back. "None of your damned business."

She makes a mental note to bag the clothes and sheets and toss them. She can't imagine ever using them again, having the shadow of such brutality close to her skin. She returns to her mother's room, but other than her mother's state, it is actually neat as a pin. Whoever it was didn't ransack that room at all. It haunts her that they knew not to go in there.

The linen closet is similarly neat, stacked with the clean towels Honey had left for Bunny, and nearly all the adult diapers as well. Which means her mother has not been changed in nearly a week. It's inhumane, worse than she could have imagined. She murmurs as she wipes her mother's body down with baby wipes, folding the hardened excrement in towels as she cleans off her mother's raw skin.

She turns on the bathtub taps and prepares a clean towel. She drags her violated clothes and used towels downstairs and tosses them into a garbage bag. She does a quick turn through the house, checking her important papers. The photo albums are gone, and her checkbook is missing. A jar of coins has been smashed and most of the silver ones have been picked out, just the pennies left behind.

Honey sits and wonders at it. How can she sink lower? How can this get any worse? She spies the walker in a corner of the room, folded up and tucked between a bookshelf and the fireplace. The books have been rifled through, but the walker gleams like a discovered treasure. She drags it up the stairs and props it next to her mother's bed, thinking to wipe it down with some disinfectant before leaving the room.

In the bathroom, she sprinkles drops of lavender oil into the water and prepares some extra creams. Her mother will likely have a pretty bad rash since she was not changed and powdered, so she puts on nitrile gloves and swirls the oil on her fingertips to soften her touch.

She turns off the taps, but her mother doesn't arrive. She waits, worrying. Then she heads back into the bedroom.

"Mama, the bath is ready."

Her mother doesn't move, so Honey comes close and lifts her off the bed. The waste, now disturbed, emits a deep pungency that stings Honey's eyes. Tears are streaming down her mother's face.

"You didn't sing. I really hoped you would sing."

Honey is so rageful, she can barely control herself. She's mad at herself for leaving, hopping mad at Bunny, mad at Gloria for making this whole stupid thing happen. Bunny didn't let her mother go on the computer, so she won't be getting checks this week or next. From Mama's brief recollection, she gathers that he fed her three meals a day and left her in her room, taking the walker downstairs. He barely talked to their mother at all. And he left on Wednesday. Wednesday!

When Honey asked her mother why she let him treat her like that, she just shrugged. "Men can't handle what women can, I guess." It's not an answer, not by a long shot. But Honey knows she too can't stand up to him, even after this extreme dereliction of duty. The deal she made was one and done. He has paid his debt, however poorly, and now he has cast himself out of her life. She wishes she could take it back, take it all back, all the way back to learning to sing. If she could just rip out her voice, stay silent, disappear, she would never have been so prideful, would have just gotten a normal job that anyone else has, a hairdresser or a retail worker.

What's so much worse is losing the income. She's not sure how they're going to pay any of the bills. She should be getting a little money, about $500 all told, in checks from her clients, but she needs at least three times that to make the monthly bills. Without her mother's Social Security and without the piecework payments, they won't make it.

Honey calls her brother, leaves messages, but she suspects he's blocked her. She tries to appeal to Cassandra. Cassandra is a nurse. She ought to understand how an elderly disabled woman needs to be cared for, not just physically, but spiritually. She doesn't have Cassandra's number and never has, but she can send a direct message from a computer.

She opens her laptop, and immediately, she knows the sight in her left eye is degrading. She closes it and tries to read with only her right eye, which is straining. She finds Cassandra's profile and sends a message.

Cassandra, I know we don't talk much, but I want to understand Bunny. When he left, Mama was not taken care of at all. Her walker was DOWNSTAIRS out of her reach, and she wasn't properly taken

care of, in terms of toileting and her special diet. He is not taking my calls. Do you know why?

She thinks to add something about the Grammy, but she ought to take that up with Bunny directly. She pushes send and waits. It doesn't seem like Cassandra is online because the little circle next to her name is black, not green. Honey stares at the screen, willing a response. She wonders how Cassandra could possibly explain it. Maybe she will commiserate and say that Bunny is hopeless at the house too. But Honey has seen herself how doting he is with the kids, and how he is the one who fixes most of their meals. It can't be that. It must be something worse. *Abuse*, she remembers. Gloria's diagnosis. Honey's back prickles as she considers what that could mean. Mama said Bunny was "all right now." All he had to do was trash Honey's things and he would be all better?

It's no good waiting for a response, so Honey decides to go back to the church. A loan would be one way to do it, or an advance on another performance. She wants to dress up for the meeting, look professional, explain about the album and her mother's needs, the loss of income, and the good she's done at the church all these years. It's all true.

She has lost weight in the last few weeks, and her church dresses hang loose on her. She cinches the belt on her checkered swing dress to the smallest notch. Her face looks sallow and dry, and she looks old.

Not having money takes a physical toll. She doesn't remember the last time she felt like she could just relax, not worry about who gets paid. There was a time, she's sure, when she could just flick a debit card at someone, but those days are so far in the rear view.

She applies some lipstick and regards herself in the mirror. She could try sex appeal. Pastor Blodgett isn't married, and he's just a few years younger than she is. He could be starstruck, and he's made it clear to her before that he might have an interest in her body. She wouldn't have to do anything with him, she's sure, but maybe go to dinner, pretend not to be repulsed by his beady eyes and squirrely attitude. Women have done it before, she's sure. She knows for a fact—well, not for a fact, but from a good source—that Henrietta Pierce got her soprano lead in the Christmas performance after being seen at Melba's Place with Blodgett. Could be a coincidence, but Honey doesn't believe that for one second. She could get lucky and run into Pastor Glendon instead. Folks are calling him "Brother Idris" behind his back because he has such a shine to his eyes, looks so fine in his salt-and-pepper fade. She takes one last look in the mirror, seeing herself through Glendon's eyes, then Blodgett's. Her tiny stick-figure frame, her buggy eyes, her hair desperately in need of shaping or a press, or even a weave if she could ever afford it. She has the inverse of Henrietta Pierce's fat and luscious figure. Well, if no one will take her to bed, maybe someone will fatten her up some and give her enough for a few weeks' groceries.

Honey loves stepping into the church when no one is there. The soaring windows, dark oak wood, ratty coral carpet. All of it, for as long as she could remember, has smelled like home. The fudge cookies after service, the smell of a century of praise and bodies being shaken or lifted by the spirit. And lemon wood oil that Sister Greta uses to wipe down the pews and the wood around the choir rail. She runs her hand along its worn grain as she heads toward the church offices.

She knows all the tears in the rug, some of them widened by her own mischievous foot. She knows where a host of discreet sexual acts had once been undertaken by her peers. Mildred confessed the first touch of her breasts by Brandon S. happened on that side of the nave, and her cousin Taisha did dirty things quietly in the back with a boy whose name she never revealed—during a service! This was the space of so much of her maturation, her flirtations with tempting fate and self-centered prayerfulness all happened in this room. When she attends services now, she sees the young people in their own worlds, unaware that the paths have been cleared for them, that there's nothing they can suffer that hasn't already been suffered by someone else in the room.

During the pandemic, this is what she missed most. The sanctuary, the belief that these arms in this room would hold her, that she was more than loved. She was cherished, adored, celebrated.

Then the tenderness she feels for the church starts to peel at the edges, turning thin and papery. She wonders how robust the love really is if her Lord would let her suffer, let her brother turn away and abandon her mother. What has she done wrong? Was she prideful for pursuing fame and fortune? Or was she just using her gift? Surely she shouldn't be selfless always. Surely she should not feel overly guilty for loving to sing, loving to share her talent. Is it possible that she's tempting fate again by making this new record, tying her voice to the talents of these other two very self-centered women? Are they dragging one another to hell, and she just hasn't felt the flames lick her ankles yet?

She shakes her head to curtail this line of thinking. It's not helpful, and she needs clarity for this ask, this prideful but necessary ask. She has no other choice.

No one in in the front office, but clearly Mrs. Sterritt was there earlier. The computer is still on, and a small brown radio is playing a commercial. She hears a cough, Blodgett's, from the back room, so she heads on back. She knocks, which pushes the door open. Blodgett coughs again and says, "Come in."

The room is familiar. Peeling green paint on the hasty drywall that had been put up back when Honey was a girl. This was the room where she used to meet her pastor when she was disrespectful for a good talking-to, and where she met Pastor Blodgett for the first time when she returned home after her first foray in New York. He was young then, full of spit and fire, and he told her then that she would have to prostrate herself before the Lord to be taken back to the flock. And she did. She knelt on this very carpet at his shiny feet, and she begged. The stink of the green carpet comes back to her, vibrant in the memory of her past tears and snot. He did forgive her with a touch on her brow, a gentleman. A true conduit for her Savior.

All these years later, she returns to the same spot, no longer so humbled, but in the same desperate need. Honey is cognizant of the close quarters, Blodgett's breath and perhaps a burgeoning illness, and her own thoughts about using her body to get what she wants. In the many years since she touched her forehead to the floor and then his waiting fingertips, she has seen women do far less and earn his blessing. She needs this. No, she is owed.

He doesn't look pleased to see her, so she jumps right in.

"Pastor, I know the last time we talked…"

He harrumphs and says, "Good day, Sister Honoria."

Cowed, she responds. "Good day, Pastor Blodgett."

He harrumphs again and moves his pen on paper, but he lifts his eyes to indicate he is listening. She doesn't make a move, given the mixed signals.

"Is this visit regarding funds for services rendered?" His voice resounds in the small room, now filled with the smell of his digested lunch and some pine-scented aftershave.

"It is," she says and sits.

"I'm afraid we've just closed out our year's budget. It's a new fiscal year, as you likely know, so we cannot reconsider any accounts that have been considered reconciled. Your account, Sister Honoria, has been duly reconciled."

"I understand, but I think we may need to reopen my invoice."

"Can't be done. Not with the budget closed. We may be able to negotiate another performance. Maybe one for the Juneteenth celebration?" He leans back slightly, and she feels his eyes travel across her body. This should not be new to her, but the violation is intense. She pulls her purse to her chest, feeling like a schoolgirl. "Oh come now, Sister Honoria. Surely you are no stranger to bargaining." He licks his lips.

Honey's face grows hot. She is surprised and alarmed by this move, even if she anticipated it, like stepping off the edge while still preparing for the fall. She sizes him up, trying to keep her face open and steady. She travels the room with her gaze as if embarrassed, keeping herself from narrowing her eyes or appearing to cast judgment. She needs to seem impressionable, open to the idea that he is just making a mistake. "I believe that the devil may be showing his face right now," she says and looks at him shyly.

He blinks and then smiles. "Of course! It was a test! The devil can come in any form, at any time, and you were ready!" He winks and wags a finger at her, and the pen drops from his other hand.

Honey sighs. He's hungry and ready to take any bait. She tries a new tack.

"I am interested in learning more about keeping myself safe in this time of need." She hopes he will ask about the need, but he does not. He seems to think her visit is more about furthering her own ambitions as a soloist, as he folds his hands and waits for her to speak again. "As you know, my mother is very ill."

He cocks his head, and Honey is reminded that Blodgett was an actor in high school and in college. His dramatic gestures are barely feigned and seem stage-ready. "I noticed something while I was going over the budget with Mrs. Sterritt last week. There was something suspiciously missing from the budget. Do you know what that might be?" he asks.

"Payment for my solo?" Honey tries, smiling as adorably as she can.

"No, that was reconciled. You and I had a conversation about that and came to a mutual agreement. It was *reconciled*." He wags his finger again. "But what was not reconciled is that we have not received your monthly tithe in several months. If I recall, the last time there was a donation in your or your mother's or your brother's name was in December. And I would be surprised if it were near ten percent. 'Tithe' *means* ten percent, as you know. And, according to Second Corinthians, chapter nine, verse six, 'Whoever sows sparingly will also reap sparingly, and whoever sows generously will also reap generously.'"

Honey knows the chapter and verse. "But it does go on to say, 'Give what you have decided in your heart you can give, not reluctantly or under compulsion.' I believe it says, 'God is able to bless you abundantly, so that in all things, having all that you need, you will abound in every good work.'"

"So it does, Sister Honoria. And yet, you have not given freely or cheerfully."

"I have need," she says, and her voice breaks a little. "I have need, and my mother has need."

Blodgett leans on his hands, bringing his face closer to hers. "You look rich."

Honey barks out a laugh. "Rich! How do you mean?"

He pushes back and stands, and though he is not a tall man, he towers over her. "You are rich with health, with talent, with family. You are endowed with one of the greatest voices in the world, and you choose to share it with us generously, but we cannot feed our poor on the fruits of your voice unless you tithe on the income your voice brings in."

"Work? I am constantly working! Working my fingers to the bone!" She tries her best not to sound desperate, to pull some righteous indignation forward. He lives off the proceeds of the tithing plate.

She checks herself. Righteous indignation lies too close for comfort to pride.

He leans down and takes her hand. Honey tries not to flinch and to leave her hand in his grasp. He pets it affectionately, running his fingers across her metacarpals, across her knuckles and fingertips. "Your fingers look strong and healthy. Robust!" he says. He brings her hand to his face, and she thinks he will kiss it, but instead, he inhales. "I detect the soap and lotion on the hand. Clean and well cared for." He peers down at her over his glasses. "A woman who has money for expensive soaps and lotions has money for her Lord."

She pulls her hand back, stands up to meet his gaze. She can state the truth with integrity. The Lord would approve. "I can't pay the mortgage this month. I can't pay it next month, and they might take the house."

"It appears you are serving two masters, and you know what the good book says about that."

Honey can't help it: She inhales sharply and leans back, jolted by the accusation and the insinuation that she should serve him. "How dare you judge me," she hisses.

He looks genuinely confused. "I judge no man, nor woman. It is simply that you have not fed the pot you wish to eat from, so I'm sorry that I cannot help you."

Honey hooks her purse over her arm. "Thank you for your time, Pastor. Have a pleasant day."

She walks out of the room in such a huff that she forgets to scan the space carefully with her gaze and runs into a chair, nearly falling. She must get her eyes checked. On a roll with her Bible quotations, another verse rises into her head: "Out of gloom and darkness, the eyes of the blind will see." She wonders when that day is coming, how long it will take until she can afford to rest, restore her sight, release the anxiety that has been gripping her neck.

When she turns, Blodgett is standing in his doorframe, shaking his head. "You're a beautiful woman, Sister Honoria. Your talent could bear such luscious fruit." She can see his shining lips and feel the leer, and she turns to the office door, certain it's the way from darkness into the light.

When she gets home, her mother is still sleeping, has slept nearly the whole day. Honey doesn't really know how the "piecework" works, whether her mother needs to be awake to receive the "tickets." She shakes her mother awake.

"Mama, do you have to get up to do your work at some point?"

"No, that's over now too, baby. That's all done."

Honey's mind races through the bills, through what she had estimated from her mother's checks. "What do you mean it's done? We need that work."

"No, Bunny called them and told them that I couldn't do the work anymore. Told them not to call back. He wanted me to send the money back, but I told him you had the checks."

The room is spinning. Honey drops down at her mother's feet on the bed. "Mama, why would he want to send money back?"

"He said it was a scam. He said there was no way anyone was paying me that much money, and that it wasn't legit. He said he sees things like this all the time at his work."

"What does he see? Did he know you were writing code? Did you show him?"

"I didn't show him all that. I just told him it was a business and I just had to do some work online for a while. But he knew right away it wasn't on the level."

Bunny always has to know what's right, always has to see things his way. He probably thought she was calling people to bilk them out of their life savings or something, but from what Honey saw, her mother was fixing webpages. It didn't look sinister at all.

"He called them, you said?" asks Honey. "What did he say?"

"He called them and told them that he could have them arrested for what they did to me."

"I don't understand," says Honey. "I don't understand."

"I don't either, baby. But you know Bunny. He's got to have his way."

"I hope I can get you back on the Social Security," says Honey. "But even if I do, I don't think that will start up again for a while," Honey's voice fails her, and almost no sound comes out as she says the next part. "We might lose the house." Her mother's eyes are closed, and Honey doesn't know if she heard or saw what Honey said. Just as well. She'll have to figure something out.

Honey goes to the computer and checks the direct message she had sent to Cassandra. There is a response.

Ask your mother about Judy.

Honey's blood runs cold. Ever since she got back, she's been trying to figure it out, and the memories have slowly come back to her. When she was in New York all those years ago, Bunny would call her sometimes, late at night, sometimes leaving messages on her answering machine, but Honey was often out late, singing in clubs or meeting with A&R reps from labels or working wherever to make ends meet. The calls all came just after Mama was let go from the county school along with her friend, when Honey had a check with just enough money to buy the house. Honey thought she was rescuing them. Bunny was thirteen? Fourteen? And Judy took the top floor, just until she was back on her feet.

Bunny's calls were brief, and, she thought at the time, petulant. *When are you coming home? Can I stay with you? Do you have room where you are? I don't like Mama's friend.*

Honey buries her head in her hands and moans. Gloria called it right away. How could Honey have missed it for so long? She looks around at the house. "I bought him a prison," she says aloud. "Of course, of course he became a cop."

Chapter 22

SIAN DANCES through Mount Vernon, testing her own memory of Baltimore's geography. She happens on the parks on Monument Street and spins around in all four directions: North to the Ottobar, where she'd lost her front tooth in a mosh pit on one of the best nights of her life, long after the Whirlygirls; east to Fells Point where she'd smashed a beer over a guy's head when he came up behind her and grabbed her tits; south to the harbor, where she hadn't really gotten into any trouble, but did have incredible sex with a J. Crew employee in a bathroom in the Galleria; and finally, west to Pimlico, where she'd been standing with James Roma, the lead singer of Backbend, and she made him so mad he tossed the cooler he was carrying into traffic, causing a huge crash that killed two people.

What a town!

She's glad to be back, taking stock of the sameness of the place and the slight differences. Same dog shit, same artsy teenagers complaining about exams, same aged buildings, different street dining kiosks, different buses, same wackos hanging out at the bus stops. Honey lives less than a mile from where she's standing, and they're due to record at a local studio. Sian has nowhere to go, so she wanders, sizing up strangers, resisting the urge to dip into a bar and grab a nerve-quelling drink.

She's different now, though. Age is catching up with her. She's trying to walk straight, not to hobble, since she has developed a slight limp and off-centered gait. She has pretty frequent back pain now, and she's exhausted, and she has grown a stubborn panel of flab covering her normally flat stomach. She doesn't want to go back to the doctor because they'll tell her to eat right and exercise. That's what they always do. Or they stab her with something and tell her she can't get the flu now or whatever. She's had enough of doctors in and out of rehab over her life. She can't really handle another one dressing her down for her poor choices. Plus doctors really don't love when you tell them you don't have a place to live. She doesn't want to have that conversation again, no how.

Her phone rings. It's Gloria, screaming about what exit and how it's not an open-carry state but that everyone is clearly open-carrying all the time because obviously, how did the murder rate get so goddamn high. Sian smiles through the rant, smoking lazily.

Most of the demos have been approved, but there are some suggested changes to the harmonies on "Yelling Wayne" that Gloria isn't going to like, if she hasn't heard them yet. They're suggesting featuring Sian as the lead vocal and Honey and Gloria on backup. The idea of Gloria singing backup on anything is ludicrous. The woman can't even share a stage with her own shadow.

They are due at the studio at six, so Sian has five luxurious hours to kick back in her old city. She adores cities like this, ones that insist they're normal but are weird as all get-out. Back in the day, she used to hang out in Hampden, where she knew of two bars that operated out of the basements of family rowhouses. She once stayed with a guy on 36th who had a rowhouse that had been rezoned as a commercial property. He kept a few things in the front window and every so often, when people asked to buy them, he would sell them. Someone once bought just a left shoe. And she had never been anywhere that had such understated hospitality. She had once woken up in the living room of someone's house after a night of debauchery. She had stumbled drunk into the right number house, but on the wrong street. She found herself buried in tow-headed kids facing a TV screen while a woman in a bathrobe flipped pancakes in the kitchen.

The mother came into the living room and passed out paper plates to all the kids. She looked Sian up and down and said, "Syrup or jelly, hon?"

Sian spies a white Corolla looping around the George Washington Monument in the wrong direction, Gloria flipping the bird out the window to a cacophony of car horns. Sian lifts an arm to flag Gloria down and she skids to a stop. Gloria's hair is spun into a loose French twist and she's wearing a spangly biker cap and a black sleeveless T-shirt that says *Grandma Ass Bitch* in sequins. Sian, who rarely wears a seat belt, buckles up.

"You look like you're dressed for senior night at a BDSM dyke bar."

"I'm incognito," whispers Gloria.

"As what?"

"A Baltimoron!" Gloria laughs.

"Turn this thing around. You're gonna get us killed," says Sian and directs Gloria up Charles Street to Hampden.

"Where did you get that stupid shirt anyway?" Sian asks.

"I made it," Gloria says matter-of-factly. As if all famous people sat around with fabric glue and sequins. She should bring Gloria to the next toddler craft project thing at Carly's school. Gloria would be directing the damn thing in nothing flat.

"You probably need a hyphen between *Grandma* and *Ass*."

"We'll see," says Gloria, nearly missing a turn and laying on her horn as a bicyclist zooms around her.

"Gloria Redmond in a goddamn Corolla. I would never believe it."

"Not sexy enough of a ride to plow into…"

Sian puts her hand on Gloria's arm. "That's enough," she says. "Please."

Gloria stops when she sees Sian's face. She nods curtly and lays on the horn again as she cuts off a bus.

Only one of them is happy to see the old neighborhood as it currently stands, and it's not Sian. Gone are the thrift stores, the teenagers smoking cigarettes and pushing baby carriages, the guys on the corner pulling out their dicks for no reason, the shady pharmacies, the mystery-meat sub place. It's all replaced with yuppie shopping and sparkly lights and grad students. Sian sneers as they move up and down The Avenue. "Fucking gentrification," she spits. She's almost gleeful when Gloria drives into oncoming traffic and cuts off some hipster to veer headfirst into a back-in-only parking space.

"I am in love with Baltimore," says Gloria as she slams her car door and turns in a circle with her arms up.

"Thought you were all incognito," says Sian, wiggling her fingers.

"I thought it would be, like, killers on every corner. Haven't you seen *The Wire*? I thought I'd have to be urban."

"You really don't understand what *urban* means, do you?" Sian laughs.

"I do. But this is what the Village used to look like before it got all soft and pricey. So I feel like I'm home." She's dancing to an Ed Sheeran song pouring out of an open-front bar.

Sian shrugs. "This used to look like Alphabet City. Now it's fucking Sesame Street. I guess you can never go home again." She pulls a cigarette from her back pocket and flicks it with her thumb to satiate her craving. She doesn't have many cigarettes left and is rationing.

They've been recognized, but people here are cool. Years ago, fans would have come up to Sian and shot the shit with her. Here, their eyes flicker, and they smile knowingly and whisper to one another, but they don't break the protective bubble. Sian sees a few surreptitious photos being taken around them. It makes her feel like a movie star, but also like a leper.

They grab a table and order drinks. Sian gets a lemonade and Gloria asks for a double-shot margarita.

"We've got to record in three hours, Gloria. Go easy."

"I am a big girl. You don't gotta babysit my ass."

"One night at a karaoke bar tells me otherwise, friend. You cannot hold your liquor."

Gloria shrugs. "I can't help it. I can't seem to build any tolerance. Everything knocks me over."

"Then go slow. I don't want to carry your ass to our gig," grumbles Sian. She's already sick of this place with its highfalutin prices and expensive-looking appetizers. She wants to kick a garbage can over or something.

"I see you plotting something over there." Gloria peers at Sian. "Why are you always so angry? Did you get raped when you were little or something?"

"Jesus, Gloria." Sian raises her eyebrows. "No. I just don't like…" She's not sure how to finish the sentence, so she's as accurate as she can be: "…people."

"Well, duh," says Gloria and knocks back her drink in one gulp.

"Can't take you anywhere," says Sian, shaking her head.

"You remind me of my second husband," says Gloria. "He was a character. He didn't like anybody. I got him one of those punching bags, and he would whale on that thing for hours. Would come back with bruises on his knuckles. He was raped as a kid. That's why I wondered."

"Jesus," says Sian. She is starting to ache for the cigarette in her hands.

"Then what are you so pissed off about? What do you wish would happen in your life that hasn't yet?"

"Dunno," says Sian. She doesn't say what is in her head because she's not sure she understands it. Her next thought is, *I don't belong here.* She's wondering if it's an intrusive thought or insightful. What would belonging mean to her? This sea of posers isn't a place she wants to belong to, so that's not it. The only time she really has felt like she belonged was in a punk band, long ago. She got a nosebleed on stage once, and she smeared it all over the gear and people in the audience and it was a whole thing. All of them bathed in her blood. Is that belonging, or just a kink?

"So tell me a story," Gloria says, folding her hands in wait.

"What story?"

"I don't know. I heard about you and the Rock & Roll Hall of Fame thing. What happened?"

"I was high, and it was stupid."

"That's a piss-poor story."

"You tell me a story. Maybe I don't know how to live up to your standards."

Gloria's phone buzzes and she checks it. "Something is happening on my feed."

Sian pulls her phone out too, since that's what happens: One person breaks social protocol, which gives license to everyone. On Sian's socials too, someone has posted a picture of the two of them together, but what seems to be happening is that it's a reshare that is trending. A reshare of the three of them at the karaoke bar. The guys who recorded the video are saying some shitty things, but one says, "That's the grandma ass bitch." Sian takes another look at Gloria's shirt.

"Gloria, did you know this video was trending? Is this a set up?"

Gloria shakes her head and smirks in that *You caught me* way. Sian realizes she's been orchestrated into one more PR campaign. Gloria is a social media ninja! Sian sweeps over to where the video is posted, and it is, indeed, called "Grandma Ass Bitch" without a hyphen. The video has more than a thousand likes, and the comments are divided roughly into people identifying Gloria and Sian, and a few who are picking out Honey, and a bunch of trolls siding with and high-fiving the posters of the video. Sian hasn't had this much positive internet recognition in years and the feeling swells into her. She may be relevant again, but this time for something good—for doing something well. It has been so long since anyone has appreciated her singing.

Gloria downs her next drink, slaps a fifty on the table, and hops down from the barstool. "Let's go make a fucking album, you grandma ass bitch!" she cackles.

Honey is at the studio when they arrive, along with Len and Orla, Sian's manager, and the session musicians. Gloria introduces herself to everyone and shakes hands, and Honey is already on a first-name basis with most of them. It turns out she went to some fancy arts school around here and knows a ton of local artists, including most of the session players. Sian takes stock of the team: She knew Marvin King would be on piano because they'd all worked with him in the past, and he's a solid player and doesn't flare up and do dumb shit. There's a multi-instrumentalist who Gloria knows, and he and Gloria are having a moment. Mal, her best friend, is sitting in the drumming seat. Sian stumbles across the wires and picks her way around the amps in the crowded room.

Mal peers at Sian, and Sian worries for a second that her hair is out of place or she's buttoned up wrong.

"Babe, you okay? You look hella pale," says Mal.

"Yeah, just down. Haven't gotten out much." This is wholly untrue, but Mal doesn't question it. The pressure on Sian's back rears up like a labor pain. It intensifies as they talk, as if sending up a smoke signal to gin up concern from Mal. Mal graciously ignores Sian's contorting face. Pain always lives within each of them, and distraction is their game.

Mal nods toward Gloria. "What the fuck is with her?"

Sian shrugs. "PR campaign. Look at you being a sesh musician!"

Mal twirls a stick. "I'm bored as hell now that I'm retired. Also, I heard the demos. Your set sounds great!"

"Yeah?" Sian can feel herself blushing like a child. She's surprising herself, worried she's opening up too much. She can feel the jitteriness that follows authentic praise. When the hell did people start being sincere, start treating her well? It's creepy and she's not sure how to take it, even from Mal who, until this year, didn't give a rat's ass about anything or anyone. Or was that just a front too? Sian sees Mal a little clearer. She's happy, or as happy as Sian has ever seen her. She's relaxed, not hopping around and crawling out of her skin. "How are your grandkids?"

Mal beams. "I never thought I'd say this, but other than play, all I want to do is hang with them. Gregory was a huge pain in the ass." Mal points a stick at Sian. "As you know. But his babies Chloe and Melanie? They're like… I'm good with them, you know? I'm good with myself when I'm with them."

"Yeah," says Sian, unsure it's the same for her. The more she is herself, the more she feels like she's somehow fucking up Carly. Lulu is the one who makes her feel that way. Or at least she thinks it is. "That's great. Being a grandmother is great." She rolls her eyes and shrugs, trying to play it off. Mal catches her and squints, but Gloria calls out for the players, starting recording from the top.

Sian warms up her voice as they all take their places, put on their headsets, and wait for their cues. She and the microphone, her most familiar lover, get ready to tango. Gloria points at her.

"One, two... one, two, three, four..."

Chapter 23

HIS NAME IS Benjamin. Gloria has tried calling him Benny, Ben, Benji, Jerry, Beebee, and Bo, and even Doctor B, but he will respond only to Benjamin. That's the first thing she likes about him.

The second thing is his hair, which is prodigious. He's half Jewish and half Italian. He has hair on his head, face, shoulders, arms, chest, back, legs, and even feet. And of course, he doesn't shave his balls like these weirdo millennials. She's seen too much of that trend on her socials. She likes it like a thicket, full of manly smells. But he's clean and properly lotioned. All that, she likes.

The third thing is that he fixes little things around her house. He's been staying with her for about a month, and he is between jobs. He used to be a doctor at Sinai, and a good one. In fact, he'd done work on Len's heart back in the day. There was chemistry between her and Benjamin back then, but Len was all Frankensteined back together and looking like a ghost, so of course she played the good wife. She was happy with Len back then, but she can't say that she didn't look.

The last good thing is that having a man around the house has run off the neighbors. Which is nice and peaceful. She hasn't seen George in some time.

Driving down to her PO box on the winding road, she thinks about Honey, wonders about how she's doing. She wonders about Sian too.

Gloria hasn't had girlfriends like this before. She's had friends over time, but ambition sucks something out of friendships. You can't be worried about other people's feelings when you're moving forward. *Like crabs dragging you back underwater*, is what Jimmy, her first husband, had said. He was right about that. Wrong about near everything else, but at least he knew how to get her to stand alone, not worry about anyone who couldn't keep up.

She wasn't lonely then. She had Jimmy and all Jimmy's friends. She was some kid from the sticks, as far as they were concerned. She learned how to laugh, learned how to tease, to talk, to shoot the shit, to make someone feel like she cared about them. Jimmy's friends were authentic Italians. They were loud and funny and boisterous and they made fun of her accent whenever they got a chance. They had all been watching *Dallas*, riveted by the question, "Who shot J.R.?" They called her Sue Ellen, even though she had grown up in a beach community as distant from Dallas as New York City was from Maine or Virginia.

She got close with one of Jimmy's friends, Rita. Rita was a total lush, packing a flask with grain alcohol and a constant supply of breath mints to keep her normal for her workdays as a dental hygienist and then her nights as a cocaine hound. They used to go to the clubs, and Rita had an endless supply of LBDs she and Gloria traded off. But the party scene wasn't Gloria's style. She wanted to be onstage, didn't want to be noticed by just a few guys who zeroed in on her on the dance floor, but instead to be adored by the whole damn crowd. Jimmy sat at a table or on the sidelines, sometimes at a bar next door, escorting them from club to club and eventually getting good at sensing the moment when Rita was going to hurl or pass out and dropping her off at her door just in time.

Jimmy started Gloria out small. He took her to open mics and small venues first, and she tried out her girl-and-a-guitar act to bored and self-involved crowds. She started working banter into her act, calling people out in the audience. Over time, she garnered more energy from the crowd, but more importantly, she learned how to deal with hecklers. At his insistence, she started playing up the Texas hick aspect, wearing little floral dresses and cowboy boots, wearing her hair with flowers in it like Charlene Tilton. There was just enough nostalgia to carry her Texas wave forward into the eighties.

Meanwhile, he was trying his hand at stand-up. He had his own gig as an elevator repairman, but he was in enough buildings during the day and had made enough friends that he knew where the basement or upstairs clubs were.

Thing was, Jimmy wasn't funny. He tried. He was more angry and sad than funny, and onstage, he could flip so quickly from a joke into self-deprecation and pure hatred for the crowd that it got scary. But Gloria, she was funny. And that threatened the hell out of Jimmy. She'd save him sometimes from a knock-out brawl with a witticism, and she had once gotten his job back with a quick line, but he resented her saving him. He drank more and more, moped about being just an elevator guy.

On her birthday one year, she waited by herself with a cake for him to come home in their ratty little apartment near Houston St. He was a tidy man, but she *cleaned*. She made up the bed, washed all the dishes, swept under some of the furniture, waiting for him and doggedly dispelling her mounting rage into chores. Finally, she opened his perfect closet, his jeans and pants hanging in a straight line. Steaming mad, she took her pinking shears and cut one leg off a pair of pants. She put them back into the closet, long leg facing out so he wouldn't immediately see what she had done.

It tickled her, the ingenuity. She put on a record and danced around, ate a whole pint of ice cream from the icebox. He didn't come home. She cut another leg and felt better. And another. All the way down the line, so that all of the pants in the closet were similarly tailored. Then she started on one arm of each shirt.

By the time she had doctored his entire wardrobe, she was filled with light, swinging happily around the apartment. She washed her face, brushed her teeth, and tucked herself into bed, carefree, her shears under her pillow, should she need them.

She awoke to Jimmy in his underwear, hangers and clothes puddled around his feet, steam practically shooting out of his ears. His eyes were red-rimmed and his lips trembled. She had cut away small parts of his world. "You did this?" he sneered at her. "Fucking hilarious. Hilarious!"

Thing was, it was. His reaction was delicious! Her serotonin shot through the roof as he stomped around with his white underwear rippling over his flat ass and he shook his hairy arms at her like a pissed-off ape. She sat up in bed and watched. In the mirror across from the bed, she saw herself, her eyes twinkling, her joy unrepentant. She knew she had cracked something in herself that day, and she saw what her persona, hardened by heartache and disappointment, was going to look like. After that, the songs flowed, the music flowed, and she started to become *Gloria*.

She left Jimmy and met Charlie. He didn't like her sass either, but he didn't complain and get sad. He beat the shit out of her. So she left him when she met a music producer who gave her sanctuary in his studio. It wasn't free, but she didn't need money. And through him, she met Len, and then she did fully become this person, Gloria.

It's not that she needed Len, she thinks now. But they were damn good for each other. He gave her little ways to shape herself into something more marketable. And she brightened his star too. She was twenty-six when they met and fifty-four when he left. And now, she's here with this hairy-ass doctor who knows from women's anatomy.

But there's something she's looking for; there's a hole she can't fill in herself with men or success or fame or even gardening. She feels it opening up inside. She worries at it with her thoughts. Is it age? Fear of failure? Loneliness? All the usual suspects?

She arrives at the post office and smiles sweetly as she waits for her mail. People around see her and don't see her. She can be any old white lady in a baseball cap and sweatshirt up here. Some of these people are rich, much richer than she is. They've traded it all in too for peace and quiet.

It was fun to stir up a little trouble with Sian in Baltimore. Get people riled up. Gloria was able to embarrass Sian Harper, Sian Star! Bitch drove into a rock and roll museum in a red Porsche, and Gloria could make her feel visible and uncomfortable. Gloria smiles to herself even more broadly.

She used to do that with Rita. They'd get into a club, and Rita would start worrying about Gloria's bold moves, clutch onto Gloria's arm like a girl. Later, Rita drank herself to death. And then it was just Gloria and Jimmy and Jimmy's other friends. That happened back then. Another girl she got close to threw herself in front of a subway train on her way home from work. Another girl she tried to befriend got hooked on smack and stole all the money out of Gloria's purse. It was hard to find friends in women.

The rotting hole pulses a little. Is it possible that Gloria isn't satisfied because she doesn't have friends? It seems so simple and stupid. She can crack up a late-night host as easily as if they'd known each other since birth. Who needs friends when you have everything else? She has no filter, tells anyone anything on her mind. Has no hang-ups. Everyone can be her friend for ten minutes or an hour or a year. What is it about those women, their interactions, that feels like it's part of a theme?

The postal clerk, a woman in her fifties with sallow skin and thinning, dyed red hair, hands her the stack of mail without making eye contact and then turns to the next customer. Gloria instinctively steps in front of the approaching customer and plants her feet. She says to the postal worker, "Thank you ever so much for my mail. You have a good day now, won't you?" and she doesn't move until the bitch says, "You too."

She spreads the mail on the table.

Her check from ASCAP is more than eighteen grand. She hasn't seen that much money in one payment in years. She is torn between wanting to call the agency and just cashing it before someone notices. There's a smattering of expected bills that she will dispatch shortly, but there's also a handwritten letter from Honey. She's thanking Gloria for the work and asking whether Gloria can recommend her for any other projects. This she puts next to the huge check, torn between the windfall and Honey's obvious need.

Her phone was dead when she woke up this morning, so she grabs it from the charger. She planned to call Len, just to confirm that the ASCAP check is correct, but she sees that since last night, both Sian and Honey have sent her texts, as well as Len. She opens Sian's first.

Did you get sick $$? I think it's TikTok. We are viral and ppl are using us as sounds. Ppl are streaming me like fuck!

Next she checks Len's texts. She scrolls and scrolls down at least fifty texts just sent since last night.

Call me.

Call me.

Call me. Late night is blowing up.

Call me. I can book you solid for the next ten months.

CALL ME!

Then she checks Honey's texts.

Hello. I sent you a letter. Please disregard. I have enough money from royalties to cover my mortgage. Thank you for the work, and I appreciate you.

Work, Gloria thinks. Honey considers everything work. She's the busiest bee Gloria has ever known.

She checks her socials and it's true. It seems like that video has caused people to dig into Gloria's, Sian's, and Honey's careers. Streaming is way up with more than 600k followers for Gloria, a million for Sian, and 200k for Honey.

That little, irritating hole flares again with the discrepancy. Why should Sian have more followers than Gloria does? Gloria is the legend, and her voice is definitely better than Sian's. And Honey, why so few? Gloria opens her own music app and clicks to follow Honey, but not Sian. Throw a few more cents Honey's way.

They haven't even pressed the album yet. It's still in production. How is this possible? How can they have so much success just from something stupid like pissing off some kids at a karaoke bar? The world is crazy. The music industry is crazy. As unpredictable as the stock market and where bears shit in the woods.

She turns on her little radio and turns to a station. Sure enough, one of her songs, "The Five Items" is playing. She kicks off her shoes and does the hand motions, singing as loud as she can in her kitchen. This is what she's been waiting for, she thinks: the world knowing her name again. That bitch at the post office can suck it. She's famous again!

Chapter 24

GLORIA'S HAIR is dyed and pressed, and she's wearing a shimmery silver and blue floor-length gown. She's had eyelash extensions and so much Botox she could bounce a quarter off her own forehead. Honey arrives in a similarly flashy number, but definitely one on the cheaper side. It's navy blue with hot pink and silver sequins in a chevron pattern along the bodice and skirt. When she heard about the album's nomination, she went all out and used the total of one royalty check to purchase this outfit from Nordstrom on Mia's advice. At least her performance costume is a stunner.

But oh, Sian. No one in the world could have expected how she'd arrive today. She's draped in luscious green silk with a velvet black wrap, stilettos, and a tiara with green jewels. Her manager, Orla, had gotten her an appointment with an up-and-coming fashion guru, one of those who'd won top prize on a reality show, and they did not disappoint. The silk drapes luxuriously. Her shoulders are bare, and her bruised and battered arms have been creamed over with foundation. Her hair is returned to its youthful bright blonde, the grays a memory, and the cinnamon red on her lips makes her smile electric. She looks like money. She looks like she's made of money, like greed, like envy, like a million ever-loving dollars.

They are seated together at the Grammys. The record has been nominated for Album of the Year. Orla and Len put them up for practically every category. So they've also garnered nominations for Best Rock

Performance, Best Contemporary Blues Album, and Best Alternative Music Album, Record of the Year, and Song of the Year for "Swan Song." The industry certainly didn't know where to put them or what to call their album.

The cameras and photographers swirl around them, and Gloria and Sian soak it in, shimmering in the lights and attention. Honey, on the other hand, appears to shrink behind them, her eyes growing wider and more anxious with every step closer to their seats.

Savion is in the audience too, and he makes a beeline for Honey. He is also nominated in three categories for the jazz album he put out earlier this year, the one Honey missed being part of.

"Beautiful Honoria Conaway! I have dreamed of meeting you on this very carpet."

Honey immediately perks up and lets herself fall into his arms. He smells like cedarwood and dry cleaning, and he's wearing a lovely black shirt with purple and blue pin-stripes under his shiny tux.

"I feel like we're back on the BSA stage!" she says, pulling back, lest she smear lipstick on him.

"Good old Baltimore School for the Arts!" He grins wildly and seems to remember something. "Oh, let me introduce you to my partner, Noemie."

Noey steps forward wearing a yellow and green shiny dress and tiny spiky heels that bring her only even with Savion's armpit.

"Oh my god, babe! Honey is the reason I met you!"

Savion puts his hand to his forehead and smiles. "Of course! You told me that. Well, I have a reason to thank you. Noey and I have been together for, what, about three months?"

Noey nods. Her eyes are not on him, but on Honey. She leans in to her and says, "I really hope you win. I hope *you* win." She blinks wetly and her smile is exploding on her face.

Honey demurs and smiles, though her cheeks feel leathery and tight. "You make a wonderful couple. I'm so happy for you." She knows she sounds like all the ladies in her church, and Savion will for sure have an echo of the "Mmmhmm" chorus resounding in her head that is purposefully impossible to decode.

Noey smiles. "I love your song 'Please, Bunny.' What a great version of the Mississippi Sheiks! We're always looking for underrepresented songs that could be brought back for a modern take!" Noey gushes.

"Yeah," says Honey. "That was Tim Karman's idea. He's the genius," she adds.

"You're the genius. I could hear the heartbreak in every lyric. You brought it, girl!" Noey puts her hand perhaps protectively, on Savion's chest. "Sweetheart, I have got to get a drink in me! Can we?"

Savion nods and kisses Honey's hand as Noey hustles them away, waving.

Honey hadn't let herself imagine a future with someone like Savion. Or really, with Savion. But back in high school, his kindness, his warm eyes, his gliding hand, his confidence… she'd thought she could grow into it, that she could catch up. Now she considers her bony figure, her silly outfit, her trust in herself. She didn't have to be anyone different back then. She just needed to be pretty. And she was. But Savion, even Savion, has moved on to little girls. What could he see in a twenty-four-year-old? Does she blow smoke up his butt about how brilliant he is? Does Noey rub his ashy old knobby feet? Does she tell him stories about their future, as if their thirty-year age difference isn't going to have any effect on the longevity of their marriage?

Honey gives her head a little shake to dispel the nastiness. People fall in love for all kinds of reasons. With a twinge, she thinks, *Yes, social climbers fall in love with legendary musicians every day.* And with a sigh, she thinks, *I wish,* looking for her own social climber among the gathered flock.

Gloria plants herself fast and angry beside Honey. "Not even going to introduce us to Savion? I mean, are we chopped liver?"

Sian is sitting hunched over on a bar chair, checking her phone.

"Who is *we*?" Honey asks, innocently.

"Christ," Gloria says and drags Sian up and out. "I'm going to have to break that thing if you don't put it away."

"Jesus, Ma. I just need to finish this text," laughs Sian.

They hustle backstage into a dressing room to get changed into their performance outfits. Honey is floored by the fact that she will stand on the same epic stage where so many incredible things have happened. Where Adele sang "Someone Like You" for the first time, and pretty much stopped the world of music and demanded it look. Where Taylor and Kanye and Beyoncé had a whole thing, and where, years later, Beyoncé performed with this insane entourage while she was hugely pregnant with twins. Where Amy Winehouse performed just before she won her Grammy, and where Christina Aguilera took on James Brown. They'll be sharing the stage with some other greats tonight, including Savion, and Honey is just awed by the power of it, the majesty of the room.

They'd decided to sing "Please, Bunny" a cappella, and in rehearsals, Honey had panicked. She hadn't worked out exactly what happened with Bunny and Miss Judy, but she knew it had to be bad. Now the song was like an open wound. She suspects that Miss Judy, who had been fired for molesting students at the school, may have touched Bunny as well, or worse. Her mother has been dodging the question, but this moment at the Grammys feels like the wrong one for a highlighting of this kind of pain. She imagines Bunny at home, holding Cassandra's hand, hearing his sister plead to him to come home, come home to someone who allowed him to be violated. She hasn't been able to stand up to Gloria about the song. As they're stepping out of their designer outfits and getting on their performance costumes, Sian, who has been staring at her phone most of the evening, snaps up suddenly, looking jolted.

"What's wrong?" Gloria asks, bored and touching up her makeup.

"Nothing, why?" asks Sian, playing it off.

Gloria turns to regard Sian. Sian drops her phone into her purse and zippers it shut. She stares at Gloria purposefully as she warms her voice: "Mi-mi-mi-mi-mi-mi-mi-mi..." Gloria rolls her eyes, still suspicious.

Someone knocks on the door, and Gloria, dressed, calls out "Come in!" Sian and Honey are both partially clad. Honey lifts her dress to cover her body, but Sian stands topless and stares at the door. Serafina pops her head in. "Hey girls!" she says. She spies Sian's breasts and plaintive stare and jumps back. "Oh, I thought I heard someone say come in!" She shields her eyes demurely.

Honey gasps and then quickly recovers. "Oh, hello! It's nice to see you again." She stretches out her hand to shake, which drops one part of her dress, revealing her saggy bra.

"Oh, it's great to see you too! I just wanted to say good luck. I'll be introducing you tonight!" Serafina wears a goofy smile that makes her look unhinged in the half-light of the hallway.

Sian slips on her performance costume and grins. "Break a leg! In fact, break both." Gloria barks a laugh, holding her eyebrow pencil in the air.

"Oh, Gloria," says Serafina. "I wanted to thank you so much for the considerate gift. It meant so much to me." Serafina's words do not betray a hint of sarcasm, and for the quickest moment, Gloria worries that she sent the wrong gift, that she hadn't mailed a pacifier to this twat. "It was a great reminder that I should be extremely careful who I partner with."

Gloria narrows her eyes. "Speaking of partners, are you still fucking that Chloe or Zoey, or whatever her name was?"

Honey is shocked. Noey was Serafina's *lover*?

"We've moved on, but I appreciate you thinking about her. If I run into her, I'll let her know you asked." Serafina backs into the hallway and shuts the door.

"What did you send her?" asks Sian.

"Just something to shut her up," Gloria responds and puckers her lips. She feels Sian's waiting stare in the reflection of the mirror. "Okay, a pacifier. But I zhuzhed it up before I sent it."

"You are one seriously calculating bitch, Gloria Redmond," says Sian appreciatively. "Remind me never to get on your bad side."

Gloria turns around to face Sian fully. "The sentiment is entirely mutual."

The performance is thrilling, haunting. The room is hushed and expectant as they lift their voices into the air in a curling intro, just as they practiced. Honey feels her own voice sailing on the wings of Sian's and Gloria's, and they take turns in a beautiful aria prelude to the song itself, giving Honey a moment to widen her operatic capacity. When the first bars land and each one has a moment to deliver the full power of her range, the audience explodes in ecstasy.

They hurry to get changed back into their designer outfits, aided by Sian's stylist who, apparently, can't resist a swipe of camel-colored lipstick on Honey, which really does do wonders. The stylist had held Sian's rental jewels for safekeeping and she adjusts the tiara so many times, Gloria threatens to staple it to Sian's head. Finally, they hustle out to watch the other performances and to wait for each category to be announced.

Sian is jumpy, crawling out of her skin, but Honey, now that there's a possibility they will win, and a stronger possibility they will lose, jitters internally, as if her bones are knocking together. Only Gloria seems cool, win or lose. She already has a few Grammys in her case at home. Honey lost the only memory of this same moment over twenty years ago now, and there's just the square of dust to remind her what she was most proud of. She knows Bunny has been watching tonight. Right after Honey's performance, Cassandra sent a DM:

I thought you should know that I never saw Barnabas cry before today. You did that.

Honey isn't sure if it's accusatory or if Bunny was truly moved by the song. She doesn't respond.

The first award, Album of the Year, they lose to Savion. Rightly so: His is a gorgeous album that defies genre and is universally beloved. They've been hearing one of the hits all summer nearly everywhere they go. Not to mention, it's technically perfect. The cool arrangements always seem to come together in Savion's hands with little practice. They easily lose the Best Rock Performance Grammy, which, in Gloria's mind, they never should have been nominated for. They lose Best Contemporary Blues Album to Savion again. They lose Best Alternative Music Album to Serafina's soundtrack to *Instinct*, the movie she shot this summer. The movie isn't coming out until April, but they released the soundtrack ahead of time. Serafina gushes for nearly twenty minutes on stage about her journey and heroes, and doesn't say a damn thing about how Honey and Gloria were kicked out of an earlier project so she could edge them out again.

"See why I gave her a pacifier?" Gloria deadpans as Serafina prattles on and on.

The performances are unbelievable. The show of the night is by a tall drink of water with red streaked black hair. Fiesta Fantozi, or just Fiesta, dances out to a heavy reggaeton beat in five-inch heels and so much fabric Honey isn't sure where Fiesta's body starts and stops.

"Gosh, she's beautiful," says Honey to Sian.

"Yes they are," says Sian. When Honey looks quizzically at Sian, she clarifies. "Fiesta is nonbinary." Honey nods as if she understands.

Fiesta has nearly fifty backup dancers, and Honey isn't sure where to put her eyes. The song contains rap, flow, and sexy stops and starts where Fiesta disrobes slowly, starting with their wig. The backup dancers also slowly disrobe, shifting into outfits that change or seem to comment on their gender, so that Honey is unable to tell who is male, female, or something else by the end. The effect is of an electric drag strip club, and Honey is moved, titillated, and impressed. The showmanship—showpersonship?—is unbelievable. Honey and Sian have their arms in the air like regular concertgoers, chair-dancing to the catchy yet haunting tune.

Gloria heaves a bored sigh. "Why does everything have to be so politically correct?"

The room vehemently disagrees with her. The cheers at the end of the performance persist for nearly five minutes, lingering even after Fiesta has tearfully left the stage.

The categories pick up. As predicted, they lose Record of the Year, so all that is left for the trio is Song of the Year. Anny Jeffers introduces the category after receiving a protracted standing ovation for having beat cancer twice. As the nominees are shared and spotlighted, the three women hold hands at the table. It's their last chance, but it's Sian's song only. If they win, she's the main songwriter and she'll be the one to keep the statue. They all know this. Honey knows her night is over, but she's here for Sian and what they created together.

Anny opens the envelope. "Sian Harper for 'Swan Song.'"

Sian cannot move for a minute. She covers her mouth, but she is horrified. She never thought she'd be the one. She turns to Honey. "Come up with me. Please." Her eyes are huge, and she's pleading. Honey nods. They stand, and Honey stretches out her arm to Gloria too. The three of them come up to the stage in a set, each taking turns hugging Anny.

Sian flips her hair back, which throws off her tiara. The audience laughs, and Honey and a stagehand both dash to retrieve it. Honey places it in Sian's trembling fist.

"I didn't prepare. I didn't prepare!" Sian says, and people clap and cheer. "Okay, well first, I want to thank these people here, Honey and Gloria. This song really wouldn't have been a song without them. I wouldn't be here, on stage, with all of you, without them." Gloria curtseys and Honey nods, smiling. "And, Jesus, Tim! I mean, just Tim Karman. He's everything. He did so much. And Lulu and Carly." Sian blinks and looks up, thinking. "And Orla, my manager. But..." She stops, suddenly serious. "Maybe Orla. I mean, Orla, are you here?" The light searches for her manager in the group. It finds her seated next to Len. Orla and he have been holding hands, but she pulls her hand back.

Gloria says, loud enough to be caught on the mic, "That goddamn whore."

Smatterings of laughter, but also a lot of silence cross the room. The light on Orla cuts out.

Sian shakes her head. "I mean, I bet most of you just knew me as the one who like, did all the drugs and crashed her car and stuff. It wasn't even my car. But I just want to say, don't let anyone judge you by your worst mistake. You didn't do that. You saw us, you saw the three of us for who we are and what we can be." She puts her hand on her belly. The pain is serious. She steps back from the microphone and clutches Honey's hand.

Gloria picks up the mic. "Len, I know you're out there. I got four words for you: You ain't worth spit." The crowd roars with laughter. She starts to put the mic back and then leans in. "Wait. Two more words. You're fired."

Honey grabs Gloria's other hand and steers her away from the mic and toward the stairs. Security is heading for Gloria, and Honey tugs her along. Gloria pulls her hand away and with the momentum of the release, spins and slaps the guard in his face. The light cuts out on Gloria and the guard and trails Honey and Sian, who are trying to get off the stage as fast as possible. But just before they reach the stairs, Sian looks at Honey helplessly and says, "I'm sorry." And she crumples to the ground.

Part III:

I Will Survive

"A rested body is a rested voice."
— Leontyne Price

Chapter 25

HONEY HAS NEVER been so tired in all her life. She's been back and forth to Johns Hopkins and her mom's place since the Grammys. The tests are conclusive about Sian, undiagnosed bladder cancer that has spread to her ovaries. Because she has no home on record, Sian has been using Honey's address, which means the bills have been landing on the carpet inside Honey's door. Her mother has been barely functional since Bunny left and won't see a doctor, so all Honey feels like she has been doing for a month is pleading with stubborn people to get the care they need.

Gloria retreated directly after the show to her home in the woods and hasn't been responding to texts, emails, or calls. Honey is lonely, pissed off, and prayerful, truly, but the last thing she can imagine doing is singing. Since she stood on stage at the Grammys, her manager hasn't called once. People don't want to work with someone who might upstage them. And though she is requested more and more for vocal lessons, it's her lowest-paying work, and her schedule is as booked as possible with the home care and visiting Sian. She feels busier than ever without the income.

She is quickly depleting the SESAC checks that have arrived. They were a godsend, certainly, but barely enough to cover the mortgage back payment and the roof, which Bunny had correctly diagnosed. She knows she'll owe taxes on the money, but she can't think about that now, not until she's through this gauntlet.

Poor Lulu. She has been back and forth to the hospital as well, but the grandbaby is with her father back in Alabama, and while Sian has been facing life-and-death decisions every moment, Lulu has been the one making them. Sian had an emergency surgery right after the show, and then after barely having time to recover emotionally from the first one, a second to clear out a mass they'd missed. Despite Sian's fierce persona in the world, Sian is not what Honey would call a fighter. Honey has known women in her neighborhood who have wrestled more with their children's hair than this woman is wrestling with cancer. Every catheter, every suggestion for a treatment, every hopeful prognosis, every bone marrow sample, all have been met with the same slack, non-committal response. Sian might as well be a corpse in the bed, waiting for the last breath.

And Honey could carry her, surely she could, if her mother weren't giving up too. Honey has resorted to sponge baths because, since Bunny left, Mama won't get out of bed. Honey has asked about the job, asked about Miss Judy, asked about Bunny's time, but every question out of Honey's mouth is like a bludgeon to her mother. She moans and writhes and won't respond.

Finally, Honey gets a doctor to come to the house. She sits by the side of the bed as he examines her mother's frail body. She's anemic, he says. She's depressed, he says. She's taking her medications intermittently and her blood pressure is elevated. Her lupus is flaring. With every diagnosis, he adds another prescription.

"Dottie," he says, loudly and clearly, though her hearing is the one thing he has not diagnosed. "What brings you pleasure in life?"

She doesn't answer. Honey wants to answer: people, life, helping others, and, apparently, math.

"What do you like to do?" he asks. "Do you like to go out? Do you like games or television?"

She answers into the pillow, but they can't understand her.

"What did you say? What do you like to do?"

Mama lifts her head from the pillow. "I don't like to do nothing. Don't you have anything in there that will kill me? I don't want to do anything anymore."

"Mrs. Conaway? Do you want to hurt yourself?" he asks again, loudly and clearly, as if he is reading from a checklist.

"Of course she does, you fool. You heard her ask for poison, didn't you?" Honey moves closer to the bed. "Mama, Mama, you have to tell me what happened. I know it happened with Bunny. What did he do to you?"

"He didn't do nothing. I did. I hurt him. He ought to have killed me when he had the chance."

"Bunny wasn't going to kill you."

"Wouldn't blame him," she says, her eyes bright and wild. "I was right in the other room, and I didn't do anything. He won't take my apology."

She sits up with effort. "And you!" she says and points a finger at Honey. Honey can see it wagging at her in and out of view. "You didn't have to go write that song. It's just going to send him over the edge."

"What edge, Mama?" Honey asks. "There's no edge that man has not already gone over."

"He was handling it until you sang that damn song. He sent it to me on my phone, and that's the last time I heard from him. You did that, you selfish bitch."

The insult hits Honey in the face, and she burns all over. She has given everything to her mother, everything for the last however many years. She's bathed the woman, taken her to appointments, gotten her drugs, gotten her new prescriptions, dressed her, fed her, managed her money, changed her adult diapers and bedpans. There isn't anything she hasn't done for this woman. She stands up and tries to walk out the door but catches the side of her body on the doorframe. The doctor looks up, alert, and asks her if she's all right.

"She ain't all right. She's blind as a bat but she's pretending she's fine. She's gotta be the only one without problems. Ain't that right?" her mother insists.

Hot tears and a roar overcome Honey's head and she slips down to the floor. All she has is problems! What is her mother going on about?

The doctor says, "Stay there. I'll get some ice. It's on the first floor?" He doesn't wait for an answer though. She suspects he just wants to get away from their crazy drama, make a phone call to have them both carted off to a loony bin.

Honey stretches her legs out onto the floor and runs her hands along her thighs.

"Mama, you have to tell me. What happened to Bunny?"

"You weren't here. You were out in the world, making your way. You don't get that story."

"Mama, please!" she cries. Honey doesn't know why she needs to hear it, but she does.

"You have your own shit to deal with. It's time you started taking care of that instead of being everyone's damn nursemaid." Her mother just sounds tired, like she's been working on this argument for months, and is tired of delivering it.

"You're impossible," Honey whispers.

"You're impossible! You think you're so holy, but you wasted what God gave you. And you made me rely on you. You think I want to be stuck in this house? Do you think I want to be in this room that don't even got any windows, while my daughter is out and working all day and living her life?"

Honey flips over on her hands and knees and moves out of the room through the hallway carefully. The ground is pushing away from her, and she's dizzy with the accusation, her sense of reality careening out beyond her hands so she can't grab it. She can navigate, but it feels good to crawl, good to be low to the ground. She pushes into her own room and climbs into her bed. She lies on her back, staring at the dim light fixture, wishing she had more light, a skylight, an overhead light. To be bathed in light.

The doctor bounds up the stairs with ice, useless now. He first dashes past Honey's room, but he doubles back and stands awkwardly in the doorframe, twisting cold water out of the icy compress. He seems hesitant to enter and hand it to her.

"I think your mother would do well in an institution. Temporarily," he says. "Or assisted living. She could make friends."

"Do you think I can afford an assisted living place?" Honey asks.

He coughs. "I'm sorry for asking this, but didn't you just win a Grammy? One of your songs was playing on the radio on my way over here. Do you not have money?"

Honey sighs so hard it rattles her whole body. She can feel air snap out of her bones as she cracks her joints and stares at the ceiling. She could sell the house now that the roof is fixed. She could put her mother in a home and herself in an apartment. It could happen. She lifts her arms and moves them to her thoughts, conducting the ideas like an invisible orchestra arranging her poorly organized life into place, a swell of space for appointments with students, a clatter of friends for her mother, the business with Bunny floating on clouds of song into the past. A heavy cadence of separation from her mother, leaving the person who knows her best, a crash and boom of the fear of self-discovery, of realization. She opens her mouth and hears the deep clear note that rises into the space, cracking all the walls and shattering the rotten roof and the foundation, bringing her own life down on top of them all. Out of the rubble, the music rises up from her chest and, in song, she ushers in her own freedom.

Honey calls Bunny from Mia's phone because she hopes he has not blocked Mia. He doesn't pick up, but she leaves him a detailed voicemail about how she has decided to find their mother a better placement, Arbor Oaks, which has round-the-clock care, laundry services, computer classes—not that Mama needs them—and plenty of people around the same age. She's selling the house, moving downtown. It's all arranged. He doesn't have to do anything anymore for either of them. She feels good and clean when she hangs up, like she's finally cleared out all the cobwebs and made a fresh start.

Within three minutes, Bunny calls back on Honey's line.

"What in the living hell gives you the right?" he demands.

"Bunny…"

"Seriously, you need to stop using that name. I'm not a baby anymore. And you know that people call me Barry. And besides, you have ruined that stupid nickname with your goddamn *Please, Bunny* shit." He mocks her singing, and she hears the venom in it. She had no idea how cruel it was. With Gloria and Sian, it seemed lighter: a commentary, not a drag.

"Barnabas," she tries. "Barry, I want…"

"I don't care what you want. I don't care what you think you need. You don't go making decisions about what happens to Mama without me."

"Since when have you cared what happens to us?"

"Since I found out that you let her get scammed. Since I found out that you have been cooping her up in that house, bathing her, never letting her get back on her own two feet. And, since I found out that you're covering for being blind."

"I'm not blind," she says. "I have a doctor's appointment. It's called macular degeneration."

"I don't care what it's called. You are not reliable. You've never been reliable."

"Barnabas, I know what happened to you."

He breathes, tense. "You don't know shit."

"I know Miss Judy was fired. I know what she was fired for. I know…"

"You don't know anything."

His words are needles under her nails. "I know you took my damn Grammy. I know when I walked into my house, my clothes and my things were all tore up. I don't know why you did it…"

"I didn't do nothing," he breathes, but she can hear the guilty child in him. He's defensive because he is lying.

"What did you do with it, Barnabas?"

His breathing is heavy and ragged. And in that moment, she knows he took it. She can't imagine what he did with it because he wouldn't have sold it. She knows it's gone. It was a solid reminder of the sacrifice she'd made for him, but also of the sacrifice he'd made for her. He probably could barely live with that thing in the world. And after all this time, though she pines for the heft of it, for its shine, for the love and appreciation it represented, she can let it go. At least, she knows she must.

"Don't matter," she says, with effort. "I know Mama let that woman live in the house, and I'm sorry. I wouldn't have asked you to come back here. I didn't know when I asked. But I know now. I am so sorry."

She gives him space, tries not to breathe as she waits.

"Do whatever you want with her. I'm done." He hangs up, and Honey listens to the space he leaves as if he will lift his voice into it, forgive her, forge a new relationship that doesn't involve mutual abandonment, one where she is again a little girl who just wants her brother's name to rhyme with hers, so she gives him a nickname that does, and nothing bad will ever happen to either of them.

Chapter 26

MAL STANDS next to the bed with Sian, who is probably half the weight Mal had seen her last time. Mal wasn't watching the Grammys when Sian collapsed, never would, and heard about it through an alert on her phone. She had to call Orla to find out that they were flying her to Hopkins, god knew why, but that she would be in good care there. And she has been. She's surrounded by a wonder of complicated machines all casting various glows and making a rhythm Mal tries not to hear and be soothed to. She wants to tear it all off Sian and carry her out of the building. Sian has been trying to leave this earth for so damned long that when her body finally agrees, all these idiots decide to plug her in while she can't fight them.

But Mal doesn't want her friend to die. She wants her friend's wishes honored, but she selfishly wants Sian alive. Despite all Sian's relapses and bad choices, Sian is the one person Mal never had to take care of. Unlike Mal's male bandmates, who always seemed to need mothering, Sian pushed herself regularly into recovery and back into the search for profound meaning all on her own. *Trademark*, Mal says to herself, an old joke between them, but Sian isn't awake to appreciate it.

They've removed much of Sian's bladder, and then forced her into menopause with medication, and cut more out, along with her uterus. Sian hasn't eaten, has barely woken. The doctors think she's in shock, but Mal assumes she's in there hiding, afraid to see what's left of her body, protecting the tiny flame of her soul so she can feel all right when she has to emerge after this horrid storm.

"Babe," says Mal, tentatively. Then, "Yo, slut."

There's no response. Mal feels unsure of herself. Sian's not in any sort of coma. She's just locked behind a door in her head, and theoretically, she can hear whatever Mal says.

"Don't die on me. Please. I know it's a lot to ask, but I kind of still need you. I definitely need you. If you can just stick around..." she says, feeling stupid. The machines hum along like daft angels, insisting on some song about recovery, like this patient drone is the actual sound of miracles. Mal supposes it is.

She touches Sian's hand, and Sian doesn't flinch. She groans a little and moves her head but doesn't open her eyes.

"It's me. It's just me. Me and you." Mal is feeling hopeful and nostalgic at Sian's slight arousal, and both emotions elicit a wild discomfort. All the platitudes of twelve-step programs come up: *One day at a time. Do the next right thing. Take what you like and leave the rest. Don't quit five minutes before the miracle.* They've never made sense before now. They don't really make sense now, but they feel good. They feel like they're working, but she's not sure if they're working on her or Sian. Or both. It hits her suddenly: They feel like prayer.

She drops Sian's hand and stands up, stretches, hops around, shaking her hands out. It's too much energy, too much shit. Where do you put this in a hospital, where every room holds trauma, every room holds the end of something unfinished that's about to be abandoned and forgotten?

Mal's mother died in a hospital like this one. Not this one, but they're all the same, really. Hospitals say they're about wellness, but they're really about killing things. Killing viruses, killing infections, killing replicating cells, killing rotting tissue, killing smell, killing pathogens, killing hope. That last one may be hyperbolic. But she has never left a hospital with more hope than she came in with, so there's that. Maybe other people get lucky. Maybe other people are better at praying and hoping and believing in things that will give them sanctuary.

Sian turns again, making a little whine as she moves, and Mal rushes back to her side, as if the outcome will be different, as if Sian will flutter her eyes and smile, take Mal's hand and say she loves her. Mal has always loved Sian. Really loved Sian. Jackie, Mal's wife, is great, perfect, the best wife Mal could have, but Sian is the one Mal would throw herself in front of a bus for. But that's the trick: If you want to throw yourself in front of a bus for someone else, you don't love them. You are living some maudlin, masochistic dream that can only end in disaster.

So Mal reserves the space in her heart for Sian while using the rest of it to make this lovely, stable home life that can support a son and his kids and a rock band full of morons she's stuck with but who don't do anyone real harm anymore. She leaves this perfect little room for Sian where they can laugh and fuck and get into fights with each other and life and talk the nastiest shit about people and lament about having to exist in a world facing an existential crisis created by assholes like themselves and people who shoot each other because every single person thinks their life is more important than everyone else's. Sian and Mal always land in the same place, like a pair of red-eyed demons watching the world huff itself into a haze and promising each other that, same time next year, they'll strip the world bare and make sense bracelets out of the pain, piss on the burn of their mutual afflictions.

Only this year, Sian's not coming. This year, Sian is tripping on her own, in her own little head, leaving Mal out here stranded and starving.

"You goddamn bitch. You better come out of there," Mal hisses near Sian's ear, and Mal detects the tiniest, most minuscule hint of a smile on those reedy, pale lips. She puts her own mouth on Sian's and there's no reaction. Cold and dead, or nearly. What Mal wouldn't give to have Sian wake and lick her nostril, shove her tongue into Mal's ear. Do something that proves she's alive and doesn't give a fuck about death, isn't afraid. That Sian wants to come back to give Mal just one more day.

Mal closes her eyes and listens, really listens, to the sounds in the room, the steady breathing of Sian's unencumbered body, the hums of the machines, the beeps, the clicks and whirs of the oxygen machine, the footsteps in the hall, distant cries and complaints. She snaps into the timing, using a three-four polyrhythm, tapping the backbeat with one hand on the bed rail and a triple on the side of the chair she's sitting in. She plays and plays until her knuckles get sore hitting the rounded metal and she feels stupid. She wishes she had some sticks or pencils or anything to drum. She stops and rubs her hands together, and Sian, without looking, reaches out backward to grab Mal's hand. Mal starts, and her heart turns liquid. Sian grasps Mal's hand and brings it to her lips. She breathes on Mal's hand for a second and then drops it. Then she taps the bed in a slow, steady four-beat rhythm with just a lovely finger, a come-on finger, a finger that has known Mal through and through. And Mal gets her. She joins in again, with Sian's fingers tapping out the rhythm while Mal pounds away, taking the backbeat and adding flair with the other. They play and play and play until Mal can't feel her hands or anything other than the reverberation of the drumming against her own pounding chest, beating perfectly in time.

Honey and Lulu drink gritty coffee and stare past the wavy green lights behind the fake wood grain panels in the waiting room. Sunlight blasts through the windows into the space, and Lulu, with her red hair and fair skin, shields herself with a magazine.

"Do you want to switch seats?" Honey offers.

"I'm fine. I'm fine," says Lulu. She is not in the least convincing.

Lulu stands and paces the room, full of other worried waiters. Every so often, someone steps in to call a family forward, but they are well past news. To abide by the one-visitor-at-a-time policy, they're dutifully waiting for Mal to come out of the room. Neither is particularly excited to go in and watch Sian slowly kill herself, so they wait out here and pretend they want to go in.

Honey stands. "Really, you can have this seat. It's in the shade."

"I don't want the fucking seat," Lulu growls. "I'm sorry, it's not you. It's, I'm just…"

"No, of course. It must be impossible for you right now."

Lulu looks up, her eyes burning into Honey. "It has always been impossible. The woman is impossible. It's not, this isn't new, you know?"

Lulu blinks wildly, seeming to fight with a deluge of memories or painful scenes, as if she's watching a violent movie she didn't ask to see. "Most of my life has been having to be rushed with her to a hospital and watch tubes be shoved into her along the way while doctors and EMTs speak slowly to me and tell me she's going to be all right. By the time I was ten, I could tell you how to spell *cirrhosis*, explain what a biopsy was for, and determine whether my mom's hep C tests were positive or negative. By the time I was fifteen, I had two cans of Narcan on my person at all times, and I asked my grandmother for a defibrillator for my birthday so I could restart my mother's heart myself in case she OD'ed again. And by the time I was twenty, I could have passed the goddamn medical board exam knowing what I know about all the damage she's done to herself."

"I'm sorry," Honey whispers. She sits and allows Lulu to pace, though others in the waiting room are leaning farther into their phones, clearly trying not to overhear the tirade.

"The woman has been killing herself for years. She's been half dead longer than she's been alive. I don't know why she's even here, why anyone is keeping her alive. I bet if we asked, she'd want to be put out under a tree somewhere and just consumed by animals until she was all the way dead and gone."

It's too much. "Don't say that about your mother," says Honey, firmly.

Lulu whirls. "You don't know her. You just met her. Who the fuck are you to her anyway?"

Honey answers truthfully, "No one."

Lulu rolls her eyes and looks up. "I'm taking this out on the wrong person. You are just joining the circus, but I was born into it. I'm sorry you're wrapped up in it now." She adopts a mocking tone: "The narcissist brings all the attention to herself, drags her daughter all the way from

Alabama, where she's living a normal, natural life that everyone is entitled to, so she can participate in *Celebrity Death Watch*. So much fun for me!"

Honey sees the daughter. There's so much of Sian in her, so much anger and frustration. Sian *did* this, but she also *is* this. Honey remembers that she said her daughter hated her. Honey reconsiders now: Sian may have been right.

She knows, however, the danger of not seeing consequences of your actions. She tells Lulu, "If she passes, you will regret what you're saying."

"You don't know me." Lulu crosses her arms. "You don't know what I'll regret."

"That's true. But she may be dying this time. Really dying."

"She fucking better be." Lulu sits back down and grabs a magazine from the rack. Most of them have headlines about Sian on the cover: *SIAN STAR'S SWAN SONG! SIAN SWOONS AFTER WINNING GRAMMY! SIAN STAR's CANCER SUPERNOVA!* Lulu throws one after the other on the floor. Then she sits and crosses her arms and her legs and rocks herself.

Honey is unsure how to approach the ragged, livid daughter, but she lifts the part of herself she calls to when she is singing in church, that little bird of faith that seems like nothing but, in an empty room and when brought forth, can flutter and make a huge mess of hopeful noise. The bird guides her hand. Honey moves to sit next to Sian's prickly child, and she puts her hand flat on Lulu's back, just resting, and then smooths in circles.

The motion brings the tears forward, and soon, Lulu is sobbing full force. The rest of the room seems similarly comforted, relaxing back in their seats or having covert, innocuous conversations.

Honey makes wider circles on Lulu's back, though Lulu doesn't move toward Honey at all. Unsure, Honey slows her breathing. She stretches for a box of tissues on the far table and holds them in front of Lulu.

"Thank you," sniffs Lulu, making judicious use of the tissues and gathering herself together.

Honey, still moved by the force of faith, ventures, "You should bring the child here. To say goodbye."

Lulu shakes her head and chops her hands to punctuate her statement. "I made a promise to myself that I would never let my daughter see my mother this way. She would only get to see the best parts of my mother. Not this." Lulu's vehemence surprises Honey.

Honey rubs Lulu's back more, but Lulu arches and Honey takes the hint. "I'm sorry," says Lulu. "I'm not great with people touching me."

"Don't be sorry," says Honey. "You know what you need." She scooches a tiny bit over on the bench, and it's incredibly hot through the windows. Honey stands and starts futzing with the cord to the blinds, which drop, darkening the room but creating the relief of some shade for her and Lulu. Lulu glances gratefully at Honey and they return to their absent stares, processing life with and without Sian.

Mal comes into the waiting room and stands in front of Lulu. "You can go in," she says. They don't make eye contact, and Lulu stands, marching off to the room. Mal doesn't seem fazed by Lulu's lack of warmth.

Mal sits and stretches out her legs, leans back and expels air and pent-up emotion that morphs into a single protracted word: "*Motherfucker.*" A woman with a child of about six cuts her eyes at Mal and stabs at her cell phone, probably reporting on social media about rudeness in hospital waiting rooms these days. The child, however, is on alert, her eyes wide and a smile threatening to emerge at the verboten pronouncement.

Honey agrees with Mal, though that's not the word she would have used. "It's hard to see her like that."

"You just got on the green. This is par for the course."

"That's what Lulu said, only with fewer golf metaphors."

"Yeah, I figured. It hasn't been easy on Lulu. Sian never wanted her, and was a, to put it lightly, begrudging mother. Lulu could have done a lot better if Sian had gotten her shit together or put Lulu up for adoption. But Sian is Sian. She's going to muscle through, even if she breaks everything in her way, including herself."

Honey tries to reconcile the quiet, nearly resigned Sian with the violent and angry descriptions. She'd heard about Sian from people in the industry and was familiar with her antics from the media, but Honey assumed her own story, one of the media making a reasonable person out to be crazy, is just the way it is. Perhaps Sian is one of the crazy ones.

"Well," Mal says. "You probably didn't know her all that well. You certainly didn't party with her, right?"

"I am not much for parties." Then Honey takes the meaning. "No, I don't party like that."

"Yeah. Then you probably don't know what she's like."

Honey turns to face Mal. "What is she like?"

Mal sits up to talk with her hands. "It's like, you know when you have a really bad shit? Like an ugly thing that is sticky and doesn't want to leave your ass? It's like, you wipe and wipe, and it's just like never done?"

Horrified, Honey blinks rapidly. "What?"

The irritated mother huffs and turns away, dialing someone who will appreciate this lack of etiquette. The child, however, nods solemnly.

"Come on, of course you do. One of those situations where you like wind up just getting shit everywhere, on your legs, on your hands, maybe on your pants? You have to like, totally disinfect yourself and the toilet and like, bomb the bathroom?"

Honey rolls her eyes. "Please, please let this be going somewhere." Her gaze lands on a woman who must be in her eighties who has been eavesdropping as well. The woman shrugs and smiles.

Mal points to the woman, newly energized by the camaraderie, and then goes on, "Right? And so you clean yourself up, maybe get new underwear? But until you take a shower, like a long, hot shower when you stay in there for what feels like a month, with really hot water that, like, peels off your skin, you just don't feel clean? You can scrub your nails, you can use like, a whole bar of soap trying to get that smell out of your nose and out of your hair, but you just can't get clean?"

"I am familiar with not feeling clean," Honey admits.

"Yeah, well, the industry shit all over Sian, and she could just never get clean."

The metaphor hits Honey hard. She deeply understands the stench of the industry on her, the ghostsinging, the begging for work, the feeling that someone else owns your body, your voice, your sex. "She couldn't find hope?" Honey asks, hearing her own question's naïveté and flushing with embarrassment.

Mal takes her point graciously. "If there was a rainbow, and it wasn't Lulu, Sian couldn't find it." Mal squints. "I thought it would be Carly. She did like that kid. But Sian was afraid that she would turn the kid to shit too. I could tell she worries about fucking up more people."

"Lulu is successful, and healthy, and bright?" Honey says.

"The one thing Sian and Lulu agree on is that whatever Lulu is doing right in the world, it has fuckall to do with Sian."

What a hopeless case the two of them are! All the encouragement her own mother gave her as a child and young artist seems like diamonds and pearls in the moment. To be raised by someone who was so self-destructive, it must have vaporized any hope for them. She thinks of the song, "Your Tattoo," and now it seems somehow sinister, even a threat. And she sees Sian through Lulu's eyes. "Swan Song," really? What a cliché!

Honey excuses herself and stands in the hallway outside Sian's room. She'll go to Sian, and she'll whisper words of grace and prayer and love to her as Sian takes this journey to the spirit world, to meet her maker and reconcile herself to the afterlife and possibly return her soul to the hosts of angels and definitely return her body to the fruit of the earth. She will do this because she owes it to Sian, and she will sing at the funeral, sing Sian's final song, and be there to hold up all those mourners who cannot hold themselves as Aaron and Hur held up Moses' arms when he couldn't do it himself. She will do that.

But right now, once Lulu steps out of the room, she and Lulu will look through the window at Sian's wrecked body, at her tortured soul, they'll have just a moment, and she will show Lulu what she can't see right now and possibly, what Sian needs her to see: That Sian isn't doing this for attention. That Sian, after this long and awful journey, is finally at peace.

Chapter 27

HUNDREDS OF INDUSTRY monsters attend the funeral, all talking non-sense about Sian's life as if they hadn't left her to die more times than not. Van Jurgen huddles with Len and Orla, now public about their engagement and about Orla's pregnancy. Jacky Jones chats with Mal's old bandmate and ex, Merlin Zaccardi of Backbend, probably about some new project. Serafina dares to attend with Seth Allen, the producer who was recently accused of molesting the soul singer Vallenia back when she was on that Disney show. Serafina must be on a PR rescue mission for Seth Allen's reputation, but only in the flicker of her eyes does she seem to be worried about what tradeoff she's making.

Lulu has organized this. She has always been incredibly detailed, and her career as a PR rep was useful as they pored over guest lists. Some of the names are a *Fuck you* to her mom, who railed against these producers for years, never providing hard evidence of any crimes against her except for signing her to huge contracts that filled her bank account. Mal wonders if there's any connection between the allegations Seth Allen faces and Sian's public and erratic hatred of him, though Sian had never mentioned him by name. Mal would be surprised if the two were unrelated, in fact.

Invited, but conspicuously absent, is Gloria. Perhaps Gloria wasn't interested in schmoozing with Len and his new wife and baby bump, but she sent condolences and promised a tribute. Lulu has made sure to have AV hookups in case Gloria or anyone else wants to patch in and share during the reception.

Lulu was cowed into not inviting Danny Dire. Not out of respect for her mother, but Mal was sitting right there while Lulu made the list, and the look on Honey's face at the thought of having to be in a room with him again, even retired and, reports had it, beset by at least one neurodegenerative disease, was too much for even Lulu on this vengeful mission.

And Lulu didn't plan to bring her own child, Carly, to say goodbye, which nearly wrung out Honey's heart.

One of the most cynical moves Lulu made was to book a preacher whose whole thing was prayer over addiction. Honey had recommended someone from her own church, Pastor Glendon, whom she described as a fine young firebrand and very empathetic to people from all walks of life. Honey contrasted him to some other pastors from her church, both of whom preferred the well-hoed rows that gave them access to fancy cars, favors from the female congregants, and a little pomp and circumstance in the community. She said Pastor Glendon wore plaits and spoke to the young cats using hip-hop references, but he could post up for white people as smooth as Obama.

Lulu dismissed the suggestion out of hand. "He sounds great! Mom would have loved him. So, no." Her finality was caustic. Instead, the psychopath they did hire charged fifteen hundred dollars and required a twenty-foot clearance when he spoke from the pulpit, which promised to be a riveting, life-changing performance.

Mal chewed black licorice as Lulu arranged the fields in her grand spreadsheet, deleting everyone her mother had ever loved, including Tim Karman and Sian's childhood friend Celeste. With a black tongue, Mal said, "You are a true coldcocking son of a bitch" to Lulu, who smiled privately and typed faster and with greater purpose.

The funeral has come together in a large, white ballroom at a hotel downtown in Philadelphia, and the pastor seems unready for the cool, rich crowd. He appears to have been misled that the deceased was in need of post-mortem faith healing, and he has next to him what people are suggesting is a box of snakes. He raises his arms to silence the crowd, and even Mal is impressed by how he commands the attention of these many self-involved fuckwads who are more worried about the paparazzi getting their best angles than the fact that Sian has left this world too soon, too soon. Mal leans back in her seat and watches as the most powerful and hated people in the music industry pretend to care about her dead best friend.

The pastor begins with a sermon about being led out of the darkness and moves into the vagaries of addiction, the twisted and thorny paths down which it can lead one, how the Lord is impactful in turning one's head away from temptation and pride and toward the true light. He gesticulates with passion, his voice reverberating in the room, but she gets sidetracked by counting the number of mentions of *eternal damnation*, six fully stretched syllables. Mal hears a buzz around her growing louder as the room's solemnity is cut by discreet smirks and the glow of cell phone screens.

She checks her own feed and finds that the handle #snakebox is live chatting its reaction to the preacher and trending on the socials. It's a little hilarious. The black metal preacher sermon regains her attention and, as she comes back to the reality of the room, she sees that in fact, a good number of the gathered mourners are on their phones, scrolling to see what other, more interesting events they're missing, whether anyone noticed that they're here and has mentioned what they're wearing or who they've talked to. They swipe down to refresh their inboxes on narrowing intervals, and the murmur swells. Mal leans forward in anticipation of something, some climax of the service. Perhaps there really are snakes in that box.

The preacher's epic rant does roil forward, growing louder and more passionate. He breaks his twenty-foot rule and moves toward the mourners, spittle flying from his reddened face and his hair damp with sweat and wild with his fervor. "You must give yourself to the Lord! Renounce your ways! You are nothing but a vessel for His love!" he yells, foisting his stare upon people near the front, who did not expect such an intimate experience. Their faces lengthen, jaws drop, hands turn up empty and forlorn. His sermon reaches its pinnacle, wherein he implores the audience to chant with him the one word that is the key to retaining dignity and love: "Submit!"

The attendees, deeply uncomfortable at being forced to chant, shuffle and demur, but Lulu, a maniacal gleam in her eye, steps forward and faces the crowd beside the preacher, chanting and using her arms to egg them on. "Submit! Submit!" she yells. She makes individual eye contact, as much as she can, and Mal is entranced by Lulu's dedication. Even the pastor seems unnerved by Lulu's passion.

Honey sits to the side, completely unable to comprehend it. Of course, Mal thinks, this would never happen in Honey's church. Honey crosses her arms and appears to retreat to the prayer box in her head. Mal has been holding her feelings at bay, living in the stead of Sian in this spectacle, trying to gather the memory to tell her later when she'll commune with Sian's ghost, just the two of them and their private language, their private sinister sisterhood. Honey doesn't deserve any of this, she sees through Sian's eyes. And the realization is so powerful, it deeply shames Mal to be part of this.

Lulu then advances on Mal with a fierce interest. She leans forward and pushes her face into Mal's hair, breathing hot into Mal's ear. "This is for Mom. You see it, right?" The room falls away, and the whole plan comes together in Mal's head with such force that she steadies herself with a hand on Lulu's shoulder. Lulu smiles and shouts "Submit!" Mal grins, finally seeing Lulu's game, Lulu's long con: It's performance art. This is not in spite of Sian. It's *for* her. It's the one way to clean the wounds for good.

They seem to share an electric moment, reaching out their hands to touch, and then Mal adds her voice to the chorus. She steps forward and turns to the crowd. Together, the three of them—pastor, daughter, lover—accuse the gathered: "Submit!"

Lulu yells at her mother's manager, pregnant Orla. "Submit!"

Mal yells at Jacky Jones, the rat fink who once left Sian out in the cold on a dark and rainy night, crying and stranded, just because she'd left the stage early with bronchitis and strep throat. "Submit!"

Lulu finds the asshole who got her mother drunk one night after she had just earned her 10-month pin, the longest her mom had gone sober. "Submit!"

Mal locates her ex-husband, Merlin, just for fun. "Submit!" He smirks and joins in.

Together, they take to task the room full of industry cogs and wheels, people who make a living crushing innocent souls in the gears. "Submit!" they yell. "Submit!" until many of them do, but the rest just leave.

Later, at the reception, with the crowd in the room winnowed down to a reasonable size, family and truly loved friends find their way into the space, and the preacher is dismissed, Lulu holds Carly's hand and circulates among the mourners. Lulu is graceful and smiling, with an open face. She hasn't had to say a word about the service to any of them because parts of the funeral were livestreamed by attendants and the events are breaking headlines all over the news: *SIAN STAR GETS LAST LAUGH* and *SIAN WON'T GO GENTLE WITH REVENGE FUNERAL*.

At last, Lulu can speak compassionately about her mother, about moments when Sian shone in her care and love. Lulu doesn't pull punches, and she is upfront about her family's damaging support during Sian's struggles, but with the clarity of an analyst, she expertly toes the line between explanation and excuse. As Lulu talks, memorable scenes from Sian's life, some familiar to anyone who had followed Sian's story and some private and compelling, appear on the screen behind her. Not once does she or anyone mention the Rock & Roll Hall of Fame, not even for the good things.

Lulu and Carly together announce the creation of a foundation in Sian's name called *Sunny's Stars*. It's a fund to advocate for and protect children in the entertainment industry, including performers and the children of performers, providing them legal fees and expert advice, as well as early intervention and mental health services and mentorship for finding normalcy within the trappings of fame. And with the recent uptick in royalties from having a Grammy-winning song and hit album, there is enough money for the foundation to launch by the end of the next year. The QR code leading to a donation site is projected on the screen to appeal to the generous, fellow survivors, and remaining guilty parties.

It turns out Lulu has privately scheduled a number of Sian's closest friends to speak; Mal couldn't stomach standing in front of the crowd and speaking about Sian, but the bassist from the Whirlygirls who reconnected with Sian a few years ago gives a brief and honest account of the highlights of their friendship. Tim, of course, shares about his time helping her on her last album before this comeback. And one of Sian's twelve-step sponsors gives a moving speech on what has been true and worked for them as well as for Sian, that the struggle is never over and that sometimes, letting God means giving in. This last bit elicits some stir, and Lulu keeps her head high as people quietly debate the relative advantages of resolve and mercy.

The last speaker is Celeste, a friend from Sian's high school whose house Sian would sometimes wind up at. Celeste is like a second mother to Lulu, but she had also mothered Sian. For as much support as she had given to Sian over time, Celeste could never catch a break. She had married young, had children young, contracted a bacterial infection that caused her to lose both feet. As a singer, Celeste had lived in Sian's shadow her whole life, but she's always been there to catch Sian when she fell. She often caught Lulu as Sian was falling too. Celeste is speaking lovingly about Sian's warmth and truth. Lulu is holding her eyes closed to keep from tears when Lulu's cousin Sara rushes over with a glowing cell phone.

Sara whispers fiercely, "It's Gloria. She's livestreaming."

"That can wait." Lulu strains to hear Celeste's voice. Celeste is describing a private moment when Sian confessed her fears about parenting, and Lulu really wants to hear this.

"She's livestreaming about Sian. She thinks she's being broadcast."

"Bitch can wait," sniffs Lulu and tries to catch onto the words she's missing.

"You don't understand. When Gloria talks, everyone listens!" She points to the room, and it's true. Heads are staring at screens and people have popped their earbuds in. It's like a private listening party, and the only one not part of it is the person speaking.

Poor Celeste. One more casualty that the dead shit cat of Sian's career swung by and hit in the face. Lulu stands and quietly approaches Celeste. She takes her hand, squeezing it to indicate a pause in the speech, a gentle interruption. Celeste, mistaking the gesture for authentic connection and a true moment, launches in on a nearly hagiographic account of Lulu.

"This girl, this girl is so fiery, so fierce, so put-together." She's pointing at Lulu, hugging her close. "Sian really never had to worry because…"

Lulu buries her face in Celeste's hair to explain. "We need to cut to Gloria. She's livestreaming. We'll come back to you."

Celeste drops her eyes and nods, the way Lulu has seen her do a million times when she wasn't the one who got the callback, didn't get a date with the guy she liked, had a kid who went to a state school instead of accepting his offer to Brown, didn't drive up in a Lexus, didn't live in the million-dollar house. Lulu wants to shout, *You're the one. You're the one who didn't get screwed over in the audition, who didn't get smacked around by that guy. You're not the one who couldn't pay the tuition because you'd smoked or lost all the savings, not the one who crashed that Lexus, not the one who lost the million-dollar house, you're the clear winner.* Celeste was doing great. Celeste was the true rock star. And Lulu is the one who had to preempt her because sadly, no one is listening to Celeste.

Lulu takes Celeste's hand and nods to Sara, who stands at the mic and announces the patch into the livestream. Heads look up to the screen, which illuminates with the too-close body and face of Gloria Redmond.

Her face squints forward into the phone and delight explodes onto her face. "Oh, I'm on! Thanks to spacekitty462 who let me know that I'm joining you live in this funeral. Well, hiya folks! I'm dropping in on this day to celebrate my good friend Sian Harper's life."

She pulls a wistful face, but then, as if she has just remembered something, she launches into a story. "When we were working on the album, Sian told me something very important. She said that this album had to be serious. It had to be important. That, to her, was everything. We dug into our hearts, really scraped out some scary stuff, she and I. And that album, I know she was proud."

Nearly imperceptibly, Honey moves backward in her seat. Lulu senses Honey being erased, and her heart stings.

"I was working on one of her songs, you might know this one. When she brought it out, it was a poem, and it wasn't getting at what it's like to be a woman in this industry, all the work it takes and, man, men, you all..." She stabs with her finger at the screen. "It's work, baby. It's work. It's work for all of us in the industry."

Lulu reaches over to Honey. "What is she doing?"

Honey shrugs. "What she always does. This ain't new."

Lulu peers at Honey in a new way, sees layers she didn't see before. The lack of traction, it's a feature, not a bug, of her time. As hard as Sian had had it as a white woman, it must have been so much harder for Honey with the Glorias of the world. Celeste, Honey, Mal. They make the backbone of the art in the shadows, and women like Gloria, and, she'll admit it, her mom, just dress it up and make a killing. They're all complicit. She's complicit.

Lulu looks back to the screen. Gloria is strapping on her guitar. Lulu hears the first licks of Sian's song, the one that won the Grammy. Lulu's mind races because they were going to close with this song, going to close with Sian's version. Gloria, in the sweet shine of her voice, begins, and with her version, she clears out the ragged strip that runs through Sian's, and, like bright air, she transforms it into a song of gentle letting go, of peace understood and accepted, of solace. Even the words, hard and brittle in her mother's voice, seem to morph into a paean.

This is my swan song
Her neck is long, a body all its own
It leans, white and forlorn
Her pond is home forever and it
Swirls with dirt and feathers
She drinks, a reminder
To be kinder
To who she's been before

This is my swan song
She is a box afloat
Heart, a stomach, an oviduct
soak the endless belly
She eats, a reminder
To be kinder
To ones who came before.

This is my swan song
Two feet in a pond
Braving the waves
Being nowhere
Going home

As she finishes up the song with a flourish, the audience claps wildly and Gloria takes a prim seated curtsey.

"Sian, all my love and hope in your great beyond!" Gloria shakes her head and blows a kiss at the screen. For ultimate effect, she picks up a candle she had out of view and blows out the flame just as she ends the livestream.

Lulu is so angry she can't feel her face. This bitch upstaged her mother at her own mother's funeral. She looks to Honey and Mal. Mal is stretched out on a folding chair with a hat over her face. Honey is seated too, turned almost unnaturally to regard some patch of ground, probably the safest place right now to put her stare. She looks hunched, deflated. And yes, erased.

Lulu feels a panicked hand on her shoulder. She spins and sees Tim, his eyes like bullets aiming out of his head. "Are you kidding me right now? Is this real?" he spits. "I have a fucking flowerpot to return to Gloria, and now I have a reason to use it."

Chapter 28

THEY DRIVE UP the mountain road to Gloria's in Lulu's comfortable hybrid, Lulu and Tim in the front seat and Honey in the back.

Honey was hesitant to leave Herbie at the apartment in his condition, recovering from cataract surgery, but she couldn't miss the opportunity to tell Gloria Redmond to her face what she thought of her. The light treatment for her own eyes has left Honey a little woozy when she travels, so she is happy sitting in the center of the back seat, eyes closed, listening to her new piece through her earbuds.

It's "Lord, Remember Me" by the Soul Stirrers. This time, Pastor Glendon was the one who helped select the soloists and approved the music. They picked a few more bluesy numbers, nothing too strident, but something that could give the elders a little groove to work with, raise some arms in praise. Honey was covered up in a choir robe when Pastor Glendon locked eyes with her and gave a coy little wink and a smile. Honey about fell out right there, but she got the solo, and she got an invitation to dinner with the man, and she got her eyes diagnosed and her dog's eyes fixed, and she's about the happiest she's ever been tucked into that little back seat swerving up these country roads to Gloria's place.

While Honey is luxuriating in her current situation, Tim and Lulu are trying to review the logistics for their confrontation with Gloria.

"We can't just, you know, come at her. What she did was unforgivable!"

"Did you see the think piece on it in the *Times*? It was gorgeous. I want it framed on my wall."

"Everyone sees right through her."

"But she's seriously making bank anyway. Check the streaming sites. She uploaded her version and it's got more followers and likes than Sian's. Fucking ridiculous!"

"I know, it's an insult to her whole legacy. Gloria is savage."

"She's a savage rat."

"A savage sewer rat in a pit."

"She can't get lower. She's at the bottom of the pit."

"There is no bottom. Gloria can always, always go lower."

They huff and cycle through old and new arguments but can't land on a strategy for confronting Gloria. Honey shakes her head and draws the music into her mind, moving the tones along her throat without sound, until finally, after ambling up a gravelly hill on a road that is unpaved yet well-tended, she can see the white, gleaming fortress of Gloria's "little cabin on a hill."

They are prepared for a guard chicken. There is no such chicken as they drive up.

Gloria is seated on the porch stairs, as if waiting for them. She is in blue jeans and a loose white top, her hair tied back in a red bandanna. She's smoking a cigarette, which she stubs out on the side of the steps, dropping the butt into the flowerpot. She appears relaxed, curious even. She doesn't get up.

Tim gets out of the car before Lulu even pulls up the emergency brake. He rushes to the house, but he does so without a plan and then stands fuming at the white picket fence. His small, taut muscles surge against his flannel button-down, and for what? This old woman who has been waiting for the drama to arrive, like a teenager who spreads just enough rumors to cause a fight? The scene almost makes Honey feel bad for her. Gloria has to push her privilege in front of everyone, make a mess and insist others clean it up, and Tim bought right into it. He stands in the street and balls his fists, intent on launching into a diatribe, but his words boil down to a simple question that, to him, encompasses everything he has ever known about her.

"What is wrong with you, Gloria?"

"I don't remember inviting you to my country cottage," she says, clear as glass. In fact, they had not directly told her they were coming, but Honey, unable to allow herself to appear at someone's house unannounced, had sent a surreptitious brief text from the car, just to be polite.

"I don't remember inviting you to my mother's funeral," says Lulu, but she's wrong. Honey recalls that Lulu did send an invitation to the service, not the reception. Glora puts her hands on her hips, and Lulu backtracks. "Or, rather, you don't show up when you're invited, but you barge in when you're not."

"Sounds familiar." Gloria extends an arm to encompass Lulu and Tim, as if Honey doesn't exist.

"So I guess you heard about the service." Lulu says.

"Maybe. I might also just have that sixth sense about that service." She taps her forehead where a third eye might appear. "Your mother hated most of the people in the room. When I heard that Jacky Jones would be there, and ugh, Consuelo Rodriguez, that heartless bitch, I did ask myself, what do these folks have in common?"

"Merlin was there. And so was Mal. Seriously, you knew?" Tim shakes his head.

Gloria shrugs. "Consider it a hunch. So, y'all just jumped in a car to tell me off or something?" She uses a come-on gesture with her hands. "So bring it."

Tim and Lulu look at each other, unable to name which wrong to right first. Honey lifts her hand. "I want to know why you didn't mention me."

Gloria shifts her gaze, confused, as if she's just noticed Honey's presence. "What now?"

"Well, you went on and on about how you and Sian collaborated. And you didn't even mention me." Honey clasps her hands in front of her stomach, channeling Pastor Blodgett's Socratic spirit.

"I'm sorry if I hurt your feelings," says Gloria, and though she appears to mean the words, she doesn't seem at all remorseful. "But it wasn't your day. We weren't celebrating you, were we?"

Tim gasps while Lulu responds, "Seriously?"

"Seriously," says Gloria. "I mean, I was working with Sian. That's how I knew her. I can only share my own experience. That's what these Gen-Zers tell me: Don't tell other people's stories for them."

"That's not..." Lulu starts. "It doesn't mean to erase them from the stories."

"Oh no?" says Gloria ever so sweetly. "My mistake." Then to Honey, "Next time, I'll tell all about how you felt when you were working with us too."

"Gah, you're impossible!" Lulu shouts.

"Now where have I heard that before?" Gloria asks a squirrel sitting in a tree that has been monitoring their conversation. She's like the fauna-bewitching princess and the evil queen wrapped up in one.

Tim holds up his hands. "You said that you and Sian *dug into your hearts*, that you *really scraped out some scary stuff*. I didn't see that happen."

Gloria frowns and mocks his tone. "You didn't see Sian give everything to that album? You didn't see her really dig down deep to give you something that mattered?"

"I did see her do it. I didn't see *you* do it."

"Ha!" says Gloria. "What do we owe you, Mr. Man? What did you want from me that I didn't give you? I think you got writing credit, and I think you got a hit album, a nomination for a Grammy. You made out pretty well just by hitching your little wagon to the stars of three exceptional women."

Honey makes a little noise. She sees what Gloria is doing, but Gloria is right. What did Tim want from them in that little house? What did he pull out of Sian, and did she even have it left in her to give?

Gloria smirks, sensing the ripe scent of Honey's conversion to her side. "That's right. We would have been just fine without you, me and Honey and Sian. We know how to make a goddamn album."

"It's not about that," says Tim. "Just listen to the schlock you peddled back in the '80s. You, with your little cowgirl get-up."

"Oh, and you would know about little girl get-ups with your ridiculous hair metal. I gotta say, I had, or tried to, a lot of hair metal guys back in the day, and very few could get it up, and of those, not for long. Bunch of drunk-ass glam wannabes." Gloria spits after this dress down and dabs at her mouth with a hankie.

"I'm from Atlanta, A-Town, wrong side of the tracks. I have my open-carry bona fides and I'm a damn good shot." Tim says, puffing out his chest. "And not once have I had complaints when I had long or short hair."

"So surprising. An a-hole from A-town. Ha! I'm from Texas. We had open carry before we had cash and carry, you fucking pussy." Gloria stands akimbo at the foot of her porch. "And if you haven't had complaints, maybe you were looking in the wrong suggestion box."

Tim's fists are balled and he looks around for anything to throw at the woman. She reaches down, picks up the pink ceramic flowerpot with all her cigarette butts in it, and looks like she's ready to hurl it over the fence.

Honey steps forward. "You have an answer for everything, don't you?"

As if to answer, Gloria glares. She puts down the flowerpot.

Honey asks again. "Why did you ask me to be part of this album, Gloria? Why me?"

Lulu steps forward. "And why did you ask my mom?"

Gloria purses her lips, and Honey puts a hand on Lulu's shoulder. "I already worked that one out. It was a favor from Len to Orla, Sian's manager. He wanted a second cut of the take, so he got Gloria's management fees, and Orla got Sian's."

Lulu makes the connection. "Oh, and the baby bump. That must make you real mad, Gloria," Lulu seethes.

But Honey squeezes Lulu's shoulder again and makes eye contact, gently. Lulu relinquishes the moment to Honey and waits.

Honey steps forward, her palms open. "But why me? Why did you pull me back in?"

Gloria takes her time with her answer, squinting into the clouds, looking for the right words. "I don't have anything against you, Honey. You're a good one."

"A good one," says Honey. "A good what?" she asks, pointedly, clasping her hands.

"Oh, now don't get all sensitive. You know I don't mean it like that."

"A good what, Gloria?" Honey wants her to say it.

Gloria throws up her hands. "A good collaborator. A good singer. A good person."

"Because I know my place, right?" She bares her teeth, hissing the word "place." She wants to hear the woman admit it.

"It's not like that," says Gloria. She fumbles for another cigarette in her pocket, but she slaps her forehead like she just remembered that she finished the pack. Gloria is squirreling around as if Honey is threatening her, daring her to say something racist.

"You don't hog the spotlight," she says.

"That's what I said," Honey deadpans. "I know my place."

Honey turns away and begins to walk back to the car, but she stops in her tracks. The largest white man she's ever seen is approaching her directly, wearing camouflage and marching, military style, with an M16 against his shoulder. She ducks behind Tim and then grabs Lulu to stand in front of her as well.

Lulu drops her cell phone. "What the fuck is that." It's not a question because she already knows the answer.

"Mornin'," the monster speaks. "Y'all appear to be bothering Miss Gloria. Let me disabuse you of the notion that she takes unannounced visitors. State your business."

"What?" asks Tim. He has his hand on his back pocket as if he has a weapon there, but the pocket is flat, and he has nothing other than his wits.

The man speaks loudly and clearly now, as if this is Tim's final warning. "State your business."

"George," Gloria starts. "No guns." Her voice is shakier than Honey would appreciate. Honey would very much like to hear Gloria's sassy tone right about now.

"Miss Gloria, I will handle this unpleasantness." He turns back to Lulu and Tim. "Since Mr. Benjamin is no longer taking up residence with you."

Gloria looks like she wants to slap him, but she keeps her eyes on his rifle. "George, I don't want you to handle any unpleasantness. This is my business, and these are friends of mine. We were just having a conversation." She flutters down off the porch to unlatch the white picket fence and usher in her visitors. "Come on in, and let's get you a drink."

George doesn't take his eyes off the trio. He squints more closely at Lulu. Then recognition dawns on him. "My oh my oh my! You're Sian Star's daughter, ain'tcha?" He turns to a woman standing in her nightgown on a porch about fifty yards off. "They're Gloria's friends! All clear!"

The woman gives him a distant thumbs-up, and the screen door bangs as she disappears into her house.

"Enjoy your morning, folks," he says. "Miss Gloria, Annie will bring you over some cardamom muffins later. She's trying a new recipe."

"Thank you, George," Gloria says stiffly from the porch, ushering Tim, Lulu, and Honey into the house.

"I'll tell her to double the recipe!" he calls, but Honey is relieved that they are already inside. She watches as he adjusts the rifle and heads back to his house, probably composing an Instagram update in his head and thinking of how many likes he'll get for coming so close to celebrity so early in the morning.

Gloria looks tired up close. She takes her time brewing a pot of coffee while the rest of them huddle and debrief in her living room. The decor freaks Lulu out, but Honey and Tim seem perfectly at home adjusting crocheted pillows on the brocade couch. Lulu wasn't raised in a home where people cared about their surroundings so much, and this room looks as carefully arranged as Graceland did when she and her mom saw it together.

When Gloria returns to the table, they see that even the coffee mugs are curated.

Lulu's reads, *The Legend Has Retired.*

Tim's reads, *Tough Titty, Bullshitty*, and milk has already been added to the cup.

Honey's is blank.

Gloria's own says, *I see the assassins have failed.*

Lulu raises her eyebrows at Honey and holds up her mug. She nods at Honey's as if they should switch. Honey understands the faux pas and claps her hand over her mouth. They quietly switch mugs.

Gloria notices and says, "I got that when I retired. Someone or another gave it to me."

"Just a little insensitive, considering," says Honey, as she leans back.

Gloria stares at the mug until it clicks in her mind. "Oh, Sian. Yeah, I do suppose you're right." She waves at them with the back of her hand as if trying to discourage a fly. Gloria turns her attention to Honey. "So, I believe you were calling me a racist."

Lulu spits her coffee back into the cup. "Jesus, Gloria."

"Who is Benjamin?" Honey asks.

"A nomad. A nomad who is no more."

Honey's eyes widen. "He didn't die, did he?"

"No, I didn't *kill* him, Honey. People don't kill each other up here. Or if they do, they don't tell people about it," she laughs. Honey doesn't seem to take the joke and sits a little more primly on her chair. "I just ran him off, like I do all of them." She waves her hand in the general direction of the world.

Lulu spies a weight, an immense sadness, pass just like the briefest cloud across Gloria's face. Then she's back, all sunshine, ready to move on. Lulu shakes the empathy out of her head. She has come here for a purpose and intends to deliver a message, a message her mother needs her to deliver.

"Well, why don't you tell me what *your* gripe is. Everyone else has felt perfectly fine giving me their criticism. *Notes, Ms. Redmond. Notes!*" She flails her hands like some dysfunctional stage director trying to get her attention.

Lulu looks up at the ceiling as she prepares to speak, but she realizes, it's to keep the tears from spilling. She needs to be strong for this. When she's got her words in the right order, she looks at Gloria. "Your timing sucks."

"My timing? I've never had anyone complain about my timing before."

"You preempted one of Sian's best friends, and then you took her song, and you rewrote it?" Lulu's face scrunches up in disbelief. "It's the most backstabby thing you could have done."

Gloria settles her face and blinks at Lulu. "You know who would have hated your stupid little foundation? Your mother."

"What? Why?" The tears come now. This woman is so cruel, but lifting her mother's intentions, insisting that her mother would have rejected her tribute? It's inhuman.

"She wouldn't have wanted a fund to help kids like her. She would have wanted one to help kids like Honey." Gloria leans back. "She was all bleeding-heart liberal."

Honey leans forward. "What do you mean, kids like me? Are you referring to the circumstances under which I was raised?"

"What, did you grow up secretly rich or something? Are you a Cosby?" Gloria titters at her own joke.

"I was raised by a loving mother," Honey says. She clasps her hands. She doesn't want to give Gloria anything more; Gloria is working the edge of a knife so closely she's bound to cut herself.

"In Baltimore, right? They got a name for kids from the ghetto: *underprivileged*? Right? Or is it *under-resourced* now? *Under-* something." Gloria takes a long drink of her coffee, and Honey can smell that it's spiked with alcohol, probably whiskey.

"Black?" Honey asks, again, pointedly.

Gloria's arm twitches slightly, and Honey can tell she's uncomfortable with the term. "That's probably the biggest demographic," says Gloria, agreeing to something other than Honey's meaning.

"My mother would have been so proud of this foundation," says Lulu, staring at nothing, making a speech to an invisible tribunal. "She always talked about how she needed an advocate, that kids can't go into this alone." She puts her hands on her cheeks. "Or maybe I just need this foundation. I would have needed an advocate because she was never there. She really wasn't there."

Honey attempts to put her arm around Lulu, but Lulu shrugs it off. "I just need…" she says and stands up. She seems unstable for a moment, keening slightly, and then she spies the back door. She goes outside and sits on a low stone wall. They can see her through the sliding glass door, her fingers tracing the grout between the stones.

"Why would you say that?" asks Tim.

"I'm sorry," says Gloria. "Did I invite you here? I was perfectly happy, living in this beautiful scenic haven without having anyone come by and tell me what they do and don't like about me. If I needed that, I would spend all my time reading comments from internet trolls."

"Those comments," Honey says and shakes her head. "I can barely open up my email because they've doxxed me. Again."

Gloria asks, "Is that when they share your email out with everyone? Yeah, they did that to me too. Now I've got all these trespassers."

They haven't seen a soul near Gloria's house since they arrived. White people have been driving slowly past Honey's house, taking pictures, freaking out her neighbors. And the police have come by more often, assuming that the white people are there to pick up drugs. They're even installing a new blue light down the street in response. Honey wishes she understood how to just be famous and happy.

Honey takes a breath. "Really, Gloria. Why did you pick me?"

Gloria is ashamed of her reason. She doesn't know why, but she knows it's the wrong answer. "Because I felt bad for you."

Honey purses her lips and nods. "I knew it. I did. I knew it."

Tim asks, "But you were struggling, right? Didn't this album give you a win?"

Honey peers at him for a minute. She thinks about how to frame it so he'll understand. "Sian called you up, right? To help with the album?"

"Yeah, so?"

"Did you need a win?" Honey asks him.

"I was getting over a breakup, and her call perked up my spirits, so yeah, I think I'd take it."

"No, I need you to listen to my words." Honey looks into his eyes. "Did you need a win?" She emphasizes both *you* and *need*.

"I think I would have been okay if she hadn't called. Something else would have come up."

"Exactly. And if someone had called you, had told you…" She cuts her eyes at Gloria. "If someone, say a manager, told you that someone asked for you specifically, would you think they were doing it out of pity?"

"I would hope not," he says.

"Well, neither would I." She pats his leg and turns her attention to Gloria. "We're all artists here. There are no echelons of artistry. There are no tiers on this cake. We made a beautiful thing together, but it was only possible collectively." Honey holds her hands together in a fist.

Gloria slow-claps. "Tell yourself whatever socialist story you need to. You've been through the wringer in this industry. And you haven't learned anything."

Honey stops. "Do you think that you contributed more to the album than I did? Than Sian did?"

Gloria shrugs. "Without me, there wouldn't be an album."

Lulu slides open the door and heads back to the couch. Honey, Gloria, and Tim are seething. Lulu has something important to say, but she doesn't know what transpired to bring them to this simmer. Still, she hopes her message, the clarity she received in the quiet outside is a balm in this moment.

"It wasn't all bad," she says.

"What wasn't, Lulu?" Honey asks.

"Fame. I think of it as net negative, but it wasn't all bad. Not for my mom, and not for me." Lulu twists her hands. It's a truth she has just come to and doesn't quite trust yet.

"Of course it wasn't," says Honey, almost acidly. "Who said it was?"

"I don't know. But all I know is I never wanted my mom to be famous. And I don't know who my dad is, which sucked. And the shitbags my mom dated, well. You can see why I would think it was all bad. But it wasn't." Her face has a serenity, a calmness that wasn't there earlier. "The only times I saw her really happy were when she was performing. I saw it that night with you three, at the Grammys. I hadn't seen that face, that luminous face, where she goes when she sings. You saw it, right?"

Tim nods. "I saw it."

Honey doesn't really know what Lulu is talking about, but she nods. Of course, she's seen other singers do that, other musicians just bury themselves in the music. She doesn't know if she does it, but that must be what Lulu wants to know.

Gloria nods too, but she did see it. She saw it, and was afraid of it. Sian had tuned into something deeper than herself when she sang, and it was what her own mother had tuned into, before Constance died. Whatever it is, it flutters away and leaves cynicism in its wake as soon as Gloria makes a grab at it. She can fake it. She can play around, but she doesn't remember how to access it, or if she ever knew. But she will never share this with Lulu. She doesn't want to give her the satisfaction of knowing that her mother had something that Gloria never did.

Tim says, "I saw it the week you three worked together."

Gloria asks, "When?"

"On 'Please, Bunny.' Whatever y'all were pulling out on that one, you were hitting it. You were in the zone."

Gloria surprises herself with the swell of pride that rises into her throat. She hasn't been complimented by a musician in a long damn time. A really, really long time, even if she still resents this fucker. People glide by and *Gloria this* and *Gloria that*, but this feels *good*. Good like a full-body hug or a warm compress on a sore neck. She smiles, despite herself. A long-ago story shakes out of her memory and demands to be told.

"One Christmas Eve, I was booked in Georgia, and I was running a fever so high they had to catch the mercury spurting out the end of the thermometer. I had snot running down my face, I was lit up like Rudolph's nose, and I was seeing everything double. I begged Jimmy to let me skip this one, let me just rest for one night, and he almost let me. But he said we drove all this way and we couldn't go anywhere, so I might as well give it everything I got. I was so mad at him, but so body tired, I figured, *All right, you real revolving son of a bitch. I'm gonna die up here on this stage tonight, and you're gonna have to sling my body back to New York in your goddamn trunk, you crying the whole way.* So I sang my heart out, poured everything into those songs, the broken window in the bedroom that whistled in the wind and froze my ass in the winter, the roaches and mice that skittered all night across our legs, the constant trashbin stink that seeped through the walls of that stupid apartment, the ache of what someone took from me, the baby I couldn't...." Her voice breaks. She shakes her head, drags her finger in a line from her legs to her belly button. "This here plumbing is shot." She holds a finger up. "That's the first thing New York stole from me."

Tim starts, and Honey blinks, holding the burn of a tear in her eyes. Gloria shakes her head. "Anyway, I sang with more power than I ever had. When I was done, Jimmy was at the bar, and he wouldn't even look at me, but there was this one woman who stopped me. At least I think she was a woman—I was extremely sick. She said that my performance made her believe in God again. Made her believe in God!" She smacks the table. "I ain't never sung like that again."

The room is silent for a minute, everyone stuck in their own swirling thoughts. Honey breaks the silence. "You gotta get yourself another real asshole to make you do some shit you don't wanna do!"

Gloria barks a laugh, surprised at Honey's colorful outburst. "Suppose I might," says Gloria. She swipes her finger against her eye to lift away a tear. "I wish I'd pushed for that when we recorded. I wish I hadn't made it light." She turns to Honey. "You deserved better."

"Sian deserved better," said Tim.

"You deserve better," says Lulu to Gloria.

Lulu stretches and takes stock of her surroundings, seeing them for the first time. So much plastic, so much color, so much curation. Gloria never pulls back the curtain. This is the most she's let anyone access, and it's just a peek. She asks Gloria, "Aren't you tired of it? Aren't you tired of, you know, fronts? Façades? Walls?"

Gloria shrugs. "Honey, this is as close to *know thyself* as I'm ever gonna get. This is my own little hideaway. I can be whoever I want here. I don't have to be what Len tells me or what Jimmy tells me. Len didn't think we could do anything in that stupid house." She leans back and throws up her hands. "Who sends someone to Staten Island for inspiration?"

"I liked it there!" says Honey. The others goggle their eyes at her. "I did! It reminded me of Baltimore, if Baltimore were all white."

"Yeah, I can see that," Lulu says, turning back to Gloria. "But also, the answer is that Len is cheap. He likes his ROI."

Gloria narrows her eyes. "Child, you have no idea."

Something is bothering Lulu. She asks, "Gloria, where is the chicken?"

Gloria squints for a moment, unsure how they would have known about the Mayor. Then it comes to her: Stavras's article. She had no idea so many people read that damn magazine. "Oh, poor Fred. Dory got him. She doesn't get to use the door anymore. I cut her off."

"Your raccoon ate your chicken?" Tim crinkles his face until he looks like a human question mark.

"Yeah. I thought they were better friends." She looks wistfully at her back door, now with a little deadbolt on it. "Guess not!" She slaps her leg and laughs.

Tim and Lulu can't really help but find the macabre laughter infectious, or maybe it's just the silliness of the drive up here, the failed retribution, the inanity of trying to force a nearly seventy-year-old woman to admit fault. Honey reflexively flicks her wrist and rolls her eyes. She wonders, *What kind of nutjob would trust a chicken to a raccoon?*

Chapter 29

HONEY'S FAVORITE forty minutes of the week are when she is working with dear Nala. The child approaches in her pigtails and her school uniform, sweet round cheeks plump with baby fat. Honey lights the candle and the girl immediately relaxes. They warm their voices with a few exercises, and then Honey nods to the accompanist.

They begin with a few standards, "Someone to Watch Over Me" and "Time After Time." Nala's eyes twinkle and she asks if she can request one she's been practicing. "But I don't want to tell you. I want you to guess," she says, conspiratorially. Honey nods, and Nala shares her secret with the pianist.

It takes just a minute before Honey recognizes the song and claps her hands, jumping in to harmonize on the chorus. It's "Atmosphere" by Fiesta, the song that blew Honey away at the Grammys. Nala's vocal range is much more expansive than Fiesta's, but she adds her own style and flair to the song, doing a little dance and ending it by leaning forward, waving jazz hands. Honey laughs and applauds, offering praise before challenging her to improve one or two transitions and correct some of her breathing.

After the session, Honey again impresses the idea of contacting Lulu's foundation on Nala and her mother. Nala's mother is unsure what to do with her incredibly talented daughter. She's just in her first year at the Baltimore School for the Arts, but she has been asked to sing at the Vice

President's house as part of a celebration of Baltimore's talented school children, and then on opening day for the Orioles in the spring. Honey has offered to accompany Nala on both trips, but she has been rebuffed. Her mother thinks she ought to pay for Honey's time, and she's right, but also, Honey would do anything for this girl. Nala has been managing her own socials, and her mother doesn't have the savoir faire to navigate nascent fame. Lulu has people who can help, Honey assures them, and money to get her to competitions and gigs. "Call Lulu," she insists, squeezing Nala's mother's hand. "She's a friend."

Honey's new assignments teaching at the Baltimore School for the Arts are funded, at least in part, by a huge donation to the school from Savion Kimberman and Noemie Valentin. They're expecting their first baby and were recently married in a private ceremony in the Virgin Islands. While Honey hadn't been invited, she did send personal well wishes to the couple in an extended voicemail where she sang the Etta James hit, "At Last!" as a wedding gift. They sent her a photo of them blowing kisses in front of an orange sunset, and Noey individually sent her a personal thank-you, Sathima Bea Benjamin's *African Songbird* with Dollar Brand. After one listen, Honey can't help humming the song "Music" to herself as she putters around, running errands.

As Honey pushes the security buttons on the door to her little apartment, she listens for Herbie. He is curled up, dead asleep on a pink, puffy dog bed. She scratches his ears and he pops up, sniffing her hand and then her shoes. She scoops him up with the mail.

She gets an email with an update about the kids from Cassandra. Bunny's suggestion that Honey had been keeping her mother sick still stings, but Honey has to admit, now that she isn't responsible for her mom's daily care, her mother is getting better. And Honey, post-surgery and with her vision therapy, has been able to see the difference. Stolid as ever, Bunny has only sent Mama a card on her birthday, signed by Cass and the kids, and nothing on Christmas. However, Bunny is months away from his twenty-year mark with the county police, and Cass has suggested that he might want to take retirement, which may give him time to draw down and find his way back to the boy she once knew.

There are two returned checks from the assisted living center, and she panics. Is her mother... gone? She calms herself, looks up the front desk number, and calls, sitting and deliberately regulating her breathing.

A receptionist answers. Honey explains the problem of the returned checks as calmly as she can. After a few clicks on a keyboard, the receptionist seems to have found an answer.

"I see here that your mother's status has changed. She's no longer listed as 'resident.' Instead, I have her listed as 'employee.' That can't be right, can it?"

"No, that must be a mistake."

The receptionist puts the phone down and Honey hears the distant clatter and ambient murmuring. In a moment, a man picks up the line and introduces himself as Dr. Kennedy, the floor manager. Honey can't imagine what is going on. She's never met this man, and he launches into a smooth explanation that raises her hackles. What has her mother gotten herself into?

"Hi there, Ms. Conaway. I'm so sorry about this misunderstanding. I thought your mother would have told you by now about our little arrangement. It's just that Ms. Dottie, your mother, well, she seemed to want to keep this news from you, and I told her that you'd need to know. But you know your mother. She does what she wants." Dr. Kennedy gives a little chuckle, as if they go way back, as if Dottie is some little inside joke they have.

Honey's mind is racing. She can't imagine what her mother could have done to get mixed up as an employee. Maybe she was playing around on the computer and changed something. "What did she do now?"

"Well, here's what happened. We had a contractor set up our website a while back, but once it was set up, we didn't get anyone to maintain it. Dottie went on our computer system, all by herself—you know how she loves the computers—and spotted all these errors. There were broken links and some things that weren't updating, and some of it had our old information. As luck would have it, we do, or we *did*, have a grant-funded position for a Website Manager. We were planning to hire someone from the outside, but Dottie, she's a firecracker, so she asked how much it pays…"

Honey sees where this is going. "So you gave her the job?"

"Well, it wasn't all that simple! We asked her to do a test that we had intended on giving to the applicants, and wouldn't you know, she passed the test. Then we gave her the admin passwords and off she went! You won't find anything wrong with the website now, and if you do, let me know, because she'll fix it right up!"

Honey isn't sure how she feels about the doctor's patronizing tone. Why wouldn't her mother be able to do a website job? She got herself that piecework job where they were paying her $600 a week. She could probably do so much more if they let her. "So she isn't being charged living expenses?"

"Oh, she is. But she's paying them! She won't be able to afford the whole year, but we did have to stop the automated payments because by now, you've overpaid your share for the full year. She can cover the rest."

Honey hears in her head the way Serafina dressed her down for not standing up for herself, and how Bunny insists she doesn't know how to negotiate. Honey screws up her courage and asks, "How much is she earning, Dr. Kennedy?"

"Come again?"

"How much per hour? It seems to me that if you've got her in residence, and she's well enough to do a job that you planned to pay someone who isn't in residence to do, well, you ought to pay her outright. How is she doing, you know, physically?"

"She's moving around great! Been going to PT and is traveling more regularly with her walker."

"So you think she might be well enough to live on her own? Not need the assisted living situation?"

Dr. Kennedy is quiet for a minute. "Well, according to her chart, she's only sixty-eight. Plenty of people work well into their seventies and don't need to be in a permanent assisted living situation. So I imagine that with some more support, she may be able to live on her own, yes."

"So how much per hour are you paying her?" Honey asks, trying to sound curious and firm at the same time.

His response is patronizing. "Well, she doesn't have the experience for a market rate. We just discovered that she has this talent and decided to put it to use. You know, to keep her busy and productive."

"Is she doing the job?" Honey taps her nails on the counter. *Give me Gloria's attitude right now*, she prays. *Give me Serafina's confidence.*

"She is," he says, noncommittal.

"Huh," says Honey. "So she's not working for her room and board right now, right? Because, Dr. Kennedy, that seems like what I might call indentured servitude. I think she should be paid a fair and living wage."

"To be honest, I think she's just all around happier here. She's made some friends, you know," Dr. Kennedy answers brightly, as if she ought to pay to have friends. His voice gets low and conspiratorial. "You should drop by and meet her gentleman friend."

"She has a boyfriend?" Honey is surprised, but she wants to keep him talking so she can google the salary the Website Manager was offered in the first place.

Dr. Kennedy sounds like he's about to pop with the news. "Yes! And it was quite the stir because a number of these women residents had their eyes on him. But it turns out that she's the lucky one."

Honey laughs, and then corrects the record. "No, Dr. Kennedy. You'll see. *He's* the lucky one!"

Dr. Kennedy laughs at her joke. "That's probably true, Ms. Conaway. Probably true." Honey laughs too, politely, leaning into the deference that she has believed in all these years, but she has made herself a promise not to assume less of her mother, and not to let anyone devalue her mother, or herself, anymore.

Honey closes her eyes and takes a deep breath. She has a number in her head, and she steadies herself to negotiate. "Well, I'll just have to meet him as soon as I can! Now about my mother's employment contract..."

Just after seven, Pastor Glendon, or as Honey knows him now, Reginald, knocks on her door, and then slips in the key and lets himself into the apartment. Honey watches him as he takes off his shoes and pads to her couch in his stocking feet. He's brought something delicious in a bag, something rich and greasy like collards and sweet potatoes. He's also brought her flowers, and he leans in for a chaste kiss on the cheek, just a firefly's promise of the touches he'll deliver later.

They take their dinner to the porch and eat under the setting sun in the lush courtyard shared by a few apartments. Honey likes her neighbors, and she likes more that they bring her baked goods and stories but leave her alone when she's with Reginald. Without the weight of the house—such an ill-advised purchase for a twenty-something—she feels unencumbered, and she thinks this is how Sian must have felt, moving from couch to couch with little more than the clothes on her back. Honey couldn't fully cast herself to the wind. As much as she cared for the woman, she's not at all like Sian.

The phone buzzes during dinner, and then buzzes again. Honey excuses herself, worried something has happened to her mother, to Bunny, or to Gloria. But it is Gloria.

"Guess what?" asks Gloria. Before Honey can answer, Gloria shouts, "Chicken butt!"

"Gloria, are you drunk?"

"No, I'm high on life! I'm inspired. So guess what!" She is hyper and silly, but she is not slurring her words.

"Chicken butt?" Honey asks tentatively, feeling silly, but her answer sends Gloria into a fit of giggles.

"Noooo, I'm moving to Baltimore! Where is Eutaw Street? Is that near you?"

Honey's head spins. "You're moving? And you don't know where you're moving to?"

"Yes! I bought a building. It looks great for a club. Oh, that's the news. We're opening a club! In Baltimore. On Eutaw Street. Did you know Baltimore has a huge jazz history? Cab Calloway and Eubie Blake and…"

"Yes, I know," says Honey firmly. "Gloria, why are you moving to Baltimore? Why are you coming here?"

"Because I live in the middle of nowhere with a bunch of ungrateful animals and creepy neighbors and Manhattan is too expensive and Brooklyn is full of hipsters." She takes a breath. "And I want to be close to someone I actually sincerely like."

Honey thinks for a moment. Eutaw runs north-south and is about five blocks from her old house, but on the other side of town. Down by the Hippodrome, Lexington Market, the Everyman Theater... It could work. The area has some nightclubs now, not that Honey has been to them. What building could she have bought? And is she proposing to live down there?

"Why now?" Honey asks. "Why here?"

"Honey, I have invited you and your boyfriend up here at least ten times, and you always tell me I live too far away. So I am coming to you. I'm Airbnb'ing this house and using it as a getaway, especially when I get sick of you. But you gotta do this with me."

"Gee, Gloria," she says. She's still reeling, and Reginald is cutting his eyes at her, gently, trying to suss out when she'll be able to extricate herself from the call and resume their intimate dinner.

"Aw, you don't want me, do you?" Gloria fake pouts. The manic energy drops. Honey can hear only the sound of her own pulse. Every bone wants to reject this woman, this crazy-ass woman who just doesn't learn. But she also sees how lonely Gloria is. This woman who hasn't really had all that many choices, who has put up walls of wit and sass and barely lets anyone in to see her real dreams, her real loves. This club may be the thing that Gloria is meant to do. Honey takes a breath and looks into the sky, as if it has the answers. In her experience, it generally does.

"Gloria, where are you planning to live? You can't live in a building while it's being rehabbed."

"I figured I'd move in with you and cutie. Have ourselves a threesome." She cackles.

"Gloria! Hush! We are Christians." Honey covers the mouthpiece of the phone as if Reginald could hear Gloria through it.

"Are you kidding? Jesus himself was born of a threesome!" She laughs again at her own joke, and Honey, horrified but also dreadfully amused, covers her mouth to hide her smile from everyone who might judge her: Reginald, neighbors, God.

"Gloria, you are incorrigible!" she laughs. "I do have to go, but yes, talk me into it all tomorrow."

"Listen, listen, listen. The best part! Here's the name: '*Mama's.*'"

And suddenly, Honey can see it: The marquee, people lined up to listen to cabaret-style singing, pictures of legendary Baltimore women like Billie Holliday, Ethel Ennis, and Blanche Calloway, but also images and tributes to all the women who have been eaten up by the game, the mothers, the women who birthed the sounds that are cherished today. As she pictures it, the stage would be intimate, powerful, and women would have space to graffiti and draw whatever they wanted, whatever was true. But you could only be a woman to mess with it.

No, she thinks, *Fiesta is a mother, a new kind of mother.* All the girls and women, and the people who aren't men. Any people that Danny Dire would want to lock into a bathroom, anyone who doesn't feel safe and who needs a space to perform, to be her whole self. Honey is flooded with ideas for events. She notices Reginald peering at her. Her smile is so wide, she covers her mouth again.

"Yes, let's talk tomorrow." She rushes Gloria off the phone and turns to find Reginald beside her, his hands on her waist.

"Sister Honoria, I do believe you have received some very good news tonight," he says, burying his face in her neck.

"Brother Reginald," she says, leaning into his nuzzle, and then collapsing into him with happiness. The gentleman he is, he dips her. From her backward lean, fully trusting his arms, she answers. "I do believe I have. The best news. The news I've been waiting for all my life."

Discuss

1. The idea of motherhood is threaded throughout the book. What resonated with you about each woman's experience with her own mother or her daughter?
2. There are very few male characters in the book. Do you feel like the book was unbalanced, or did it make sense to focus on the women's experience in music?
3. What did each woman sacrifice for her art? Do you think female and female-presenting artists always have to sacrifice more than male or male-presenting artists do?
4. Who would you say is the main character of this book? Why do you think so?
5. What did you notice about how Honey's experience in the music industry is different from the experience of white women in the text? What systemic challenges contribute to those differences? Or, if you don't see differences, why not?
6. Throughout the book, Sian is exhausted by life. Do you think she had the right to let herself die? Or do you think she ought to have fought harder and dying was selfish?
7. How do the different generations of women interact throughout the book, and how are they represented similarly and differently?
8. What is an audience's responsibility to a female artist (or any artist), especially when the artist is unhealthy, she is caught in a scandal, or her beauty is fading?

Acknowledgments

This book has been on such a journey. First, big ups my publisher, Chris Kosmides, for being open to my work on my very first day joining the Hampden Writer's Group in Baltimore. He has also graciously put up with my insistence on revisions for everything from the font size to the front cover, and dealt graciously with my forthright attitude. You're a saint, dude. And speaking of revisions, thanks to all my earliest readers who helped me shape this book: my daughter Eve, my partner Michael, and fellow writers Charles Cohen, Jennifer Emrick, Sarah Hendess, Katherine Pickett, Debra Whittall, Ruth Ticktin, Elisabeth Cohen, Jane Delury, and Ed Doyle-Gillespie for their insights and gentle but targeted suggestions. Also, so much love and thanks to my friend and editor, Tess Hoffman, who improved so much of the flow and untangled those stumbly, jumbly moments.

The people who ran next to me in this marathon: My GM writers group (Amy Snyder, Michele Lundin, Agnes Bannigan, Pat Mohr, and Brenda Bryant, Ellen Goldstein) and the Hampden Writers' Group (Mark Charney, Jonathan Tomick, Emily Dernoeden, Amelia Franz, and Joseph Maria, among others) who read several chapters and gave me excellent advice. Thanks to Christine Grillo and, again, Elisabeth Cohen, for editorial and publishing advice.

I have to thank my Aunt Doris and Paula LeVere, the inspirations for some of the stories in this book. Also huge thanks to Hassan Aziz, whom I pestered about music theory, harmonizing, and collaborating with other musicians, and who always gave me an answer I could use. And thanks to my cheerleaders, my book club gals, Tina Cavaluzzi, Sharon Menefee, Ava

Schweikert, Kristin Hermann, Bibi Medina, Kate Gehr, Kim Ledgerwood, and Ellen Montoya.

Going way back, thanks to Mike Garry for always knowing what I should be listening to, from Mother Love Bone to Luscious Jackson, and always being right, and to Geoff Legg, who made sure his Michigan library had a copy of my first book, published 25 years ago and not worthy of a library barcode. I hope this one makes up for the trouble!

The documentary *Trio* about Dolly Parton, Emmylou Harris, and Linda Ronstadt provided the inspiration about how three women from distinct genres could find their way into collaboration, and *20 Feet from Stardom* gave me insight into the hustle of making it as an artist in an industry that wants to pay artists for as little as possible and automate the rest for quick profit. Bless the epic Merry Clayton, and I hope she sees herself in Honey's striving life. *The Righteous Babes* by Pratibha Parmar illustrated how difficult it is for women in music, but also a reminder, as Tori Amos says in the movie to young female performers, to "just fucking fly!"

As a non-musician, I had to do a ton of research to ensure this book rang true. Many details are supported by the following materials which enriched both the life and work of the artists portrayed in this book and my own storytelling: *Playing to the Crowd* by Nancy Baym, *Soul Mining* by Daniel Lanois, *The Performing Life* by Sharon Mabry, and *Rebel Girl* by Kathleen Hanna. Some inspiring fictional stories about the rock & roll life are *The Final Revival of Opal & Nev* by Dawnie Walton, *Mary Jane* by Jessica Anya Blau, *Daisy Jones and the Six* by Taylor Jenkins Reid, *Utopia Avenue* by David Mitchell, and *This Bird Has Flown* by Susanna Hoffs.

If you will indulge me, everyone should read *Here Goes Nothing* by Eamon McGrath, a micro-meditation on being cramped in a van for a month of gigs. While it didn't inform too much of this book, you can expect echoes of it in my next books, despite the perfection of the slim volume itself. And the writing of Hanif Abdurraqib (all of it, all of it) implores me to hold music reverently in my writing, for music is neither decoration nor soundtrack; it is existential. It tells us about the deepest parts of ourselves, much like poetry, and that in our darkest times, it is essential to our survival. (And I hope he agrees with all that!)

There are several institutions that supported my work, though most of them might not even know it. Baltimore School for the Arts provided a waiting room where much of this book was drafted, and where I could watch teaching artists and uber talented high schoolers move through the hallways singing, dancing, or practicing a horn or two with an open door. The talent nurtured in this high school is phenomenal, and I hope I did it justice in the leaves of this book. And Professor Solomon always checked in on the progress of this novel! Enoch Pratt Free Library provided books and a grand working space, and the Baltimore-based radio station WTMD provided a rich soundtrack and a lot of inspiration for the songs in this book. Deejays Alex Cortwright, Kelly Bell, Megan Byrd, and Brooks Long, among many others, provided stories that may have alchemically been turned into fiction within these pages. The Bun Shop hosted me quietly for hours at a time, and I picked up albums from Mt. Vernon Records just down the street. The online writers' community Gutsy Great Novelist Writers Studio has also provided me with tips and encouragement as I've polished this novel, so thank you so much for hosting it and including me, Joan Dempsey!

For massive amounts of support and time to write from my family, Michael Craven, Sage Craven, Rain Craven, and again, Eve Craven. And for cheering me on, thanks to Dad and MaryAnn, the Craven Clan, Heather Nixon & her girls, and Pam Robie, and Mom, who I hope is reading this book from heaven. All my love and thanks.

If you don't find yourself being thanked here, I'm so sorry, I knew I was going to miss someone. I'm sorry it had to be you, and I offer my deepest thanks for how you have shaped me over time. I am because we are, friends. Nothing beautiful is created alone.